Keith Waterhouse, bo ... ds
coster-monger. He wo ... k-
er's and a garage be ... nd
becoming a writer. *M* ... el.
The brilliantly success ... as
published in 1960 and has been filmed, televised and turned into a stage play. Mr. Waterhouse has written extensively for the theatre, cinema and television. He is a frequent contributor to *Punch* and, since 1970, has had his own column in the *Daily Mirror*

'Mr. Waterhouse is not only among the funniest writers of our time, he is also among the wittiest and most observant.'

—*Evening Standard*

'He must have a claim to be the most entertaining novelist now at work on contemporary British Society. He laughs with it, he lampoons it, he peoples it with characters well observed, exactly drawn and obviously thought about.'

—*Punch*

'Keith Waterhouse is funny in the pleasantest way; tolerant, even-tempered, unmalicious, but with the sharpest of ears, the twitchiest of noses.'

—*The Financial Times*

MAGGIE MUGGINS
OR
SPRING IN EARL'S COURT

KEITH WATERHOUSE

CORGI BOOKS
A DIVISION OF TRANSWORLD PUBLISHERS LTD

MAGGIE MUGGINS
A CORGI BOOK 0 552 12063 4

Originally published in Great Britain by
Michael Joseph Ltd.

PRINTING HISTORY
Michael Joseph edition published 1981
Corgi edition published 1982

Copyright © Keith Waterhouse 1981

Conditions of sale

1. This book is sold subject to the condition
that it shall not, by way of trade *or otherwise*,
be lent, re-sold, hired out or otherwise *circulated*
without the publisher's prior consent
in any form of binding or cover
other than that in which it is published
*and without a similar condition including this condition
being imposed on the subsequent purchaser*.

2. This book is sold subject to the Standard Conditions
of Sale of Net Books and may not be re-sold in the UK
below the net price fixed by the publishers for the book.

This book is set in 9½ pt. Caledonia

Corgi books are published by Transworld Publishers Ltd.,
Century House, 61–63 Uxbridge Road,
Ealing, London W5 5SA

Made and printed in Great Britain by
Cox & Wymans Ltd., Reading.

Contents

1

Tears Before Breakfast

Maggie didn't know where she was. That made it morning.

Even when legless, and she had been legless in her time, she always knew where she was going. But she didn't always know where she had been.

It would be a bed-sitter, unless it could prove otherwise. The curtain, no more than a rag really, of the kind of slime-green you get by mixing blue with yellow, certainly pointed that way. It hung from what might have been a broom-handle wedged lopsidedly into the window-frame. By borrowing a saw and taking—what?—an inch and a half off that makeshift curtain rod, someone could have made a really neat job of it. Neat but shabby would have suggested a proper home. Lopsided and shabby suggested a bed-sit.

It was possible, of course, to be both—a bed-sit that was a proper home, a proper home that was a bed-sit. Nothing to do with who owned the furniture, it was which person a stranger waking up in that room got the strongest sense of —the landlord or the tenant. Only the smallest touch, and one of them was there to the exclusion of the other. Take away the shelf of paperbacks and it was a bed-sit, add a potted plant and it was home.

Speaking as a bed-sit tenant herself, Maggie was not a big reader, and vegetation made her sneeze.

What she had thought was another friendly warning from her liver was not spots before her eyes after all, it was dust flecking the sunlight that penetrated the slime-green curtain where it had grown threadbare. That made it late morning, with people about, instead of that demolition-site acre of time between dawn and the first newsagents' shops opening. If Maggie ever killed herself—seriously killed herself, not just got 'very wet' as on the night of 'my drowning'—it would be in that two-hour vacuum between the last all-night bus and the first early-morning one.

Going not so much by the angle of the pencil-beams as by their brightness, she guessed it would be about half-past nine, Muggins Mean Time. Maggie didn't own a watch, although several had passed through her hands. The only one she wished she'd kept was the little square one with the crocodile strap her Mum had given her for her twenty-first. She'd sold it for eleven quid in the French Pub one morning, then got maudlin pissed on the money and felt a right bastard all next day. If she'd hung on to that watch she knew where she could have got forty for it.

Muggins Mean Time meant give or take, usually take, one circuit of the big hand starting and finishing at half past the hour. All Maggie's appointments—the appointments she made herself, not those forced on her by people who sat behind desks—were for half-past. Half-past, she always thought, was far less committed, far easier-going, than the fixed, chiming numbers that got counted out by armour-suited figures whirring out of little doors with hammers: at the twelfth stroke, boyfriends standing under public clocks all over England shot back their cuffs, checked their watches and fumed. But those on-the-hour 'dates' (yukky word) that you saw typists and shopgirls scurrying to keep were at least preferable to the ones green-inked in big diaries by the people who sat behind desks, who in their finicky, grapefruit-knife fashion divided the day into dainty quarter-hour segments and wanted you punctually in their waiting-rooms at a quarter-to or a quarter-past.

Half-past nineish, then. So much for the time, now what about the place? It did matter, for Maggie had to arrange her day. She didn't like to get up until she knew what she was getting up for.

Very definitely bed-sitterland. Wardrobe you could put to sea in, bedside kitchen chair flecked with whitewash, top-heavy chest of drawers, born to be second-hand, with soup-pan rings burned into the polish. Chianti-bottle lamp on the floor, its flex tightly stretched across a jigsaw puzzle of bits of underfelt and offcuts from some other room's fitted carpet all curled at the edges like stale bread and butter, the fraying wires only just making it to a lopsided thirteen-amp socket in the skirting of a hardboard wall. Maggie could tell it was hardboard without having to reach back and rap her knuckles on the scuffed patch of buff distemper above her pillow. A plaster frieze of melted icecream flowers dripped along the perimeter of the ceiling where it met three of the walls, but vanished where it met the fourth; the melted icecream blob of laurel leaves or whatever, that must have surrounded a central light-fitting at one time, had been unceremoniously scythed down the middle by the hardboard partition. Two rooms made out of one room. It was often so.

In fact it was always so, in Maggie's experience. She couldn't remember, in all her ten years in London, ever having been in a room, and most certainly she'd never lived in a room, that wasn't really half a room. Everywhere you went had been divided, chopped up, partitioned off, with tall thin doors that you had to go through sideways, and T-shaped kitchenettes without any windows, and lavs where your elbows brushed the walls when you pulled your drawers up. The only wasted space was between the top of your head and the far-off ceiling with its lozenge of detail from some grand ballroom design of melted icecream grapes or melted icecream fleurs-de-lis, and that was only because the cowboy builders hadn't yet found a way of splitting rooms up horizontally as well as vertically.

It was like living in bloody Hong Kong. Even the shops, or anyway the shops that Maggie used, had been sliced up and then vacuum-sealed like processed cheese, your average fair-sized grocer's having become a long thin launderette, a long thin dry cleaner's, and a long thin mini-supermarket where the only way to squeeze between the checkout desk and the crates of long-life milk was to hold your carrier-bag of goodies at tit-level and breathe in. Even the police station where they'd taken her after her drowning: the room she'd been questioned in had been reclaimed with roughly cemented breezeblocks from the dead end of a wide corridor. Even the Social Services day centre she had to go to, which wasn't in a clapped-out building at all but was housed in a cluster of Portakabins so you would have thought they could easily expand as the need arose, kept splitting itself up like a flaming amoeba. Maggie really thought it was a bit much when the interview rooms in a sodding Portakabin had hardboard partitions down the middle. She had sat in one sliced-off compartment facing the woman who sat behind the desk, and at the other side of the hardboard with its poster of a pregnant man had sat another woman behind another desk, and facing this one, to complete the mirror image, had been a West Indian woman by the sound of her in the other sliced-off compartment. And Maggie had been able to hear every whining word about how her man come home Saturday from that Rainbow Club and give her 'this'—bunch of fives, presumably—because he want to know her but she wouldn't know him when he have too much rum. V. biblical. Maggie could still remember the juicier bits from her school scripture lessons. *And Adam knew his wife again; and she bare a son*.

'What I'm urging you to do,' the woman who sat behind the desk was saying (Maggie had christened her Miss Roberts, although she was a Mrs. something-or-other in real life), 'is to take these leaflets and a copy of the adoption memorandum form home with you to go through at your leisure, but not to commit yourself at this stage, because you've got all the time in the world.'

'The usual nine months, actually,' muttered Maggie, trying by her own example to make the woman keep her voice down. But Miss Roberts evidently had a lot of customers who didn't hear very well. She could no longer open her mouth without sounding as if she were trying to get through to a deaf old-age pensioner.

'Much longer than that, my dear, because no one can stampede you into making any final decision until six months after the baby is born, whatever you may have signed in the meanwhile. Now what I'm saying is that you could *very well be* in a much different frame of mind after you've seen your baby and held it.'

Own fault, Mags. Before taking refuge in this broken-down borough, she really ought to have checked that they had a full-time adoption counsellor with a proper office—all right, half an office: done—where you could slink in and out unseen. Miss Roberts doubled as one of a harassed scrum of social workers, so that Maggie had to take her turn with the tower-block depressives and other urban shellshock victims who daily streamed through the Portakabins. She could see herself being stared at, next visit, for if she could hear what was going on in the West Indian chick's cubicle, the West Indian chick could certainly hear what was going on in hers.

'Look, do you mind, this is my private business you're shouting from the rooftops,' she wanted to protest. But she didn't want the West Indian chick and the duplicate Miss Roberts behind the other desk on the other side of the partition to hear her voice, which was her private property.

If Maggie ever had need of a passport, she hoped they would let her enter 'Private person' as her profession.

So, then: the wardrobe that looked like a family tomb carved out of railway sleepers, the Junk City chest of drawers, the kitchen chair that had doubled as a painter's ladder: she certainly hadn't strayed out of her own social class last night, that was for sure. Not that that gave her much to go on. At one time if you were in bed-sitland, it usually meant Notting Hill, Paddington, Camden Town, no more than half a dozen West or North-West postal districts. These days it could be anywhere. Clapham for God's sake, she had woken up in before now. She had even seen that wardrobe's twin brother as far out as Raynes Park. That was the only time she had ever gone home by Green Line bus—wearing, as she recalled, a borrowed black number with rather more cleavage than she had cleft, and the ritzy pillbox hat with the royal-funeral veil that she'd found down the Portobello, on account of one of the faces she knocked around with had wangled an invite to the opening of another of those chrome-and-cocktail joints in Covent Garden. A right nana she'd felt, tottering down the bus aisle on her stilettos at half-eight in the morning, with all the punters squinting up from their crosswords to clock her purple fingernails and fishnets. She must have looked like the touring version of *Breakfast at Tiffany's*.

The anonymous room gave no clue: could be anybody's ('Couldn't we all, dear!' responded Maggie to herself in camp tones like Sean's). Anybody's, any place. Where?

There were no traffic sounds, but what did that prove? You could be in the back doubles behind the Harrow Road and there would be no more noise than in the middle of Epping Forest. And vice versa. A blackbird sang, but what did that signify? There were blackbirds in Earl's Court.

She would have to try remembering. A drastic step,

Maggie would agree, but it was the only thing for it bar getting out of bed and looking out of the window. Once she knew how far off she was from base, she could make her plans.

Base was Half Moon Court ('Named after my half-brother,' she used to joke, but the joke fell flat because so few knew that Moon was her real name) off Berwick Street market. Maggie liked to start her day either in the Half Moon itself or in the Leather Bottle opposite if for any reason she and the Half Moon were not on speaking terms.

If it turned out that she was in somewhere like Streatham or the ratty end of Wimbledon, and that melted icecream ceiling certainly did suggest one of the farther-flung Victorian suburbs, she could get herself together at leisure and make it to the Half Moon by opening time. Maybe waste a few minutes over a cup of coffee at the Nosh Bar first—it wouldn't do to be seen pacing up and down Half Moon Court like a Soho brass on the early trick while waiting for Sid the Squirrel to unbolt the doors. But if she was in say Barons Court, Kilburn, North Ken., somewhere civilised, she could get back to Balmoral Gardens and do—well, *things* for an hour or so before going out again. She was always telling people she had *things* to do at home and the opportunity to do them didn't come up nearly often enough, not that it was possible to pin Maggie down on what *things* there were to be done. Certainly not lining drawers with newspaper or getting a pillowcase of laundry together. Lying on the bed smoking, the same as she was doing now, was about the only *thing* when it came down to it.

The truth was that Maggie just liked going back to her room and being there. Within reason. And not for long periods.

Had she been home yesterday at any point? Well, take it in easy stages—was it home that she had set off from in the morning? Maggie twisted her head to look for her knickers, and located them half-in and half-out of the crumpled ball of tights on the floor near the window. Oh, those. Then she hadn't set off from home, because she'd definitely been wearing those on whatever day it had been the day before yesterday. Maggie tried never to wear the same knickers two days running, although it didn't necessarily follow that the ones she'd changed into had been rinsed out.

She was trying to remember where she was and she didn't even know what bloody day of the week it was. God, she must have given the vodka a right going-over last night.

Unexpectedly, like a shaft of sunlight in a cellar, his face flashed back into her mind. Sandy-haired bugger, looked younger than he probably was, with the kind of crooked grin that didn't half fancy itself. Freelance journalist, so he claimed (Oh, yes, then what was he doing out of bed before half-past nine in the morning?) Given her the eye once or twice in the Half Moon and other places, and they'd finally been introduced by Sean—where?

'He's fucking potty about you, kitten,' Sean had murmured. 'You mean he's potty about fucking me,' Maggie said. She remembered that.

Simon, that was his name.

She had no recollection at all of the dirty deed being done. It could have been statutory rape for all she knew, although the disposition of her clothes—tights and knickers in one heap, corduroy strides in another, dusty velvet jacket slung over the end of the bed—suggested that at least she had undressed herself. When men undressed you, they always impetuously hung your things up.

Where was her jumper, then? She caught a glimpse of green: she was half-lying on it. Must have been feeling the cold and come to bed in it, how practical. Still: bare bum and cable-stitch, quite a turn-on for a certain class of face, and he'd probably needed one after what they must have put away yesterday.

Was that a love-bite or a flea-bite? Hard to say.

And it wasn't what had taken place but where it had taken place that was the important thing. Think.

Try putting it together slowly. She had presumably started in the Half Moon. No she hadn't, the first piece was falling into place, for once in her life she had never even set off for the Half Moon.

Sean. She had woken up on Sean's broken-down sofa with a coil of wire stuck up her bum, having zizzed off the night before. Overcome by tiredness, she'd been, after they'd staggered back and seen off two quarts of cider, after reeling out of that club in Queensway at Christ knows what hour, after—

Never mind raking up ancient history, the point was that

she'd spent all yesterday morning around Ladbroke Grove. Had a bath while Sean made some of his endless phone calls, then gone across to his local boozer to cash a cheque, then all round to Hagerty's Bar in the Portobello, where they'd got in a school and stayed until closing time, although Maggie hadn't meant to.

Then where?

Maggie crushed out her cigarette in the empty packet she was using as an ashtray and wondered why she never got hang-overs. Was it a good sign or a bad sign? She sometimes pretended to feel rough when she surfaced around lunch-time, making the regulation comic grimaces and crooking her elbow against the glare of daylight, but she didn't feel rough really, it was just that everyone seemed to expect it after what she'd put away the night before. Could women get cirrhosis? At pushing thirty?

If there were no more ciggies in her bag she was in deep trouble. It was lying open on the whitewash-flecked bedside kitchen chair. She reached into it, found a half-full packet of Rothmans, and saw that tucked into the cellophane wrapping was a scrap of card scribbled over in felt-tip.

Ahhh, his bread-and-butter note, bless him. Magic evening, had to dash, didn't want to wake you, must have a replay, all that crap. Signed Peter called Simon.

Of course. Joke. Another flash of light in the cellar. His name wasn't Simon, it was Peter. Sean had introduced them: 'This is Peter,' and she'd said, 'You introduce people and you don't even know their names. He's not Peter, he's Simon, anyone can see that'—because he looked, or she affected to believe that he looked, more like one of life's Simons than one of life's Peters. And after some joshing they compromised. He became Peter called Simon.

It was a game Maggie played, but only with those she didn't know very well. It gave her something to say when she first met people, that was about the size of it she supposed. 'Sorry, I see you definitely as a Malcolm.' Bloody tiresome they must find it, some of them, though most got so much into the spirit of the thing that she usually wished she'd never started it.

Oh, and people she didn't like—Miss Roberts, Sid the Squirrel: she did it to them too, without them knowing. Stuck labels on them. She never did it to mates, though. Not proper mates. Proper mates—Sean, Riggsy, one or two others—got their proper names. Proper mates, and proper bastards. Ken.

She fished in her bag for matches—the disposable lighter she'd picked up somewhere had flickered and died. Another bijou surprisette: this time her fingers closed on the velvety texture of high-grade paper money. Two tenners. Twenty quid.

If Peter called pigging Simon had bunged her twenty quid for his night's entertainment she would personally stuff it down his throat. The cheeky sod. She might be anybody's for a bag of crisps, but she wasn't on the game yet.

Not being on the game was an important moral demarcation line for Maggie. It was, she'd decided, her last frontier: cross it once and she might as well stagger off into the sunset with a mattress strapped to her back.

There had been several frontiers, or perhaps it was the same one that she'd kept on steadily pushing back and back. It had been a long slide from losing her virginity—losing it? She'd taken it for a walk in the woods and abandoned it—to being anybody's and perhaps she hadn't finished sliding yet. But she never did it for money, ever.

She found the matches and thought fleetingly about setting light to the two ten-pound notes, but that was against her principles too.

Cheeky sod.

Would it be possible, Maggie wondered, drawing angrily on her cigarette until sparks flew off it (serve the bugger right if she set the bedclothes on fire), to get hold of twenty quid's worth of horse manure in sacks, and somehow hump it up to Peter called Simon's room and—

Sor-ree! Take it all back. There was so much light in the cellar it was dazzling.

Slowly now. Hagerty's. Sean. That Irish mate of his, the AC-DC one who fancied both of them. Had asked them both for a quid but wouldn't tell them why. 'Will you trust me now? I'm asking you, you're both lovely people, will you trust me?' he kept on saying, and Sean gave him two quid for the pair of them and he took it off to the betting shop and came back with twenty-three quid apiece for Sean and Maggie and a roll of notes that thick for himself. He'd only backed, hadn't he, a Christ-knows-what-to-one outsider called Nimrod for no other reason than that he and Sean had once won the jackpot in an afternoon drinking club of that name in Fulham Palace Road? So naturally, since it was chucking-out time by now, where else would they take a swift cab to but the Nimrod, where they drank themselves stupid on bottle after bottle of fizzy wine that Sean's Irish mate called poor man's champagne and Maggie called rich man's Andrews Liver Salts? And naturally, Sean's Irish mate thought he'd bought them both for the night (why had she still got two crisp ten-pound notes left, don't say she hadn't bought a round all day, mean bitch?), which wouldn't have been her scene and wasn't Sean's either so far as she knew; so when they fell out of the Nimrod and into that big Victorian pub across the road, and ran into Peter called Simon, Maggie made it plain to Sean by their code of little nods and winces that he could please himself but she was rowing herself out. So Sean wheeled his Irish mate off to one of those faggoty pubs of his, and Peter called Simon took her to that Chinese throw-up where the lav was so filthy disgusting that she wouldn't use it, and he said there was always his place, but she was wetting herself so they went back to the pub and had a brandy and a pee, and then he chatted her up and bought a bottle of wine to go, and there it was on the yellow-painted mantelpiece over his boarded-up fireplace, unopened.

They must have been in kip before eleven o'clock. World record?

And then it really did go blank. She must have passed out on the poor sod. Why had she got so paralytic?

Maggie wanted to pee again. She wanted to more than pee, as a matter of fact, but she would have to see what state the lav was in. Maggie didn't like strange lavs, didn't like lavs at all, if the truth be told. Having to go once a day (not that she did, she was often constipated) was a monstrous imposition by nature, like the curse.

Maggie was secretly proud that when she served four days in hospital, having the babe, she didn't go once, not seriously went that was, after the first bleak evening when they shoved plastic pellets up her bum.

Had she been last night? Couldn't remember. She had a vague mental picture of a clean-enough lav on a half-landing, and a landladyish-looking woman on the stairs sniffing at her as if she'd crawled out of the drains, but you often got that.

Where was it she'd thrown up, then, and hadn't had time to lift the seat? The pub? No, the club, earlier.

The main thing was that she could now remember getting here. Everywhere they'd been since taking that fast cab from Hagerty's had been within walking distance, right? They'd never gone more than fifty yards off Fulham Palace Road. Putney Bridge Station must be right round the corner, which meant she was only four stations on the District Line from home, or ten stations on the District and Piccadilly Lines from base.

Bingo. Who's a clever girl, then?

Putting Peter called Simon out of her mind for ever—she doubted that their paths would cross again, he was the Half Moon's newest ex-customer if he ran true to form—Maggie sat up in bed and blew the ash from her boobs and put out her cigarette stub in the empty packet on the bedside kitchen chair. She dug her seven-years-bad-luck bit of mirror out of her bag and found a not-very-used Kleenex and dribbled spit on it and started to dab at the eyeshadow that was caking her skin. She couldn't remember washing yesterday, must have gone on painting and repainting herself like the Forth Bridge.

She could remember everything else, though, by now. It was surprising how long it sometimes took, considering. How long did it take a waking hunchback to remember his hump?

Maggie pushed the soiled Kleenex under her pillow, remembered it wasn't her pillow and retrieved it and stuffed it in her bag, looked for her jumper and remembered she was lying on it and tugged it from under her and began to put it on, then stopped with it round her neck with one arm in and one arm out and began to cry.

Too brightly she told herself, 'Tears before breakfast!', not that she ever ate any. Slow, cheap tears, they were. Maggie had remembered her life.

2

A Shoulder to Piss on

By 'home', Maggie meant in the first instance the forecourt of Earl's Court tube station. At whatever hour, it was her stopping-off place before she walked the few yards to Balmoral Gardens.

No one was ever allowed to escort her further, her room was private. If they didn't have a room of their own to go to, it was their hard luck. 'Drop me off at the piazza,' she would say, very firm with it, and inventing a room-mate if pushed. Nor did anyone pick her up at home. 'See you on the piazza at half-past. If wet, in the galleria.'

The piazza was what Maggie called the few yards of pavement in front of the Earl's Court Road entrance to the tube station. The galleria was the covered forecourt itself with its glass arcaded roof. Very Eyetalian.

Not that she'd ever set foot in Italy, never been further south than Brighton on that clean weekend with Sean, but she could imagine it.

All human life was there. Not at this hour, of course. At this hour the station was still milling with mere punters, wave after well-trained wave of them pouring in across Earl's Court Road as the pedestrian lights changed from WAIT to CROSS NOW. Late typists who had had no breakfast hurried out of the minimarkets with their Virgin Records carrier-bags stuffed full of fruit and crispbread; clerks looking like sex murderers emerged blinking into the daylight from their garden flats, unpeeling Kit-Kat bars as they shuffled along the ticket queue; world citizens with the world on their shoulders, an Atlas-load of quilted bedrolls and girdered rucksacks and climbing boots, created a bottleneck under the blue-glass London Transport canopy as they traced the

Victoria Line to its source from YOU ARE HERE; and sauntering, round-shouldered Arabs—the camels of the desert, Maggie called them—browsed through the freebie Aussie mags they'd found in the tin stands by the news kiosk, where liberated Turkish girls jotted down addresses from the pegboard cabinet of advertisements for clean hotel chambermaids.

But by half-tennish, when the crazy old ladies who called themselves 'residents' began to venture out to walk their dogs, most of the punters would be gone, off to peel oranges in their big glass crates in Vauxhall or sit on the lions in Trafalgar Square, and the piazza with its galleria would come into its own.

Then it began to look a bit like a market place, though not like a market place on market day. There might be a pusher or two, a tout for one of the leather clubs and another for a dodgy abortion clinic, sometimes a moneychanger undercutting the bureaux de change, and of course Henry was always there like a bent package-tour courier directing incoming punters towards the network of rip-off 'hostels' and 'holiday flatlets' that paid his commission; but most of the faces you saw there had oozed up through the cracks in the pavement for no more than a smoke and a breath of air. Maggie wasn't saying that if you stood in the middle of the galleria with a fistful of fivers, the Earl's Court Mafia wouldn't produce a prospectus for relieving you of your money. In the main, though, if they had any business at all it was with each other. 'This,' Maggie had said, 'is where the grapevine ends.'

You couldn't expect the punters to notice what went on. They knew they were living where it all happened but they didn't know what it was that was all happening because they didn't notice. Not unless it was the Filth frogmarching a pick-pocket out of the Piccadilly Line lift, or a body (usually nothing violent: someone been using bad gear, nine times out of ten) obstructing the bank of ticket machines.

That was what Sean had been on their first encounter: a body obstructing the ticket machines.

But the crazy old ladies wandering backwards and forwards between their mansion flats and the Asian dellies where they bought their petfood, they noticed right enough, if they weren't too crazy. They noticed everything. Noticing was what had driven them crazy. One of them, pausing by the pedestrian lights until her straining King Charles spaniel had expelled enough raw material to enable the next wave of feet to fan compass-needles of dogshit over a twelve-yard radius, saw Sean stumbling to his feet and clutching his cramped stomach as if about to spew. 'Oh, aren't there some dirty pigs!' was what she said to the first person to catch her eye, who was Maggie. A few years ago she would have asked, 'Is he all right?' The crazy old ladies had learned about metropolitan life by now, they knew where they didn't belong.

Maggie felt very sorry for them. The Old Brompton Road memsahibs, she called them: there must have been nannies pushing Silver Cross prams through the squares when they came to live around here, and shopkeepers in straw hats who would slither halfway up their arses to sell them a quarter of a pound of cheese. Now in half the drawing-rooms where they'd poured one another afternoon tea you saw pingpong tables or rows of airport-looking chairs facing a telly, and the basement areas were stacked with sheets of plywood waiting to be room-dividers, and there were seasidey boarding-house names on square plastic canopies over the grand doorways. And all their silver teapots had gone to the antique shops, and the antique shops had sold up and been turned into doner kebab houses. They'd gone out to buy more cheese and been served by black men who couldn't understand what was being shouted at them, then they'd gone home with their lips twitching and found a swing-bin liner brimming with empty milk cartons and gnawed fried chicken portions on the front steps and a cowpat of vomit on the pavement, and every day something of that kind had happened, and they'd gone crazy.

We've driven the poor old cows round the twist, Maggie told herself, meaning herself, the pushers, the touts, the pimps, the moneychangers, the black men, the Arabs, the Aussies, the foreign students with their bright orange rucksacks, and Sean, at that time a stranger, who had staggered to the ticket booth and was trying to make himself understood to the Pakistani behind his thick glass grille.

She wasn't living in Earl's Court then, where was she living, oh yes, Maida Vale, not such a posho address as it sounded, it was in her very brief squatting period. Maggie wasn't one of nature's squatters. 'I don't mind hanging my bedsheets out of the window, but I can never think of anything to write on them,' she told anyone who asked what she was whining about. So she'd been flat-hunting and then she'd been on her way to the Half Moon.

Come to think of it, it was that same day, that same evening rather, that someone had told her about the shared room that was going in Islington: so if she'd gone to the Half Moon when she first meant to instead of getting tangled up with Sean, and then gone somewhere else in the evening as she always did because going twice to the same pub on the same day always looked as if nobody loved you, she would probably never have heard about the shared room in Islington and so would have been handed on a plate the once-in-a-lifetime and now lost-for-ever opportunity of never meeting Ken. But if the day hadn't happened at all, if she'd stayed in the squat listening to all those student buskers tune their guitars and watching that face with the hairband paint HOMES NOT OFFICES on every flat surface he could find, she wouldn't have met Sean. And what would she do without Sean?

Maggie wasn't superstitious, although she quite enjoyed the morning Horoscope Half-hour in the Half Moon, when whoever had a newspaper was expected to read out what the stars foretold and everyone had a good chortle. But what she did rather believe in was fate or destiny or whatever you liked to call it. You were allowed to think that you were choosing your own course but in reality you were being corralled along like cattle. Something like that.

Sean had managed to buy his ticket by now but was having trouble getting through the automatic barrier: he was trying to feed his ticket into the slot the wrong way up like a mug-punter down for the Cup Final. But he definitely wasn't a punter, he was a face.

Difference between punters and faces: faces knew their way about, punters didn't. Sean knew his way about, even if at this immediate and precise moment he didn't know what planet he was on. The poncy schmutter might be too pricey —everything Maggie stood up in was v. likely worth less than the label on Sean's blue jeans, and that black cotton top had never seen the inside of an Oxfam shop—but there was no way the King's Road had seen him coming. He had been given that gear as prezzies or a little friend had staked him, you could tell. He was a lend-us-ten-quid face in around two-tons'-worth of gear and about the same round sum in medallions and bracelets.

He looked terrible, as white as a clown. So white that the dribble of saliva trickling down from one corner of his full lips should have left a mark, like tears on face powder. His eyes, which even if this hadn't been one of his off-days must surely still have looked their best behind a pair of shades and clearly rarely saw daylight, were red and marbled. His black hair glistened unhealthily, as if hair could sweat. His sense of balance was shattered: he had to paddle the air with his arms to keep upright, like an amateur tightrope-walker.

Stoned stupid, obviously. Put a kite-string on him and he could fly.

Wrong again, Mags.

He had dropped his ticket on the ground and would have keeled over in his efforts to retrieve it if a turbaned postal worker going off the morning shift hadn't helped him. The postman got him through the ticket barrier and helped him to the lifts. Maggie, dawdling on the concourse so as not to get involved, saw Sean accosting the one or two waiting passengers like a Glasgow drunk, and she saw the postman go down the steps towards the ground-level platforms as if he wanted the District Line, but she bet he really wanted one of the underground Piccadilly Line platforms and was making for the distant escalator beyond the fruit-stall to avoid having to go down in the lift with Sean. She didn't blame him. She was about to do the self-same thing.

Normally, as she was often to remind Sean, if someone had said to Maggie, 'Can you get me to Charing Cross Hospital, it's an emergency,' she would have made an excuse and left. If you did it for one you had to do it for them all. Sean dropped lucky, that was all.

What happened was that a punter who shouldn't have been let out, who thought that Charing Cross Hospital was still at Charing Cross, was trying to put him on the wrong train. As Maggie followed the turbaned postman off the escalator and on to her platform for Leicester Square, this middle-aged business punter with a briefcase—he looked like the kind of geezer who wrote letters to the *Daily Telegraph*, but say this for him, he was the only one who would have anything to do with Sean—had got him to support himself against a chocolate machine and was telling him loudly, as if there was a better chance of getting through to him by shouting: 'Should really be on the District Line and walk up from Embankment! Or change on to Northern Line if you can't manage! Quite a steep hill! Change Northern Line, get out Charing Cross!'

'Can gemme Charing Cross Hospital, emergency?' slurred Sean. That must have been what he'd been repeating, like a mantra, as he was reeling about upstairs.

'Yes, that's what I'm telling you!' bellowed the business punter, who clearly meant to shove Sean into a carriage and then get into a different one himself. Still, that was Good Samaritanism gone raving mad in Earl's Court terms. 'If you want to take this line you'll have to change at Green Park! Jubilee Line! Or change at Piccadilly and it's one stop on the Bakerloo Line!'

His wife probably bought him one of those tube-map tea towels for Christmas, thought Maggie. He learns six new stations every night while he's doing the washing up.

Knows sod-all about London, though.

Nor, apparently, did the other few punters who were drifting about the platform, taking it all in but keeping their distance, including the turbaned postman who'd directed the poor bugger down here in the first place. Either that or they didn't want to know. Neither did Maggie, but someone would have to put him straight.

'He's going the wrong way,' said Maggie.

'So I've been saying! Much quicker on the District Line! But he'd have to be got up to platform one or platform two!'

Though addressing Maggie, the business punter was still shouting, presumably to keep Sean in touch with any developments that might affect him. But if he thought he was going to offload the stupid young sod on Maggie, he had another thing coming.

She didn't know why she was bothering, anyway. Up West was just about the best place for any face on a bad trip to be, if he could get there without flaking out. He'd just have to lie in the middle of Piccadilly Circus and wait for the van, and if he missed it there'd be another one along in a minute.

'He wants to go in the opposite direction,' persisted Maggie. The train was coming in. Maybe there'd be someone getting off it who'd want to help. She'd known stranger things happen.

'No! Embankment! Walk up to Charing Cross or better still take the Northern Line! He wants Charing Cross Hospital!'

'The Charing Cross Hospital's in Hammersmith! It's moved!' Maggie was shouting herself now, against the noise of the train. As for Sean, he didn't seem to be hearing either of them. He was feebly embracing the chocolate machine as if he were its spent lover. His eyes were so wide and still that he looked like a blind man.

The business punter began to make a great production number out of slapping his forehead and saying how stupid he was for forgetting where Charing Cross Hospital was. Maggie glanced towards the train. The doors had hissed open and the few passengers trickling on to the platform were making for any remote exit they could scurry for rather than having to go past the sick-looking face by the one nearest the escalator.

It had taken Maggie only a second to look round but it was one of life's golden moments she had lost to the business punter. Already he was backing away, still babbling his apologies. 'So very stupid of me, I really should have known, *thank goodness* you came along, *could* you take care of him, most kind . . .' and the crafty bugger was on the train.

It moved off. The platform was empty. Sean stirred, as if coming out of sleep. Maggie caught his arm as his long thin legs began to fold up like a whooping crane's.

'Can get me Chair Cross Hoss, mercy?'

Maggie gave the whistling little sigh that acknowledged she had stood for it again. Maggie Muggins, that was her. 'Come on, sunshine.'

What a day.

So. An overdose, wasn't it? Sleeping pills. Your actual stomach-pump job. Bleah.

Maggie could have done without all that, thank you very much, but she really was lumbered this time. Really really lumbered.

It was one of those situations that aren't funny at the time but you laugh at them later, even though they still aren't funny. Sean and she subsequently worked up the events of the day into a twenty-minute act for their own private amusement, using comic voices to exaggerate their encounters with all involved in the saving of Sean's life (including

Maggie herself: Sean did a wicked imitation of Maggie that made her piss herself), and they always ended up falling about. Maggie was aware that on some of these occasions Sean was on the knife-edge of hysteria; probably she was too, but she hid it from herself better. She never had been a one for throwing fits.

She had meant to dump him in Casualty and toe it to the Half Moon for a very long much-needed drink, but getting shot of Sean was like trying to put down a sheet of clingfilm, you pulled it away from one hand and it stuck to the other. Not that Sean himself tried to detain her, he was so far gone that they took one look and wheeled him off at once to do disgusting things to him, but there were index cards to be written on and forms to be filled in and people sitting behind desks to be kept happy, and they seemed to think that Maggie was more involved with him than she was.

Yes, yes, she could just have said she'd found him in the tube station and please could she kept him if he wasn't claimed in ninety days, and then buggered off. But she couldn't do that, they might row Old Bill in if he looked too much like a mystery, and she didn't want to land him in it.

Maggie knew nothing about him except what he'd managed to mumble while she was piling him into the cab she'd been forced to lash out on at Hammersmith Broadway: that his name was Sean, he'd taken these pills, and he didn't want them bothering Lionel.

Lionel, she could never remember his second name, QC or something. Had a flat near The Boltons where Sean, although he still kept on his room in Ladbroke Grove to crawl back to if one of their screaming matches went too far, was more or less living. Had another flat in Brighton where he kept a waiter from one of the posho restaurants down there. Sean hears about waiter and takes pills to scare shit out of Lionel. Lionel supposed to be coming back from Brighton that morning, doesn't turn up. Sean himself now shit-scared, daren't ring for an ambulance and give Lionel's address —apparently Lionel had the habit of thumping him a bit—so staggers down to the Earl's Court tube and into Maggie's arms on platform five.

She met Lionel once, although he had long ago rowed Sean out by then. It was when Sean suddenly decided to become the last of the big spenders and take her on that famous clean weekend to Brighton. Why, knowing Brighton's reputation, she didn't care to ask—it was a bit like taking oil to Newcastle, she thought. Perhaps Sean was hoping to make Lionel jealous.

They went to a party in one of those Regency squares, where Maggie's impression was that she was the only straight face there, not excluding the few other chicks present who mostly turned out not to be chicks at all when you looked at them close up. She wondered if she had stumbled on the origins of the word poufy as applied to gays: half the men there had such puffed-up flesh that you thought it would fall away in flakes. Lionel's features were bronzed but blurred: looked at sideways, he was like a croissant with hair. It came from a lifetime of swigging champagne on verandahs and pulling sailors. He was chatting up some of the rough trade who were the other half of the guests and Sean became very pissed and quarrelsome and got him into one of the bedrooms to pick the bones out of their dead friendship and try to stab him, not very effectively Maggie would have imagined, with a wire coathanger. After that Sean was completely dropped by his upmarket chums and began to spend all his time with the kind of faces Maggie herself mixed with. 'Don't forget,' she would tell him, 'I dragged you down from the gutter.'

The casualty clerk pulled a nice clean card out of a box file, placed it nice and squarely on the desk in front of him and poised his ballpoint expectantly, and Maggie heard herself giving her name and address and telling this pratt that her relationship to Sean was sister.

Well, no one was going to believe she was his bird, were they?

Why she was giving them her real address she would never know, it was not the kind of thing you usually found Maggie doing in circumstances like these. Perhaps she was more unnerved than she thought. Anyway, it didn't matter, the Maida Vale squat wasn't really what you would call a real address, and it would give her all the more incentive for moving on.

What she didn't sus until the clerk started writing it all down was that she was now lumbered all ways up, because she couldn't leave Sean in it, could she? She would somehow have to let him know that he had inherited a sister plus a new surname and change of address. Were there any particular visiting hours for patients who had tried to do away with themselves? Maggie didn't know the form at all.

They kept her hanging about until nearly pub closing-time and then solved the problem for her. A nurse came out to tell her that Sean would be all right but was not a pretty sight just at present, could she come back in the morning with a complete change of gear as he had thrown up all over his top, jeans and sneakers?

And thank *you* very much, said Maggie aloud as she walked out into the unfriendly road.

At any rate it would make a story to tell. You kick off the morning putting some punter right about trains and you end up at Jean Junction buying schmutter for a non-existent brother.

Strangely enough she never told it, not that night in the Half Moon, not ever, except to Sean himself when they went into their act in private. She knew why: too near home. She didn't yet know why he'd taken his overdose but she could guess, it was because he was the kind of person who takes an overdose. Being a potential suicide was enough to make anyone kill himself and it didn't bear talking about over the shepherd's pie at the Half Moon. Definitely a touch of the there but for the grace of Godsville.

She didn't recognise Sean at first, and he didn't recognise her at all, when she trolled back to the hospital with his nice new things in their shiny carrier-bag. That was a good start, considering they were supposed to be practically Siamese twins, but luckily nobody sussed. She told Sean how she came to be there, tarting the story up a bit to make him laugh, and he cried and hugged her.

They were old friends at once. 'It's as if we'd known each other all evening,' mock-marvelled Maggie when he gave her a thank-you dinner at the Italian restaurant in Soho that became 'their place'. Sean knew, and Maggie knew that he knew etc etc etc, that it was more than a quip, she was saying they were on the same wavelength.

They got to know one another. Maggie told Sean nothing at all about her own background and he gave her several versions of his. In all of them he came from a shopkeeping family in Leicester but the shop got smaller or larger according to Sean's mood and what he'd been drinking.

Sometimes there'd been the means to have him privately buggered at a boarding school, sometimes he'd left home at the age of fifteen to lose his own way in the world and had been sleeping rough until a Member of Parliament took up his case in a public lavatory cubicle in King's Cross. 'Down to our last penny, were we?' asked Maggie deadpan, but his only response was to make kissing noises at her, he didn't give a monkey's whether she believed him or not. If she did try to catch him out, just to make him wriggle, he could always make two opposite stories match somehow: yes, poppet, he *had* been a steward on a cruise liner but that was *before* he was Clive's houseboy in Malta—that was how they'd met, surely he'd told that story, about jumping ship?

Maggie didn't give a monkey's either. If nothing he said was completely the truth, nothing was completely a lie either, and anyway he was very droll with it. All he was doing was putting in highlights, touching up, missing out the flat bits, like a painter. Well, Maggie did that too, so did a lot of other people she knew. 'Larger than life,' eavesdroppers might think when they heard the gales of laughter at some of Sean's improbable stories. No, dears, smaller: that was why he had to add the monosodium glutamate.

Without either of them putting anything into words they formulated the ground rules for their friendship.

The first rule was not to intrude. Maggie never called on Sean unexpectedly, nor he on her. They rarely telephoned one another. If either of them vanished for a few days the other was not to ask for an explanation except joshingly—'God, you look terrible, where were you when you needed me?' became one of their catchphrases. Then an account of the absence might be given, but only if it made a good tale.

They hardly ever made a formal arrangement to meet. When they did, perhaps three or four times a year, it was to have dinner at their Italian place when in effect they briefed each other about any important developments in their lives. Only then were they ever allowed to talk seriously—that was the second rule. It was over one of these meals that Maggie told Sean she meant to have Ken's babe, and over several of them that Sean reviewed the ever-changing options that would be open to him if only he could summon the reserves of character needed to change his lifestyle. He never would, of course, and Maggie was selfishly glad of it: she knew that she got from him the inner strength that only a really weak person can give.

The third rule was not to overdo it. Although they saw each other nearly every day, at the Half Moon and such places, it was not usually for very long. A wave, a kiss, a quickie, 'the loan of a quid across a crowded room' as Maggie put it, and they would go their separate ways. Unless.

Unless one of them needed the other, really really needed, no mucking about, and then they used a code. A double code: it had to be deciphered twice. 'You don't feel like coming out to play, do you?' meant 'Let's get monumentally pissed' and that meant 'I need you'. That would happen about once a month. Sometimes, like yesterday and the day before when they had got themselves legless, it was Maggie needing Sean, but more usually it was Sean needing Maggie. Either way round, it did them both good.

'I don't know what we'd both do without a shoulder to piss on,' Maggie said to Sean once, but that didn't mean to say that they whined to one another or that they either asked one another's advice or offered it—rule number four. Each was expected to sense what the trouble was and kiss it better. Since telling Sean her decision about the babe she had never mentioned it again, except when retailing the latest hilarious instalment of her encounters with the Portakabin women. But he knew why she had needed him these last few days, of course he did, and he knew that it wasn't as straightforward as she would have had to make it sound if she'd been made to put it into words.

Sean always knew what was bothering Maggie, even when she didn't know herself, and she always knew what was bothering him, even when he didn't. Partly that was because of the bank of information they'd built up from their occasional briefings at the Italian restaurant, but mainly it was instinct, the shared knowledge about one another's feelings and susceptibilities they'd had from the start.

Maggie had been wondering, between Peter called Simon's place and Putney Bridge station that morning, if you could have that kind of understanding with someone who wasn't gay. If you could be as she and Sean were, and screw one another as well, it would be terrific. Really.

3

The Milk Round

The surge of punters was thinning now and little by little the cast of characters was changing. Maggie watched with the same idle fascination as when she and Sean had watched the ebb-tide on Brighton beach change contours with each receding wave.

More punters with rucksacks, fewer with those flat black executive playboxes, more rolled-up foreign newspapers and fewer *Mails* and *Telegraphs*. A tall blond boy, American or Scandinavian, on roller-skates with fluorescent wheels, a spade chick wearing headphones, a fruitcake with shaved head and Belsen candystripes carrying on his shoulder a gibbering radio receiver in black metal, like a heavy-duty parrot. They didn't fool Maggie, they were still punters. Twenty minutes and half a dozen tube stations from now the spade chick would be answering the intercom on an advertising agency reception desk. And the tall blond boy and the fruitcake were tourists. Welcome to Earl's Court, the gateway to Pizzaland.

The last of the morning crowd buffeted a studenty-looking young man hired by the hour to give out handbills for a carpet sale (rottener job than it looked: Maggie had done it herself when desperate, and she knew he was fighting the urge to shout 'Go on, take one home and shove it up your arse' at the punters who shrugged him off). A breakfasting Aussie dropped a McDonald's carton on a pavement already lapped by a tidal scum of squashed styrofoam, flapping sheets of newspaper, carpet sale handbills scuffed into shreds, and the overspill from the Keep Earl's Court Tidy litter bins. The first of the crazy old ladies walked her dog past, mouthing her disgust. A commuting Paki moved cross-grain through the rearguard of late late typists to place an empty Fanta can very carefully on the telephone-directory shelf of one of the battery of phone booths scrawled with rent boys' numbers, where Maggie had taken refuge.

V. useful public service, that bank of phone booths. When one of the blowers rang you saw punters looking startled, they had never rumbled the pay-phone's potential for incoming as well as outgoing calls. The form was that, say, if you were advertising an old van for sale or you were looking for a fourth on an overlander to India, you nicked one of the galleria numbers, 'ring afternoons only'. Saved the expense of a permanent address.

Henry's personal blower, keeping him in touch with his spider's web of flatlets and roomlets, was the end booth nearest the street where Maggie had installed herself to ask him, when he had a free minute, if there'd been any calls. He didn't like taking messages for other faces, thought it a diabolical liberty in fact, but he would make an exception for a mate. Maggie would rather not have been his mate, there was a lot that was bleah about Henry, but it did save her having to give anyone the Balmoral Gardens number.

She had sighted him across the galleria: he was chatting up two chicks who had staggered up off the Piccadilly Line with Heathrow tags on their luggage. That was their first mistake: Henry thought all air passengers were rich. If they had come over on the ferry, or pretended to Henry that they had come over on the ferry, he would have recommended somewhere a bit cheaper. Not smaller, cheaper: even if they'd flown in on Concorde they were still about to wake up tomorrow morning thinking they had spent the night inside their own suitcases. He was probably sending them to that rabbit-warren in the Cromwell Road that Maggie had christened the Samsonite Light-weight Hilton.

Henry clocked her and gave the curtest of nods. Message. Hang about, Maggie.

There was one amenity the galleria lacked and that was lavs. You would have thought that London pigging Transport could have run to a Ladies, considering all the punters dying to spend a penny they must be shipping backwards and forwards every day of the week. Maggie was beginning to wish she had gone, properly gone, when she'd had the chance back at Peter called Simon's. She would just grab a quick word with Henry and then whizz round to Balmoral Gardens and stage a little sit-in with her crossword book. Or not: the urge sometimes wore off if you left it long enough. Bit like sex, really.

Wanting to go apart, Maggie had started to feel a bit better—not a lot better, considering what day it was, but a bit. Her bijou excursionette from Putney Bridge had quite perked her up. She was very fond of that stretch of line: it was almost like a country railway, with the open-air platforms and their fretworked wooden canopies like market town halts. Of course, the Steeple Bumpsted effect at Putney Bridge had been rather spoiled by the chalked blackboard notice in the old-fashioned booking hall: *Trains subject to delay due to* BODY ON LINE AT FULHAM BROADWAY. Now that was the kind of treatette they didn't give you on the Bluebell Line. It was last night's notice, not this morning's, they just hadn't got round to rubbing it out yet, but Maggie did wish they wouldn't do that, it would have fair brought up her breakfast if she'd had any. Trains subject to delay due to ACCIDENT would have been more than enough, thank you very much.

She wished she hadn't remembered that, it made her tiny upsurge of high spirits sink again like a soufflé left out on a window-sill.

Maggie still hadn't mapped her day out properly apart from what she knew had to be done, and she began to consider the case for investing her twenty-quid windfall from Sean's Irish friend on getting, if not roaring pissed once again, then in the region of feeling-no-painsville and perhaps a shade legless by nightfall.

There were things to be said for this plan and things against it. In favour, she needed to get pissed today of all days; she certainly couldn't see herself sitting face to face with Miss Roberts or whoever in that portable welfare echo-chamber stone-cold sober. Not this time. Plus, she needed to get pissed for the third day running because of the depression caused by getting pissed for two days running.

But she could make out just as strong a case for remaining vertical, if she worked on it. One, she didn't want to be slurring her words again when she met her Dad off the Doncaster train after lunch, not that she had anything to say to him that wouldn't sound better slurred. Two, there was no one she felt like getting legless with except Sean, and it really would be a case of the gone too fars to make him come out to play for three days on the trot. Three, it would leave her skint for the weekend unless she did some grafting tomorrow, and if she went on getting legless she was going to feel less and less like grafting, which was never the strongest of Maggie's impulses to begin with. Four, not that she blamed herself but wasn't she overdoing the elbow-lifting of late?

Maybe she should keep her head down and do the milk round today. She'd been promising herself for a while to get the milk round done again and there would never be a better day for it. Or how about doing some grafting? Bad thinking: if she went anywhere near the Portobello it would be all round to Henekey's with tongue hanging out before they had even opened the doors.

No, the milk round. Keep her nose clean.

Maggie wasn't too concerned about her drinking. She had no real fear of becoming an alcoholic, she couldn't afford it with the price of vodka as it was. Anyway, she was never home long enough. (Maggie believed that although drink might become a problem in time, it would never become a problem-problem unless she started knocking it back on her lonesome, like Riggsy.)

It did bother her what she might be doing to her guts. She really ought to start eating more—if you got a good knife-and-forker down you every day to line your stomach, it was supposed to be far less damaging. And she would have to start worrying one of these days about what she was doing to her looks. Weight was no problem: she could sink a barrel of Guinness a day and they'd still be able to use her to rod out drains with, but it went to your face in time. It already had. That flush around the cheekbones, which sometimes prompted people who didn't know her to ask if she spent most of her life in the country, was nothing more nor less than boozer's rash.

She would go like Riggsy in the end.

In the end? How old was Riggsy? Fifty? Maggie would be her dead ringer at forty unless she did something about it.

Raddled: stupid word, it was one of those got-it-out-of-a-book words that didn't ring true, like blanched, faltered, apoplectic, dour, but it was what Riggsy was, she was raddled. She had the kind of lines on her face that made it look not so much lived in as slept in.

At forty, looking raddled, Maggie would be, like Riggsy, the woman you always saw perched on the high stool at the end of the bar, chainsmoking through a holder and flashing too much leg and swigging her 'usual'; and everybody was darling, and it was always her birthday, and she was the last of the peroxide blondes, and she talked in such an exaggerated, dated drawl that it was like pulling a Mars Bar apart, the syllables stretching out in long glucose strands; and no one knew for certain how many times she'd been married but she certainly wasn't now; and she knew all the doormen and half the waiters and most of the guvnors in the West End; and to look at her once you would think how sophisticated she was and later tonight she'd very likely be propping up a gaming table or getting groped under a pink tablecloth by a punter down for the Motor Show—but to look at her twice you could tell that she would be going home to a gasfire and her moth-eaten night-club teddy bears with a quarter bottle in a paper bag, and ringing up the phone-in programmes and rambling on in her Mars Bar voice about immigrants or bus conductors' manners or any bloody rubbish that came into her head just so long as they didn't hang up on her, because she was lonely, and too raddled to be anybody's or even everybody's any more.

Yes. V. strong argument for the milk round today.

The two chicks from Heathrow, looking like the Babes in the Wood with luggage, were catching shins on the dented corners of their suitcases as they zig-zagged off along the Earl's Court Road with their faces buried in their Visitors' Map of London where Henry had marked the route to some rat-trap hotel. He was sauntering across to Maggie now, though still keeping a swivelling eye open for potential trade.

God, he really was a seedy bugger, was Henry, in spite of his flashy turnout. No, not in spite of, because of: that thick coating of smarm served only to preserve and contain and reveal the inner seediness. Under the black sucked-licorice hair, the grey nailbrush 'tache, the gold tooth, the bow tie, the velvet collar, the pongy aftershave, the tin cufflinks and the two-tone shoes, there was a man who slept in his underpants. Another bet you could make on Henry was that he never pulled the chain when he came out of the lav. Still, he had his uses.

Henry didn't waste his bad breath on wishing her good morning, just gave her a quick flash of his gold tooth as if it were something he was exposing on a canal bank. 'Tone get you, did he?'

Tony who ran the Waiters' Club on Gloucester Road. 'When, yesterday? No, I was out all day.'

Leered, that was another of those words like raddled. Henry leered. Maggie could feel him mentally running his hand up and down her bum. Bleah.

He was trying to think up something suggestive but witty. 'Out, was you? Not the story I heard,' was the best he could do without the usual month's notice.

Maggie gave Henry her har-har look. 'Does he want me to ring him?'

'Yeah, give him a bell.'

It was really nice of Tony to do his Ansaphone bit for her, seeing that Maggie didn't go in the Waiters' from one week's end to the next. She ought to start going in there more often, give the Half Moon a rest, break her routine, it would do her good. And she could try out the high stool at the end of the bar for size.

The message would be from her Dad, confirming his train arrangements as he always did, you would think he was arriving from Vladivostok instead of a hundred and seventy miles up the road. If it wasn't her Dad she couldn't think who it might be, he was the only one who ever rang her at the Waiters'. She'd given him that number rather than the Half Moon or the Leather Bottle or any one of a dozen other haunts or God Forbid the Balmoral Gardens number, because the Waiters' Club kept peculiar hours and Tony wouldn't mind answering the blower at three or four in the morning, the time Maggie was convinced men of her Dad's age were most likely to be wheeled into the intensive-care unit with heart attacks. Balmoral Gardens, she'd persuaded her Dad, wasn't on the phone: it would only have needed some starch-arsed night nurse reporting back to him that they'd rung his daughter and apparently she was still out on the tiles, and they might as well switch off the oxygen and put pennies on his eyes.

Maybe it wasn't about his train arrangements at all, maybe he'd had his heart attack. (Maggie thought of 'his' heart attack, or sometimes for a change 'his' stroke, as if it had already been booked and confirmed like a package holiday, and all that had to be done now was to wave him off. There was no history of heart disease in the family.)

No. Tony would have mentioned it to Henry, and Henry would have got a big kick out of telling her himself. He liked nothing better than being first with the bad news. (But would it be bad news? She wouldn't know until she got it. When her Mum died she had felt a bit wretched, and a bit scared at death being so close to home, but mainly relieved. It was one more burden off her shoulders: Maggie liked travelling light.)

She gave Tony a bell.

The line was terrible; like all the galleria's pay-phones, it was as if it was still plugged in to some rucksack-gastropod's reverse-charge call to Melbourne. Honestly, Maggie would have been better off climbing on the tube station roof with a couple of flags and trying to get through by semaphore.

'Sorry, Tone, we've got a crossed line with a chip-pan on fire, what's that again?'

Father . . . later train . . . cccrrrsssppp . . .

'Didn't quite get it, Tony, which later train again?'

Pppsssrrrccc fifty-scccrrr . . .

'Which fifty what?'

One. Three ssspppprrrccc, gets in rrrssscccppp . . .

Three fifty-one train gets in five-fifty, or did the last time he caught it when she'd had to maroon herself in the Odeon Westbourne Grove till half-past five for fear of acquiring slurred speech in the afternoon drinking-clubs. Bugger.

'Bless you, Tony. Cheers.'

And Maggie . . . cccrrrsssppp . . .

'What?'

Sorry about pppsssrrrccc . . .

'Can't hear you, Tone. All this crackling.'

About ssspppprrrccc. Dreadfully rrrssscccppp.

Dreadfully sorry about something. Who dreadfully worry? Dad, could be, for being such a pain in the arse, but she would never know now because the pips were peeping and she had no more small change and Henry wouldn't give her the time of day without a quick grope, never mind five pee. Anyway, he was chatting up another prospect. Never interrupt Henry when he was chatting up a prospect.

Five-fifty this afternoon. Afternoon? Night, practically. Bugger bugger bugger.

The briefest whiff of Henry's bad breath, the dirty sod had been standing so close he'd practically had his tongue down her throat, had induced in Maggie a strong need to wash her mouth out with vodka and tonic. He usually did have that effect. And anyway, sod the milk round, she wanted a drink. She didn't mean to get legless, promise. Just a few sly ones before going into the Portakabin—God, she was making it sound like the gas chamber—and a few sly ones when she came out. Pace it very steady. Glass of wine, pub lunch, then knock it on the head. Tube of Polo mints, swift cab to King's Cross, and remember not to slur.

Bugger. Pacing her drinks was one thing but she couldn't be expected to make a bloody funeral march of it. If she started gulping them down this morning there was no way she wouldn't be in falling-aboutsville by ten to six. Bugger bugger bugger shit bugger. This really did put the hermetically sealed tin lid on it.

The milk round, there was nothing else for it.

When Maggie told people she had been doing her milk round they usually took it to be her fancy way of saying she'd been spending a day on the wagon. It could mean that, though it didn't necessarily, and it never meant only that. Sean was the only one who knew (because she'd once taken him on it and far from keeping out of mischief they had turned it into a gigantic metropolitan pub-crawl) that the milk round was for real, if you didn't take the milk too literally.

Postman's knock would have been a better name for it. She did it every six months or so and it was a grand tour of most of the permanent addresses she'd had since coming to London, or such of them as were still standing, with the object of picking up her accumulated mail.

Whenever Maggie moved she never left a forwarding address. She found it more convenient to keep the address to herself and make her own arrangements.

The milk round was far more nearly foolproof than anyone who hadn't tested it could imagine. In all the wasps' nests of half-room 'flatlets' and 'studio apartments' that Maggie and her kind had lived in, there was always a communal entrance hall with a cheapo table or sometimes no more than a shelf, where letters and bills and brochures and trade cards for twenty-four-hour emergency plumbers were scattered in gritty little heaps. Every once in a blue moon the housekeeper or caretaker or even a disgusted tenant might make a clean sweep of the junk mail when taking a brush to the stairs and hallway; but proper letters, lettery-looking letters, stayed there for months, years. These places were always run by foreigners who were terrified of tampering with 'Her Majesty's mails' by putting them in the dustbin, but too bone-idle or ignorant to scribble 'Gone away' across them and bung them in a pillar-box. Maggie had recovered letters over a year old on her milk round. You just walked in and helped yourself. If the door was locked—it rarely was—you unlocked it. Lesson one for anyone about to live in London: never give up a front door key, or not until you've had it copied. Maggie by now had a bunch of keys in her shoulder-bag to rival a Holloway wardress's.

She had been operating the scheme since the year dot. It had started when Maggie moved out of the first room she had ever had in London, in St. John's Wood she would have you know. Nor was the posho address the postal equivalent of just a pretty face: it was a proper block of flats with a proper porter, the only purpose-built flat she had ever lived in, except of course that many years after being purpose-built it had been purpose-rebuilt, so that what had been a spacious company pied-à-terre for dirty executives to bring their mistresses to had become a crowded 'business-girls'' apartment for five sharing. Maggie had chanced by a vacancy on the friend-of-a-friend-of-a-friend network but she couldn't take the girls' dorm atmosphere with everyone forever ironing and giggling and taking one another's phone calls and covering up for each other with Roger or Nigel and leaving little balls of hair in the sink; and so she found a back basement off North Gower Street, more of a cellar really, and gave the Chums of St. Hilda's a month's notice. But she found it prudent not to pass the news on to her Mum, who was already sending her long whingeing letters about eating properly and not taking drugs and not looking on the Pill as a licence to get screwed, and who would whinge even more if she knew that her dear little Margaret was no longer shacked up with those nice centrally-heated friends of Fiona Tightbum but was living on spoonfuls of cold baked beans in the white slave belt. Far easier to call in at St. Hilda's once a fortnight, bung the porter a packet of ciggies, and extract Mum's latest whingeing letter from his nest of pigeon-holes.

It worked like clockwork until the Chums started taking the hump at Maggie ringing up to ask if there were any messages. 'Your Mama rang again and I told her you'd gone off with a black man,' said the Chum who answered Maggie's final call. The cow wasn't joking, either. But if you didn't let people know your home phone number, and Maggie was very picky about whom she gave it to after that, the embryo milk round idea was worth developing.

Its potential dawned on her fully when she came to leave North Gower Street for Camden Town. Maggie's standing with her bank was not such that she could be confident of her account being successfully transplanted to another branch. She decided not only to leave it where it lay but not to trouble the manager with her new address in case of future nastiness about her overdraft. For the next two years, until the house was pulled down, she went back periodically to collect her bank statements plus the occasional chilly request to call in and get her account sorted out. On her final visit, when there was a sheet of corrugated iron where the front door had been, she found a thank-you-Maggie-and-good-riddance letter from her bank manager among the top layer of plasterboard and dog-eared telephone directories in the demolition skip. Nice touch.

In Camden Town Maggie ponced unemployment pay and supplementary benefits for a while: a third-floor room that was now mercifully a heap of bricks and laths remained her address for the benefit of those social security investigators you read about in The Screws Of The World, who were supposed to pop up on your doorstep with binoculars around their necks. Two other homes in Camden Town—Château Despair East and Château Despair West as she had since dubbed them—still yielded the odd long-time-no-see post-card from faces long married and moved on, who'd known her in those days. She was doing her old mates a favour in never sending out change-of-address cards: think of the mess the M pages of their little black books would be in by now.

Each passing address held a small walk-on part in her life. Moving to Chalk Farm for a while she went raving mad and filled in a tax return; she was still there so far as the Inland

Revenue were concerned. She let whoever dealt with her National Insurance go on sending their stiff little reminders to Chalk Farm too: even though it had become too dodgy these days not to buy their bloody stamps at the death, it comforted Maggie to know that they couldn't find her if they came looking for her.

So it went on. The milk round grew and grew. New addresses were added as Maggie hopped from one neighbourhood to another, and a few of the older ones were dropped as the purpose of revisiting them became obsolescent.

Maggie's motives for building up her milk round were varied and sometimes shadowy. There were some places, such as a briefly-occupied room in Paddington that was her last recorded abode on a TV rental agreement, which she preferred to keep an eye on in case of any unpleasantness that might be brewing: if there was a summons in the offing she would sooner pay up than have it hanging over her, for the thought of someone glooming around the West End hoping to push a blue paper into her hand gave her the horrors. One or two former pads she kept in touch with because you never knew, there might be a windfall: an income tax rebate in Chalk Farm, ho ho likely story, or her premium bond coming up in Notting Hill. As often as not her motivation would be what her Mum had always called 'simple idleness' but which Maggie had argued was never as simple as that, because it took twice as much effort not to do some of the things she hadn't done as it would have taken to do them. Perversely, she had waited until she moved to her most inaccessible address ever, on 'the wrong side of Shepherds Bush' as she obscurely called the area, before getting round to registering with a doctor: it was a great drag traipsing down there but it would have been even more of a drag to go through the hassle of re-registering and filling up forms. So that remained her address for matters of life and death, except attempted self-inflicted death, for which she had registered at Parsons Green.

The milk round itself could be called a drag, if she wanted to look at it in that light. By now she had more calls to make than a flaming rent collector, and it cost a fortune in tube fares. But it suited her. She could cover her tracks, compartmentalise her life. And it kept her mobile. Having roots isn't for me, Maggie had decided: I'd rather have branches.

Henry had drawn a blank with his prospect and was rabbiting to a rent boy who sometimes hung around the galleria. Probably quoting him a rate for a broom-cupboard by the hour, standing room only.

The boy drifted away and Henry came over and leaned familiarly against the hood of the phone booth where Maggie was studying small parallelograms of flesh in her seven-years-bad-luck mirror. An Indian punter was waiting to use the blower but sod him, and anyway, if the bloody thing couldn't cope with plain doorstep English, think what it was going to do to Hindustani.

'Do I look a sight?' she asked Henry. She didn't feel a sight: she'd had a cat-lick at Peter called Simon's and put some more slap on. Her hair was too short and straight ever to look a complete mess: could do with a wash, she supposed, but even a Vidal full-treatment blow-dry wouldn't stop her Dad asking where she was playing principal boy this year. One of his five jokes.

She didn't need to go to the lav any more, it was passing off true to form, but while in the area shouldn't she go home and have a go at going just to show willing, and while she was about it, change? But what into? She had nothing that would make her look like the girl on the Ovaltine tin, which was Dad's idea of high fashion. Not that her own idea of high fashion was all that many rungs up from his. The one question Maggie asked herself when buying clothes was: if you go out in it tomorrow morning and don't get home till Friday, will it have bagged at the seat?

Some people, to name but Sean, thought she could look quite smart when she wanted to. Others didn't. Once when she'd met her Dad at King's Cross he'd said: 'Oh, there you are. I thought you were one of the porters.' That was that squashed peak cap she used to wear. She had a good mind to dash back to Balmoral Gardens and put it on, if she could find it.

'Yeah—sight for sore eyes,' Henry managed to come up with, after struggling for an appropriate gallantry. Still, ask a silly question.

'Do I look as if I've been up all night?'

'Up who?'

Gone too far, Henry. Maggie didn't like that kind of banter, even when she indulged in it herself. She sometimes thought she could be a bit of a prude if she worked at it.

'Ask a silly question,' she murmured, aloud this time, and hitched the strap of her bag up over her shoulder.

Bugger the squashed peak cap and bugger going home. Maggie delved into her bag for her tube fare. It would have to be one of the tenners Sean's Irish mate had won for her. A good thing that horse had come up or it would have been a case of hoofing it down to the Portobello and tapping someone.

Come on, Henry, on your bicycle. There was no way she was going to squeeze out of the phone booth and brush her tits against his sleeve, so he could take that look off his boatrace.

Wrong again, Mags, it wasn't that look, it was another look. Suppressed excitement. Henry's bad news look.

Fractionally jerking his head towards where the rent boy had been standing, Henry murmured in the conspiratorial tones of one face to another: 'Just had a word with Barry. *You* knew Sean, didn't you? Shocking.'

Knew. Past tense. Shocking.

About ssspppprrrccc. Dreadfully rrrssscccppp. About Sean. Dreadfully sorry.

He's killed himself. Again.

What a pity she couldn't have heard it from Tony, instead of this creep. Why couldn't they ever get these sodding phones mended and keep them mended?

Maggie didn't want to ask Henry what had happened, not because she didn't want to know what had happened but because she resented him standing there like an undertaker's mute waiting for his tip and willing her, forcing her to ask.

After the quick lurch of dread, that was her first emotion: resentment against Henry. That and the banal thought that persisted: if the phone had been working properly I could have heard it from Tony.

She managed 'What—?' and the rest of the words slid up and down her throat like regurgitated gristle.

Henry sighed elaborately, corrugating his brow and permitting himself a slight just-one-of-those-things wag of the head. 'Went under a tube, story Barry's heard. Fulham

Broadway, midnight last night. Pissed out of his skull, apparently.'

Trains subject to delay due to BODY ON LINE AT FULHAM BROADWAY.

She hadn't asked if he was dead, she wasn't going to ask if he was dead, of course he was dead, she didn't want any more details.

Henry was saying something else. '. . . practically cut in two, apparently. Still, couldn't have felt nothing. Out of his tiny Chinese.'

You bastard, you're enjoying this. You really want to spin it out, don't you? And why did you make me wait for it, why did you let me rabbit on about bugger-all then chuck it at me like an afterthought? You were saving it till last, like a kid with the biggest strawberry, weren't you?

No, that wasn't fair. Henry didn't know she'd spent the last two days with Sean, didn't know what good mates they were, didn't know even that they knew each other all that well, why should he? He would have seen them having a drink together in the Waiters' once or twice, but so what? Maggie must have had a drink with a dozen faces in there and Sean was just another face. Faces died all the time, they took overdoses, got cancer, crashed cars, fell under trains or out of windows, had heart attacks, got mugged, set their beds on fire, electrocuted themselves, gassed themselves, drank Paraquat, drowned, got run over, they shot themselves and occasionally each other, and it was just a thrill of gossip that enlivened the day; and tomorrow there would be something else to talk about, a small wave following the big one, then another small wave and another and then another big wave. She couldn't blame Henry, it was the best offer he was going to get all week.

Why was she thinking about Henry, resenting Henry, hating Henry, blaming Henry and then not blaming Henry?

So as not to think about Sean.

Body on line at Fulham Broadway. Pissed out of his skull, apparently. And who got him pissed out of his skull?

What was he doing at Fulham Broadway? Was he going home? Was his Irish mate with him? Why did his Irish mate let him fall?—he wasn't half as pissed as Maggie and Sean had been.

He didn't fall under that train. Sean never fell under

trains. Even when he took his overdose, when he was a zillion times worse than legless, he didn't fall under a train.

There would be an inquest, she would have to give evidence. If they could find her. Was she in Sean's address book?

She still wasn't thinking about Sean, she was thinking about herself.

Maggie needed a drink. She said something to Henry, she didn't know what she said, just a breathed word, 'Terrible' or 'Shocking' or 'Kiss my arse' for all she knew, and brushed past him, brushed her tits against his sleeve, and went out of the galleria and stood under the blue glass canopy over the stretch of pavement she called the piazza and stared across the Earl's Court Road at the bread shop opposite, thinking 'Bread shop'.

If she had a drink now she would fall under a tube train.

Today of all bloody days, Sean. As if she hadn't enough on her plate.

Practically cut in two, apparently.

Bleah.

Oh shit.

Oh God.

Oh fucking hell.

Oh Sean.

Oh dear.

Oh Jesus.

Oh Christ.

Oh no.

Oh. Oh. Oh. Oh. Oh. Oh.

4

Just Not Her Day

There was Big John down the Chelsea Flea Market, there was that chick behind the bar at Kemble's Club who'd thought she was going to marry a film producer after he got his divorce, there was Vic in the front basement at Chalk Farm, there was what was her bloody name now, never out of the Leather Bottle at one time, always used to buy her dachshund a packet of crisps, anyway her. Hanged herself. Mary.

Maggie was counting all the suicides she'd known personally. Including doubtful cases, where no one would ever know whether they had meant to wake up next day or not, she could think of fifteen. Sean would make sixteen, whatever the inquest verdict.

That crazy old sod in North Gower Street, light years ago, who chucked his bike in the Regent's Canal and then climbed in after it, he was another one, seventeen.

Molly, or was it Polly? Used to do the sandwiches in that coaching-inn-looking boozer up Highbury, the one there was all the stink about when they pulled it down. Razor blade in the bath, that one. Bleah. Eighteen.

Oh yes, and Maggie herself. Eighteen and a half.

A fruitcake in dinner-jacket, jeans and ruffled shirt with a Paisley cravat secured by a cameo brooch was staring dead-eyed at her across the carriage, his earring bobbing with every lurch of the tube-train as it rattled through the electrified catacombs of Kensington. Maggie stared unblinkingly back, thinking: 'And *you* look overdue for the marble slab to me, chucky-egg. Between us, we could bring the score up to the round twenty before nightfall.'

Poor Sean. He'd always worn an earring too till Maggie told him it made him look like a woofter.

'But demented little kitten, I *am* a woofter! The whole world *knows* I'm a woofter!'

'Not the *point*, Sean. The whole world knows I'm a slag but I don't ponce up and down Old Compton Street with a silver chain round my ankle.'

Sean surprised her by slapping her face, quite hard. The next second he was hugging her, his wet cheek to her wet cheek. Then, sniffling and gulping, he was wagging his finger at her and admonishing her, in a voice that was supposed to be mock-stern but which he couldn't keep from breaking: '*Nobody* gets away with calling Maggie Muggins a slag. Not even Maggie Muggins.'

Quite right, Sean. Quite right.

She licked her finger and gently dabbed at his cheekbone where her eye-make-up had rubbed off, and after a bit of gulping said softly, her voice breaking too: 'Who's a silly bugger, then?'

Sean took a deep, brave breath and gave her a watery smile. 'Ah, now that's different. You can call yourself a silly bugger as often as you please.'

Two silly buggers, by dawn's early light, and too raving pissed to say good night. It was a long time ago now.

Eighteen suicides was a lot. What percentage, though, would it be of all the people Maggie had ever known —wouldn't that put it into perspective? If she had a pocket calculator and was riding round and round on the Circle Line instead of the Edgware Road branch of the District Line where she would have to get off in a couple of minutes, she could probably come up with the answer.

Say it was as low as nought point one—and even that seemed on the high side when you thought of all the alternative methods of dying, not to mention the great majority of friends and acquaintances who tended not to be dead at all. That would mean knowing what, eighteen thousand faces by name. Ridiculous.

All right then, say she knew eighteen hundred by name, which was pushing it. It came out at one per cent. High.

Maggie often did calculations of this sort in her head, and whether she was totting up the number of real one-hundred-proof drunks she could name or the number of faces who'd had abortions or been divorced or finished up inside or were obviously mainlining like the fruitcake opposite, her conclusion was always conventionally the same: 'Bloody terrifying.' Privately, though, very privately, few of these lurid statistics frightened her at all, truth to tell she could be quite blasé about them. 'If you can't take a joke, you shouldn't have joined,' Maggie would tell herself. And they did separate the faces from the punters, say what you like. If Doncaster had boasted a suicide rate of one percent or over, would she ever have left it?

Stop it, Mags. Not funny.

One sum she would never do, unlike some chicks she could mention who kept meticulous tallies and got positively turned on by reaching whatever pin-table score they were aiming for, was to tot up all the guys she'd ever laid. She'd started to work it out ages ago, just out of curiosity, but had given up at the fifty mark because it was beginning to sound vulgar. As an antidode, Maggie had then started to add up all the guys who had never got to first base with her and she was very quickly into three figures, if you counted block bookings like the theatre companies she'd met at backstage parties. The result pleased her, she'd felt quite a virgin for the rest of the day.

Well, then, maybe she ought to be concentrating on all the faces who hadn't killed themselves instead of the eighteen who had. Think positive.

That wasn't going to get her very far. Maggie thought and thought and she couldn't think of anyone she knew who didn't qualify for instant suicide, with herself at the top of the list. If they all really faced up to their inadequacies there would be so many of them jumping off Chelsea Bridge that the Town Hall would be sounding flood warnings. The only difference between them and Sean was that Sean had taken the plunge and they hadn't.

The train emerged from the labyrinth of shunting-yards beneath the mansion flats of Kensington and swayed between smoked brick cliffs into Notting Hill Gate. The fruitcake opposite Maggie got up in a sleepwalking way, breaking her abstracted stare. She too rose, for the first time taking in the other few passengers. The usual collection of weirdos and loonies you got on this bit of line: an African laughing raucously to himself and slapping his thigh, a twitching dwarf who was often to be seen in Gloucester Road directing traffic, a rich-kid punk chick in Charlie Chaplin gear, and one of the Old Brompton Road memsahibs who looked as if she would have everyone in the carriage gassed if she could have her way.

Maggie asked herself why she was bothering her head about the high suicide rate among her friends: there probably wasn't a single soul on this train who wouldn't be better off under it. The whole town was full of misfits; at least the ones she happened to know socially didn't charge through the streets waving their arms about.

The train was gliding off into the canyons of Bayswater before Maggie realised that she had stepped off it and was aimlessly pacing the platform, as if waiting for the next. Then, for a second, she thought she was in Paddington, which was where she had been intending to get off. It was because the arched glass roof over the District Line platforms at Notting Hill Gate had a mini-Paddington look about it. This was yet another station, or anyway this part of it was, that looked like a proper railway station, but a town one, not a country one like Putney Bridge. It wasn't all that high on Maggie's list but she was quite fond of it.

But she had meant to leave Notting Hill out of her milk round. Bar her six-monthly dental check-up reminder, which would remind her only of that one petrified visit to the dentist the time she broke her tooth, there would be nothing for her unless by a zillion-to-one chance her premium bond had come up. Maggie hadn't read her stars that morning but somehow she doubted that it would be a day when Lady Luck smiled on Sagittarians. What really was all too likely, though, was that she would run into someone who'd heard about Sean. Notting Hill was very much Sean's patch, not to mention her own from a grafting point of view. She wouldn't want to be cornered by some bloodthirsty face wanting to hold a blow-by-blow autopsy. Couldn't be doing with that. Not now, not ever. He was dead. Finish.

Another train had pulled in. The punters on it looked even madder than those on the one she'd just left.

Bugger it, she was here now. And the Paddington-type roof really did look nice with the watery sunshine trying to get in through its murky glass. Maggie felt a momentary flicker of the small exuberance that Putney Bridge had aroused in her that morning. A feeling of—what? Anticipation, was the nearest she could get to it. The feeling that something exciting might happen.

Trains subject to delay due to BODY ON LINE.

No, not that. Finish. Something nice, exciting. Promise—that was the word. The sun on the arched glass roof promised something.

Well yes, ducky, it was to be supposed it did: it promised the sight of Notting Hill flaming Gate, didn't it?

Never mind. Maggie knew what she meant even if nobody else did. And there were worse places to arrive at than Notting Hill Gate. At least you *could* arrive at it, and by three different tube lines at that. There were some places in London that you could reach only by changing buses twice and then phoning for a mini-cab.

Maggie would agree that she had got practically everything wrong that could be got wrong in her life, but the one thing she had got right was deciding never to live anywhere that couldn't be reached by tube, and furthermore never to live south of the river, further north than Kentish Town, further west than Hammersmith, nor further east than the Angel, Islington. She'd lapsed but once, in her wrong-side-of-Shepherds-Bush period, and loathed it. Hated the zombie lines of stamping feet at forlorn and freezing bus-shelters, with the sodium lamps turning everyone's lips purple if the frost hadn't got there first. Bleah. Not her style.

Nowadays Maggie might claim that it was that experience that had sparked off her deep affection for tube stations. But it wasn't really, there was a much soppier reason for it. She had told only Sean, who knew at once what she was talking about because he had been smitten the same way. It went back to her first visit to London on a school trip when she was fifteen, and she'd been enchanted to find that beneath King's Cross Station there was another King's Cross Station with sleek red trains that would carry you off under the streets to exciting-sounding places such as The Strand and Surrey Docks. It was like being let in on a big secret and she'd been a bit potty about tube stations ever since.

Well, perhaps not about all of them: there were tube stations she knew and could not love, like some of the outlying Central Line ones where she'd occasionally found herself: they looked like pre-war vacuum-cleaner factories.

You walked out of one of those stations and found yourself on a shopping parade with mums carting sets of twins about in double-fronted pushchairs, grovelling news vendors with rosebuds in their buttonholes giving change for telephone calls, and kids in grey flannel blazers buying giant-size iced lollies that were supposed to resemble moon-rockets but which looked to Maggie more like vibrators on sticks. Perhaps the little sods got down behind the privet hedges with them.

No: Maggie's idea of a tube station was one that decanted you—either via a clattering flight of metal-tipped wooden stairs or a miners'-cage-type lift with a disembodied voice telling you to stand clear of the gates—on to a ratbag London thoroughfare with a Salvation Army citadel on the corner and a hardware shop opposite where you might see your future landlord browsing among the sheets of chipboard and plywood and cheapo light-fittings. As for the news vendors, they had big chalked signs up: NO INFORMATION OF ANY KIND GIVEN or THIS IS NOT A CHANGE KIOSK. They gave Maggie a warm feeling inside, those signs did. (People thought she was joking when she said that. But she meant it. It was London's unfriendliness that had first appealed to her. She took to it at once, and it fitted her like a mask.)

She didn't mind the flashier, big-production-number tube stations like Piccadilly and Leicester Square, with their stairway-to-heaven escalators that should have had Fred Astaire and Ginger Rogers swanning up and down them, but she used those only when she was going to or coming back from base. They weren't for living with, or on. The ones Maggie felt most at home with had scratched, varnished woodwork, like the captain's cabin on a disreputable tramp-steamer, and corridors of tiles in different colours according to what line they were on. Her favourite was Camden Town with its tiles in blue and white: it looked like a great underground Express Dairy.

It was Sean, not Maggie, who had made that comparison, when she'd taken him on the milk round that day. And the dairy-cool look of the tiles on a hot afternoon had aroused in Maggie such a tremendous longing for icecream that despite or perhaps because of being three-parts cut, she made him take her all the way back to Chalk Farm where they'd just that minute come from, and buy her some at Marine Ices no less, none of your sweetie-shop freezer rubbish.

'That's a symptom if ever was, deary,' said Sean knowingly. Then, clapping a hand to his forehead as if smitten by a tragic thought, he shrieked, 'My Gaaad! It'll be craving lumps of coal next!' This was only a few days after she'd told him she was pregnant. He was the first of her mates to know and he was still full of it, bless his cotton knickers. To the point of boredomsville in fact: earlier on the milk round there'd been sharp words about Maggie smoking. Just because she'd asked him to help her cut down, there was no need for him to carry on as if he were the pigging father, that really was taking his responsibilities too far.

But you had to hand it to Sean. Once he got going he got going. By the time they got back to Chalk Farm he had developed his pregnancy-symptoms conceit to such a point of silliness, asking after her back pains and pretending to support her because of her poor little weak ankles, that Maggie was in stitches. As he propelled her out of the tube station lift and she collapsed with laughter against the brown wood-panelled wall, Sean begged bystanders to take no notice, it was just her morning sickness coming on—the poor dear never got it till four in the afternoon because she was a very late riser. In the icecream parlour he made a great camped-up song-and-dance about wanting cushions for her, then asked if they had such a thing as a flavour-of-the-month anthracite sundae or perhaps a nutty slack ripple, because his lady wife had this passion for sucking coal. It all went far too far and Maggie laughed so much that she had to go out into the street in case she threw up. In the end Sean bought two vanilla cones and they had a game to see whose would last the longest. They walked up Haverstock Hill nibbling daintily all round the edge of their cones and pushing the icecream further and further down with their tongues as they could both remember doing as children, so that no matter how much smaller the nibbled cones became, there was always some icecream left. What a silly day. Maggie would never stand in Camden Town Station again, with its icecream tiles, without thinking of that day.

Or on any tube station platform at all without thinking about Sean. Trains subject to delay due to BODY ON LINE.

She could kill Sean, she really could. If he hadn't killed himself already.

Suddenly, no not suddenly, she had felt it coming on all the way from Earl's Court and had been fighting it back, she felt so angry with him, not for being dead but for being dead in the way he was. Body on line dead, that style of dead. Was she never again to be allowed on the tube without being reminded of Sean cut in two? He knew her so well, why had he done it that way? Why couldn't he have had himself run over by a bus?—she hated buses anyway.

Steady, Mags.

No, she was sorry but it was true. She really was angry. Furious. Livid.

It didn't make her a monster, Maggie knew that, because she'd read about bereavement in the agony columns and she knew it was a fairly common reaction. It was just that she appeared to be going through the various stages of grief like a dose of salts. First, it seemed, there was straight, uncluttered anguish. Yes, she'd had a moment or two of that, though not a lot: too much on her mind, probably. Then there was the why-me self-pitying stage. Done that. Followed, when it dawned on you what you'd been left to cope with, by hate. You fuckpig, you have let me down by dying. That. And finally you were supposed to give your nose a good blow and 'pick up the threads', whatever picking up threads might mean.

Fine: but wasn't the fuckpig supposed to be your husband, your lover, someone of that order? It certainly couldn't have been meant to be Sean. Sean didn't qualify, he was Mr. Nobody, he was a friend, he was her best friend.

The offence was greater for that reason. He was her best friend and he had betrayed their friendship by dying on her. That was it. Unforgivable.

Before her mood had time to take the easy way out by reverting to self-pity, Maggie was relieved to find that she had a bijou practical problemette to occupy her mind. She was walking in the wrong direction. She had come up out of the tube on the opposite side of the road from the one she wanted, like some bewildered tourist, and had automatically headed into the back-doubles without thinking where she was going. Honestly, she wasn't fit to be let out of doors without *Nicholson's London Streetfinder* stuffed up her knicker-leg.

'It's just not my day,' thought Maggie drily, and smiled at her own bitter little joke. She wished Sean was there to share it. She could just hear him saying, 'Ooh, you are wicked, you'll be smitten down deadikins one of these days.' She was glad she wasn't angry with him any more.

She was in an area of little dolls'-house terraces, all paintbox pink and blue and white like a Cornish fishing village, with varnished front doors and bay trees in tubs, and cats on the windowsills instead of beer cans. The streets were cobbled. It was all so pigging charming that it was like wandering about in a completed jigsaw puzzle.

Not a Mags-type scene at all. She turned, and was heading back towards the shabby sanctuary of the Bayswater Road when she saw a woman of about her own age looking curiously at her from a midget-sized front garden where she was doing something with a trowel.

Maggie registered the tailored pants, the too-serious-for-W8 gardening wellies that you could bet were shuttled backwards and forwards in a hatchback between here and a country cottage, the cute it's-my-husband's-really jersey with the sleeves too long, the headband keeping a 'hair-do' in shape for tonight's dinner-party, the rubber gloves protecting Camay-soft hands, and particularly the handsome, properly-proportioned, vicious face.

That was a right Royal Borough face, that was. It was the kind of face you could see any morning in the King's Road pastisseries, buying croissants and florentines. You could see it any afternoon outside the South Ken prep schools, rabbiting to other faces just like it but keeping an eye peeled for the headmaster so as to get in a word about Jason's asthma or his hopelessness at maths. You could see it perched on car bonnets on Sunday evenings with a Pimms No. 1 in its tiny fist, outside the kind of pub where they serve crab sandwiches and the landlord wears a blazer. That face was perfect casting for the cossetted, manicured, expensive little street it was in. It was a real me-me-me face, that was: a tough-as-old-boots, ban-the-juggernauts, save-the-playgroup, residents-association, PTA, Jason's-down-for-Westminster, we-paid-forty-thousand-and-now-it's-worth-double absolute selfish cowbag face. Given time, when London's human flotsam began to wash into this tailored backwater as it had done in others, those hard eyes would get the glaze of fear in them and their owner would finish up just another crazy Old Brompton Road memsahib, but for the moment she was on top.

And Maggie knew her. Not just her type, but her personally. From somewhere, way back, but couldn't place her.

The woman had broken into a hesitant smile. The hesitation, Maggie divined at once, was not due to uncertainty of recognition but to the uncertainty of the wisdom of recognising her.

'It *is* Maggie, isn't it?'

Good Christ. Fiona Tightbum.

Maggie went into what she called her human-being act. '*Fio*na! Good heavens!'

The hesitant little smile became a now-I'm-rather-hurt little smile. Maggie remembered it from the days when she used to nick Fiona's razor blades and then swear blind she hadn't.

'Nearly but *not quite*. You're allowed one more try.'

No use looking at me, sweetheart.

Sodding hell, what were they all called now? Even when living among them Maggie had always had trouble remembering—it was like trying to put names to the Seven Dwarfs. As far as she was concerned, collectively they were the Chums of St. Hilda's and individually they were all Fiona Tightbum.

They'd all given each other stupid nicknames, that was partly the trouble: they might just as well have gone around in stocking-masks.

Maggie thought hard. The real Fiona, the one that the cow now cocking her head expectantly had denied being, was known as Fe-Fo. There was one called Barbara who was known as Boo, and Elizabeth who was Liliboo. How many was that? Including Maggie herself—there had been a move to christen her Moo, which she had firmly sat on—that made four. And this one was the fifth dwarf.

Grumpy?

The smile that had started as hesitant and then become hurt, had by now run through anticipation, impatience and condescension, and had probably completed its repertoire.

'No, I mustn't, Maggie, after all it's been a *very long time*. I'm Alison.'

Of course. Aliboo, as was. They would have dropped their nicknames now they'd left St. Hilda's.

Their weddings must have been like school prizegivings. What did this one get for coming top? Merchant banker? Stockbroker?

Irrelevantly, Maggie remembered Boo's convalescence after she had let herself be put up the spout, got rid, and then been flat on her back for weeks because something Maggie didn't want to hear about had got into her bloodstream. The image that jumped into her mind was of Aliboo tripping into their common living area (Nail Varnish Alley, Maggie called it) and announcing: 'Boo has emerged from sleep and is crying piteously for Lucozade.' Fetching the stuff was down to Maggie Muggins. She hadn't minded, even though it was Sunday and the chemist's was shut and she had to walk for miles. She had found herself, at last, in one of those ratty districts where all the shops, run by Asians or Cypriots, stay open more or less round the clock but no one can afford to buy anything. For the first time since arriving in London Maggie felt at home. She started flat-hunting the next day.

'How are the others? How's Boo?' asked Maggie after Aliboo had taken how-nice-to-see-you and you-haven't-changed-a-bit just about as far as spontaneous pleasantries could go without the insincerity shining through like the tin in an electro-plated sugar-dredger.

'Barbara? How very funny, I never knew she was a special favourite of yours. Well now—*she married Nigel*.'

'I imagine you all did,' Maggie nearly found herself murmuring cattily. Better not, she would only have to explain it and that would keep her here all day. She remembered something else about the Girls of St. Hilda's: they were all thick.

Hang about. Nigel. Wasn't he the one who put Boo in pod?

Aliboo seemed to read her mind. 'No, another Nigel. Nigel Mark Two we used to call him, until it became deadly serious. Nigel's in advertising, the same as Peter. That's Elizabeth's Peter: *very* grand house in Holland Park, not five minutes away. And Fiona *when last heard of* was alive and well and married to Michael who farms in New Zealand. So it would have been very strange if you *had* met her in Notting Hill today. Instead you met me and I'm married to John who's very sweet.'

Maggie, maintaining her human-being front, obediently supplied the feedline. 'And what does John do?'

'*Well may you ask*! No, he's what used to be called "something in the City". Though quite what, one will neeever know!'

They really and truly were all married to Nigels.

Maggie took stock of Aliboo in her posho gardening schmutter, comparing her with the Aliboo who used to wear pink. She was in better nick now than she had been ten years ago, it had to be admitted. She was like an overblown butterfly that had changed into a slinky caterpillar. The whole gang of them probably were. Maggie could not imagine their puppy fat having turned to real fat, or their dinner-dance nervous neckrashes not having been soothed away for ever by creams in thick white pots, or them still having hair under their arms. They had come a long way, but only in the sense that a first-class passenger on a QE2 round-the-world cruise has come a long way. They had had open tickets all along: all they'd had to do was to confirm the booking when they were ready to go. And now they must control between them about half a million quidsworth of property with matching wardrobes, and their sons, all with butter-coloured hair, would be expelled from none but the best public schools for smoking cannabis, and they had Georgian candlesticks on their Regency dining tables, and his-and-hers cars, and they no longer had to squeeze their own blackheads. They were so dim that job-creation schemes had had to be hatched by their parents and their parents' friends to get them taken on as receptionists and flower-arrangers, yet between them they had hooked four Nigels. Mr. Right cloned.

And was Maggie envious? Not in the least. But she couldn't wait for World War Three.

It occurred to Maggie that they had been talking for three or four minutes, they were standing within half a dozen feet of Aliboo's front door, which was half open, and the cow had yet to invite her in for a cup of coffee.

To be fair, Maggie could appreciate her position. In this immaculate Toytown environment—'urban village', they probably called it—it would be like inviting a turd into the house. If one of the neighbours dropped in to borrow a cup of gin or get Aliboo to sign a petition to stop people staring through the windows, she would be socially sunk. But upwards of ten grandsworth of good breeding had been invested in Aliboo. You would think she could offer some excuse.

Again Aliboo seemed to divine what she was thinking. No great feat of extra-sensory perception, for Maggie was staring pointedly into the neat little hall with its Chinese vase of cut daffs on a marble console table. Arranged all those flowers yourself, did you, ducky? What it must be to have a profession to fall back on.

'Maggie. I know this is dreadfully rude and I'm sure you must be dying for coffee but I *daren't ask you in*. We have a sick brat on our hands, mumps poor darling, and it—has—taken *hours* to get her down after a thoroughly sleepless night. The slighest breath and she's yelling for her mum.'

And crying piteously for Lucozade. Nice one, Aliboo. Right on cue—everything had always worked like clockwork for Aliboo, it was so out of character for God to trouble her with mumps—a Far East-looking chick in a lilac smock, one of the Earl's Court boat people very likely, flitted down the stairs into the hall, pressed a finger to her lips as she saw Aliboo on the garden path, and tiptoed off to the kitchen or somewhere.

There was a short, awkward lull. Maggie was supposed to have asked Aliboo how many children she had, but her human-being mask had momentarily slipped and she wouldn't. Sod it, it was Aliboo's turn to ask *her* something. Didn't she want to know where Maggie was living, who she was screwing, what she was doing wandering across this brick-and-stucco patchwork quilt? Apparently not.

Aliboo was embarrassed, that was it. She didn't want Maggie in the house but she didn't much want her hanging about outside the house either. It must be obvious to the neighbours by now that the slut chatting up Mrs. Nigel hadn't just stopped to ask the way to the nearest pregnancy-testing centre but was one of her long-lost friends. The Thing That Came Out Of The Past.

Maggie put on the kind of smile she had seen on crazy old

women when they looked in prams. 'And how many children have you got?'

Aliboo gave a small gasp of relief at the correct procedure being followed after all. 'Two, bless them. Debbie who's already at nursery school and this one, Ginny, who *can't wait* to start. We'll probably try once more for a boy and then shut up shop.'

'How about the others?'

'Ah. Now Elizabeth's waaay ahead of us with *two-oo* boys *and* two girls, no less. And Fiona when she last deigned to write had one of each. She sends us snapshots—they're *exactly* like piccaninnies. I mean,' added Aliboo hastily, 'with the sun.'

'And Boo? Barbara?'

Aliboo revealed that she had not, after all, exhausted her complete range of tight little smiles. One corner of her lips turned up in a spasm of rueful sympathy.

'Poor lamb. Miscarriage after miscarriage. I think something went *dreadfully wrong* when—well, we both remember when, Maggie. But I'm glad to say they do have the sweetest little babby, adopted. A boy.'

'So do I.'

'*No*!'

'Yes I do.'

Maggie was not aware of having spoken. When the two short sentences echoed back in her head on mental playback, they didn't sound to Maggie like Maggie at all. They could have been thrown into her mouth by a ventriloquist.

Aliboo, arching her plucked eyebrows and allowing her mouth to fall open in a controlled collapse of the jaw, was registering comic incredulity.

'An adopted babby? Maggie! You haven't! I didn't even know you were married! Do-oo *tell*!'

'I'm not married.' Again it wasn't Maggie saying it. She was listening to these things being said on her behalf, and watching Aliboo's reaction to them, as if she had suddenly become an invisible spectator of this whole cringe-making encounter. She'd had this sensation before, when everyone, including herself, seemed to be seen through glass. It would pass.

Aliboo had gone through looking shocked (though not surprised), then trying not to look shocked. She had had a brief stab at trying to look progressive, which was beyond her histrionic talents. Now she stumbled on just the right community-service phrase that would get her off the hook.

'I *seee*! A *one-parent familee*e!' Aliboo was so relieved at having jumped a difficult hurdle that she gave a licentious half-shriek, implying that of course, knowing Maggie, she wouldn't expect her to be anything else but. She was probably looking for an inoffensive way of expressing such an offensive thought when a frown stamped itself upon her brow. Pretty face still, but as easy to read as a Janet and John book.

'But adoption? Surely that's . . . I mean aren't they awfully, well . . . ?'

The Maggie who was watching from behind glass would have left her floundering. The Maggie who had taken over the conversation with Aliboo said steadily: 'No, you've got it the wrong way round. It's my own baby, but it's being adopted.'

The glass between them shattered, and the Maggie who would never have started to say these things was in control again. Except that now she could see that she had wanted to say them all along, and wanted to go on saying them.

Come in, Mags! She had thoroughly misunderstood her own motives, that's what she'd done. She'd thought she was having a little game with herself, posing as a human being and asking all those nice polite tea-time questions, yet all the time secretly pissing herself at Aliboo's absurd rich-girl posturings. Now she suddenly realised that she had just been sucking up to Aliboo, making all the right noises, in the hope that Aliboo, in turn, would suck up and make all the right noises to her.

Shaming though it was to admit it, Maggie wanted someone to talk to.

Yes she *did* want to be asked in for coffee and yes she *did* want to sit on a prune-coloured plush chaise-longue and yes she *did* want to look through Aliboo's family album with its permutated matt-finish Polaroid snaps of them all at one another's weddings, and Fe-fo's brats looking like piccaninnies. And then, abstractedly crumbling a biscuit on a delicate bone-china plate and forming patterns with the crumbs, she wanted to tell Aliboo all about herself. About Ken, about the babe, about the Portakabins, about her dead Mum and half-dead Dad, about such a lot of her life, probably even about Sean. But she didn't want her to sympathise or offer advice or say anything at all. Aliboo wouldn't even have to listen if she didn't want to, although it would certainly give her something to pass on to the other Chums. 'You'll never guess who I had round for coffee the other day . . .' Maggie didn't care about that, so long as the silly bitch sat there sewing name-tags on the brats' tiny gym slips or doing whatever she wanted to do, while Maggie talked. Just as she used punters in tube carriages as thinking-posts, to the point at which they sometimes thought she was trying to get off with them, she wanted to use Aliboo as a talking-post. Oh, yes: and it would be nice to be shown where the lav was. That really would make her feel wanted.

She could see that Aliboo thought she was mad. Completely off her trolley, my dear. Arrived out of the blue and started rambling about her babby. Sad.

What Aliboo wanted now was to get the front door of her little Wendy-house between herself and Maggie with all possible speed. But she didn't know how to go about it. Grimsville.

Aliboo opened her mouth: a hysterical little laugh came out of it, but nothing else. Tough buns. Maggie wanted to feel sorry for her, but couldn't. Instead, as the need to ingratiate herself with Aliboo passed over like a cloud, she felt a twinge of power. The stupid cow was afraid of her. She knew that out there beyond Toytown there were the Wicked Woods with beasties and ghoulies and she thought that Maggie had come to carry her off in a sack.

Aliboo, despite the veneer of sophistication that fitted her like a cocktail dress, was probably still as immature now as she had been ten years ago at the age of twenty, when she was playing sixteen. She just didn't have anything to be mature about. She had her Wendy-house and her pop-up-book children and her clockwork Nigel, and once a week she would spend her chocolate pennies in Harrods and once a month she would hold a dolly's dinner-party, and nothing worse than mumps was ever, ever supposed to spoil it for her. She couldn't cope with real life, any more than a Mabel Lucy Attwell toddler clattering around in mummy's shoes could cope.

Am I real life? Maggie wondered. Flattered, I'm sure.

Aliboo had another stab at recovering herself. 'Now I'm *sure* I've got hold of the wrong end of the stick—' she began, placing the index finger on her right hand on the outstretched palm of her left. She wanted to break Maggie's bewildering news down into manageable parts, ticking off each segment as she began to comprehend it.

Maggie, calmly and cruelly, did it for her.

'No. You haven't. I got pregnant, right? The guy wouldn't leave his wife, right? So. Had the kid. *Didn't* see myself as single-parent material. Had it adopted. And I'm just on my way to sign the final papers.'

Aliboo, hating Maggie, loathing her, for coming up out of the drains like this, said with a magnificently hopeless shrug, 'Very *commendable—*'

'—but why didn't I get rid, like Boo? It's a long story.'

The get-out. Aliboo did a quick fork-lift movement that scooped up her trowel and trug from the garden path, at the same time propelling her on to the doorstep. 'And one which I'm dying to hear. How*ever* . . .' A deep sigh, with accompanying regretful shake of the head, conjured up a diary already overloaded with the thousand daily tasks of efficient household management.

Maggie, who all through the encounter had been standing out on the pavement, put her hand on the latch of the garden gate as if she meant to follow Aliboo into the house. 'I lied about the length. Actually, it's quite a short story.'

Safe behind her front door now, so that it could be slammed in an emergency, Aliboo risked a touch of the old St. Hilda's acid. 'And I'm sure you tell it beautifully. *But* . . .'

This was the cow who had told Maggie's Mum that she'd run off with a black man. She wasn't going to get away as easily as that. She wanted to shut the door in Maggie's face but that ten grandsworth of good breeding wouldn't let her. She would have to babble on about how nice it had been, *lovely* to see you, *really* unexpected pleasure, and then she would make the mistake of vaguely suggesting coffee one of these mornings when she was less rushed off her feet. And Maggie would say: 'Fine. When?'

Aliboo was standing in the doorway with her face clamped into a rigid smile. Yet another one from her repertoire: that was a smile of fear, that was. She looked at Maggie and saw a threat to everything that she was and everything that she wanted. Good. If you can't join the bastards, beat them.

From behind a curtained upstairs window, a childish wailing commenced hesitantly like a faltering motorbike engine and then filled the little house. Ginny had emerged from sleep and was crying piteously for something or other. Whatever she wanted, it would be in stock.

'Coming, darling,' called Aliboo over her shoulder.

Maggie, still with her hand on the gate latch, looked across the little garden path into Aliboo's eyes, locking glances with her so that Aliboo couldn't look away. 'I didn't tell you, did I? My Mum died,' said Maggie.

'Oh, did she?' Aliboo's fixed smile had become even more fixed. 'So did mine. Of *lingering cancer*, Maggie, if that makes you feel any better.'

Softly she shut the door, leaving Maggie feeling a bit of a Charley.

5

The Scum Also Rises

Maggie crossed over Bayswater Road and went the way she should have gone in the first place, and it was like stepping out of one day of the week into another.

Aliboo's pretty little patch was Sunday. It was little girls coming home from parties with balloons and prezzies, it was cub scouts washing cars, it was men smoking pipes and reading colour supps, it was nutmeg trees. Shift two hundred yards north, into the traffic-choked thoroughfare that was the flightpath for the Portobello, and it was always Saturday. There was never any sense of aimlessness here: all the punters seemed to be going somewhere, they had shopping lists in their heads And no matter what side of the street they started out from, they seemed to have a pressing need to get to the other. The big red buses, nudging through the criss-crossing throng, looked out of scale.

Every district, Maggie supposed, must have its day, like every dog. Earl's Court was permanently Friday. Kentish Town, with all its rain-streaked posters for mental health projects and consumer aid centres, was Monday, and a wet one too. Camden Town, with an Irish drunk brandishing an empty bottle in every doorway, felt Thursdayish: somehow it was never quite payday in Camden Town. Chalk Farm was Sunday, but a far more downmarket Sunday than Aliboo's. And the wrong side of Shepherds Bush was always Wednesday half-day closing.

Maggie liked the Saturday feel of Notting Hill Gate. Sometimes, hurrying through on her way to do a quick bit of grafting down the Bello, she wondered why she didn't still live here. It was only when she was on her milk round, and actually came face to face with her former home with its stucco falling away like dandruff, that she remembered the strong case for living somewhere else.

Pegboard Manor, Maggie had nicknamed the place. It consisted of three floors over an antique shop that was never open and an Indian restaurant that was never closed. The whole house stank of curry. Maggie wouldn't have minded a reasonable background of Tandoori chicken, after all it was only the nasal equivalent of Musak, and if you were going to be choosy about smells you would end up in a sleeping-bag in St. James's Park. What she did think went over the top in the pong line was the booster effect injected by the peculiar nature of the building's conversion specifications. Ten Rillington Place, she concluded after living with it for a bit, must have smelled like this.

As usual, what had once been about a dozen fair-sized rooms had been split up into three times that number of 'flatlets'. Fair enough. But where all her previous landlords had employed nothing less substantial than plywood to honeycomb their rattraps, Mr. Veerekananda had opted for pegboard. Finding himself with an enormous quantity of this material after gutting the former sex-aids shop that had occupied the ground floor when he took over the lease, Mr. Veerekananda had thought it a pity not to recycle it when refurbishing the residential floors.

Thus two out of the three inner walls of Maggie's room were constructed of pegboard, painted vivid yellow. Mr. Veerekanandra had believed, or hoped, that a good thick coat of paint would effectively seal the pegboard's one-per-square-inch perforations, from many of which still hung the rusty hooks that had lately supported strings of porn mags secured by clothespegs. But he was an optimist. It was exactly, thought Maggie, like living inside a Gruyère cheese.

Tarting herself up ready to troll off to base on her third evening at Pegboard Manor, Maggie became aware, through the closely-punched pattern of tiny holes all over the party wall, of movement in the adjoining room. 'Standing there in me coms,' as she put it to Sean when she told him the story, she sensed a voyeur.

Her room was lit only by a table-lamp which, for want of a table, stood on the floor, its dented shade tilted to cast the light upwards. Yes, right up her legs: the punter next door couldn't have got a better view if he'd paid ten quid for it and something for the maid.

Sitting on the edge of the bed casually brushing her hair, Maggie searched for the lamp flex with her foot, found it, and tugged sharply. The plug came out of the socket and her room was in darkness. Pressed to the pegboard wall was a naked man. With his legs and arms slightly apart, and the light from his own bedside lamp highlighting the outline of his dumpy body, he looked like an overgrown gingerbread man.

'He must have been a fat bugger,' Maggie told Sean, 'because you could actually see all these hundreds of tiny blobs of flesh where he was pressing himself up against the holes in the pegboard. I'm not kidding, he could have gone downstairs and passed himself off as a waffle.'

'But kitten! You must have been scared shitless! What did you *do*?'

'Borrowed one of Riggsy's knitting needles.'

'Ooh! Ouch! Ooh, don't! Ooh, you are vicious!'

True story—except that she lied about the knitting needle. Riggsy would have done it but not Maggie, she was too squeamish. What she did do was to cadge some end-rolls of wallpaper from a mate who did a bit of moonlighting for a builder and decorator, and stick it up with drawing pins. V. daring colour scheme it was, though she said it as shouldn't: four yards of yellow and gold Regency stripe contrasting with three yards of embossed crimson velvet tea roses, with just a hint of simulated bathroom tiles and a patch or two of Snoopy and Woodstock. Maggie was so pleased with her first venture into interior decorating that she almost forgot the purpose of it.

Now why did she feel a pang, remembering that Joseph's-coat-of-many-colours wall of hers in Pegboard Manor? Oh, because it was the kind of thing Sean would have liked helping her do, she supposed. It would have been a giggle, doing it together. But that would have meant letting him into her room, and after all, the whole point of the exercise was to preserve her privacy.

It was odd, but what upset her most about the Peeping bloody Tom next door was not that he had seen her boobs and things—she wouldn't cross the street to see them, personally—but that until she put the mokkers on him he was able to press himself against the wall and stare into her room when she wasn't there. That was really creepy, someone staring into your room when you were out, and you not knowing. It was almost as bad as being watched while you were asleep.

But Peeping Toms, like flashers, rapists, bum-pinchers, pick-pockets, muggers, Jehovah's Witnesses, fruitcakes, winos, heads, dykes, the Filth, football hooligans and absolute psychos were all but twiddly bits in the rich pattern of London life. If you can't take a joke you shouldn't have joined. Once her wallpaper screen was up Maggie should have been (as she recollected nostalgically to Sean only a few weeks later when he came back with her to Pegboard Manor on her milk round) as cosy as a pig in shit. It was a safe house—one floor was used as a knocking-shop, which meant you got police protection from a Maltese pimp—in a nice area, and it couldn't have been handier for the tube and the Portobello: it was just that the stench of curry, seeping up from the ground floor through all the pegboard walls and stalely lingering in their thousands of perforations like herbs in a pomander, began to make her vomit.

Still vomiting, Maggie packed her things and moved out as soon as the few weeks covered by her advance rent had expired, even though—quite usual for her: Maggie believed in that old proverb about putting off till tomorrow what you didn't do yesterday—she had not yet found anywhere else to go. At once she was in problemsville.

It was summer, always a dodgy time for finding somewhere to live, and made even dodgier by the pound sterling doing whatever it was that the pound sterling did to fill the town with Scandinavians. Even Henry, who never turned away a prospect even if he had to prise up manhole covers to see if all the sewers were fully-booked, was finding it hard going. There was, or would have been if she'd spoken up a bit sooner, a room in the house Sean lived in, in Ladbroke Grove: he would have put in a word for her and if she'd had any sense she would have gone round and greased up his Polish landlord. But she didn't want to live in the same house as Sean, didn't want to meet him going up the stairs with a big butch cruiser and didn't want him to meet her coming home at five in the morning with her knickers in her handbag. Didn't want to intrude or be intruded on, was the size of it.

Feeling too rotten to work through the postcards in the newsagent's windows, which anyway were worse than bloody useless unless you thought you should try every experience once including getting ripped off, Maggie's only resort was to hump her gear down to the Half Moon in the hope that some face propping up the bar-counter would wave a magic wand. Scoff not: stranger things had happened.

Riggsy, a bit early even for her, was perched on her usual high stool by the frosted partition dividing the saloon bar from the snug. She was on the gin already, which meant she could go either way. You never knew your luck, maybe she would invite Maggie back to Parsons Green for a bijou stay.

'God, you look *awful*,' was Riggsy's greeting. Sympathy yet: that put her in with a chance. With keep-your-pecker-up chirpiness Maggie said: 'You know what they say—if you've got it, flaunt it,' and dumped a suitcase pointedly at Riggsy's feet. Riggsy laughed, clocked Maggie's gear, made an excuse and left for the Leather Bottle, a full hour ahead of schedule. And she called herself a mate.

Maggie was feeling even worse than Riggsy said she looked, all she wanted was to nurse a vodka-and-ton and vegetate for a while over the *Daily Express* word-game. Sod looking for a room: she had bunches of time and if the worst came to the worst she would just have to flutter her eyelids and pull someone. So long as he didn't mind her closing her eyes and dying for England while he got on with it.

Sean came in and started fussing over her: was she all right, would she like a brandy, had she looked in a mirror lately, had she seen a doctor, where was she going to spend the night, why didn't she come and stay with him until she got sorted out, and on and on and on. He was breaking their contract: she had to tell him to put a bag over his head in the end and he too toed it to the Leather Bottle, mortally wounded.

At the death it was Sid the Squirrel, the Half Moon's guvnor, who got Maggie fixed up. She hadn't unburdened herself directly to Sid but then you didn't have to: prowling restlessly round and round the circular mahogany bar, like a squirrel on a wheel, he earwigged every word spoken, regarding himself as having a floating invitation to add his tenpennorth to any discussion that caught his fancy. 'The only man in London who can kill six conversations stone dead simultaneously,' Maggie had once said loudly to the ceiling when he joined her group; so he was not overfond of her, and indeed sometimes barred her for short periods when she went too far. On the other hand it was getting on for three o'clock, it had started pissing down outside, Maggie was on her tenth vodka, she had a canvas grip, a zip-up wardrobe and two suitcases, and the handle had come off one of them while it was being unloaded from the cab. Sid either had to help out or resign himself to the fact that she was going to use the Half Moon as a left luggage office. He wouldn't like that.

Sid the Squirrel, hugging his waistcoated chest and twanging the last pair of expandable chrome armbands in Soho as he restlessly circled the bar, beckoned Maggie to follow him round to the screened-off waiters' dispense bar where favoured faces cashed cheques and those whose daily doubles hadn't come up were interviewed about cheques that had bounced. 'The Confessional,' Maggie called it.

'How do you feel about being an illegal immigrant?' Sid asked, without moving his lips much, but with a backward-directed spasm of his head to establish that the question was confidential. A lot of that went on: Maggie knew very few faces who didn't regularly feel the need to talk out of one side of their mouths as if the other side had been jabbed with Novocaine. There were days when, to an outsider, the Half Moon must look like a dentist's waiting-room.

Maggie shrugged elaborately to tell Sid that she was open to any offers, however bizarre. Sid, this time jerking his head in one more definite direction, towards the snug, went on: 'See the one with the cab-badge? Alfie his name is, nice lad, don't know whether you know him. How would you like him to do you a favour?'

Maggie woozily sized up the homely-looking, good-to-his-mum apple dumpling of a man in the black leather bomber jacket who was leaning over the snug bar and swirling an inch or two of Guinness around in a half-pint glass. He, for his part, was craftily sizing up Maggie.

Their eyes met and he winked. Seemed harmless enough. 'What's he want?'

'Well, his old lady's only looking for a lodger, isn't she? *But*. He's got some good news and some bad news. The good news is it's a very nice room, very quiet, very reasonable. The bad news is it's council property. Housing estate. So you'd be a whatever you want to call it, unauthorised tenant.'

Alfie himself, evidently taking the view that Maggie and he had become well-acquainted during these preambles, chimed in from the snug in ringing confidential tones that everyone in the pub could hear: 'See, darling, word gets out she's entertaining a sub-tenant, even if they don't serve her notice to quit which they have got *every right to do* under their rules and regulations it's got to affect her rent rebate, know what I mean? So if you do take the room then there's a bit too much of that'—with fingers and thumb he mimed a mouth compulsively opening and shutting almost as much as his own was doing—'she's in schtuck with the council, I'm in schtuck with her, you're in schtuck with me, we're all in schtuck with one other, know what I mean?'

'She'll keep schtum,' guaranteed Sid, who as well as being squirrel-like in his movements was chameleon-like in his speech.

Maggie, feeling ill and pissed, had been nodding her head gravely and repeatedly while Alfie outlined the conditions of his offer; she was only being polite but both he and Sid seemed to take it as signalling her agreement to a verbal contract. In a haze she heard them making elaborate arrangements—far more elaborate than could be justified by the simple task at hand, as arrangements in this quarter so often were—for Alfie to fetch his cab round to the front and load up her gear.

'Worth a drink, would you say?' broad-hinted Sid the Squirrel, no doubt in his mind that he had done her a good turn. There weren't many landlords with the nerve to cadge drinks in their own pubs, she'd say that for him.

Maggie bought him a brandy and one for herself. 'Not sure I want to live on a housing estate, Sid,' she protested feebly.

'Beggars can't be choosers, my dear.'

'But I'm not a beggar.'

Sid the Squirrel didn't seem to see the point of that rejoinder, and Alfie's engine was running, so she went. Well, that was the way life sometimes took you over.

Considering that Maggie threw up all over his back seat while they were bombing along the Westway, it was very nice of Alfie to take her to his mum's, and very nice of Alfie's mum to accept her as an illegal sub-tenant. What with Alfie having to hose down his cab and Alfie's mum having to hose down Maggie, she couldn't have made a very good first impression. But to even things up a bit, the housing estate —Sid the Squirrel had called it that, but actually it was more of a housing folly, just a single tower block with some boarded-up shops and a vandalised communal laundry, set down in the middle of what looked like an enormous but empty coalyard—didn't make a very good first impression on Maggie, or a good second impression either. Still, Alfie's mum was nice. Liked her: hated it. Four weeks of that and it was all on to Earl's Court, but not before she had made the second biggest mistake of her life.

Well, not second biggest perhaps: exaggeration. All right, say the fifth biggest mistake of her life. Certainly in the top twenty.

Maggie couldn't stop vomiting, and her travel-sickness pills, prescribed by herself from the wide range available at the Valium and Mogodon outlet that was one of the neighbourhood's few thriving shops, didn't seem to be doing a lot for her morale. At last Alfie's mum marched her down to her own doctor who had a surgery behind a steel-mesh-protected window in the row of boarded-up shops. Maggie peed in a bottle and soon had confirmed what she already knew but hadn't much wanted to think about: that she was in the club. What came of being on the Pill and on the piss at the same time. The quack gave her a card to the local hospital—local being a relative term in this neck of the woods: it meant you had to change buses only once—and before she knew what was happening, because she had a few other things on her mind at the time, they had her down for a maternity bed and a calendar of visits to the ante-natal clinic.

What she most had on her mind was Ken: whether it would be possible to blackmail the bugger into leaving his wife, and whether she would want to shack up with him and raise a family even if it was.

The shacking-up part had been quite a little ambition of hers at one time, though she had never voiced it, and Ken had always discouraged any pressuring in that direction by treating her to regular soliloquies about his wife as he nursed his half pint of real ale: 'I'll tell you what it is in a nutshell, Mags. If Helen turned out to have a lover and wanted to leave *me*, I'd be over the moon. But I really would feel like nine kinds of ess-aitch-one-tee if I was the one walking out. You see, from her point of view, she hasn't *done anything to deserve* it, there'd be *just no reason* for it, at least no reason she could understand. Do you see what I'm driving at, Mags?' Oh, sure.

There was a reason now, though, wasn't there? But was that what Maggie wanted? Ken, his guilty conscience, and a playpen full of squeaky toys and sodden rusks? Would *he* want it, or to put it another way, would he want it when he'd got it?

Maggie rather thought she could rely on those questions to answer themselves before long.

She hadn't seen him for a few weeks. They had been keeping out of each other's way—perhaps he was keeping out of her way more than she was keeping out of his. It was a policy decision: we can't go on meeting like this and all that. They had got to the point where they'd been seeing each other just about every evening and every lunchtime, and Ken, so he claimed, was finding it harder and harder to crawl back home each night with metaphorical lipstick on his collar. Maggie herself, tell the truth, was beginning to feel exhausted by it all, and a bit hemmed-in by the restrictions that an affair in full swing imposes on one's everyday movements. Perhaps they were just running out of steam, she didn't know. When Ken suggested a change of pace, it seemed not a bad idea on balance.

He was going up to Derbyshire on some kind of educational course that would keep him away for the first half of the summer term. Originally there had been some talk of Maggie joining him up there and more or less living with him: she had grown quite excited at the prospect, not only of playing houses with Ken for a while but of having a change from London. Looking back now on her excitement, she must have seemed quite pathetic, like the chick in that film *Gaslight*, or was it *The Barretts of Wimpole Street*, who wets her knickers with rapture because she thinks she's going to the theatre. If the thought of six weeks in pigging Matlock gave Maggie an orgasm, it really was time she started getting further than the pub of an evening.

She was disappointed in one way but relieved in another when Ken's wife's non-job as a community service adviser or something fizzled out of existence and the cow decided to go up to Derbyshire with him. It did mean she could lead her own life for a while and do some of the things she'd been missing, like the occasional jaunt with Sean.

Then Ken came out with his plan. Instead of just taking up where they'd left off when he got back from Matlock, why didn't they treat his absence as a kind of cooling-off period? He outlined the scenario. The way they usually played it when he'd been away for a while was that he belted round to her place with a bottle of wine, and they were at it like rattlesnakes while she was still looking for the corkscrew. There'd be none of that. It would all be very laid-back and casual. Maybe he wouldn't see her on his first day back at all, perhaps not even on the second or third day. What they would do would be to bump into one another sort of accidentally in the pub where they'd first met, the Duke of Clarence, and take it from there. Wooing her all over again, to use an upchucking phrase, was what it boiled down to, but on a less frenzied level than before. They'd arrange to have lunch a few days later, in some out-of-the-way place where they wouldn't be recognised. They would probably be fancying one another like mad by this time but Ken would have to get back to work, so they would get no further than the knee-trembling stage on this occasion. Finally he would take her out to dinner, somewhere with chequered tablecloths and candles stuck in bottles she would imagine, and at last they would go back to her place and screw the shit out of each other.

It was a highly romantic concept, typical of Ken, but it had a lot going for it. It meant they could break the cast-iron mould of their existing relationship and go for something altogether more flexible. Sometimes they'd see each other twice or three times a week, sometimes not at all. Sometimes they'd sleep together, sometimes they wouldn't, they'd play it by ear. It was, of course, the perfect recipe for Ken having his cake and eating it, but it suited Maggie too. If nothing else, it would mean she had time to wash her hair occasionally.

She not only agreed to the new arrangement, she even complimented Ken on sussing instinctively her fear of getting painted into corners, and on having worked out the best thing for her as well as for himself. But once he had trolled off to Derbyshire with his wife and their matching luggage, the new deal began to look far less attractive, especially when examined through a vodka glass in the Half Moon.

Resentment set in. He really did want jam on it, when you gave it five minutes' thought. First off, he didn't have an exact date for when he was coming back to London so she was expected to hang around like a spare part, waiting for him to turn up. Then they were going to get out their little diaries and arrange a cosy lunch, like a couple of junior executives. Why didn't they go the whole hog and wear plastic lapel badges with their names on? After that, Maggie was to go back into cold storage until they had a cosy dinner a few nights later. What was she supposed to be doing with herself in the meantime? Knitting a willy-warmer for her vibrator?

Sod it. If that was the way he wanted it, fine. But there was no way he was getting Maggie on a plate with mint sauce and new potatoes. Bugger standing about in that bloody great draughty balloon-hanger the Duke of Clarence, a pub she didn't even like. And bugger sitting at home reading *My Weekly* and waiting for the thrill of Mr. Wonderful turning up, as she was sure he would if she left it long enough, with a single red rose and a litre and a half of Augustus Barnett Soave. Maggie liked living in Islington even less than she liked its pubs: she would move, all the way back west, Notting Hill probably. If he wanted her, he would have to come looking for her. Shouldn't be difficult: she had taken him to the Half Moon a few times so he knew where to find her. Unless she'd struck lucky and scored that particular evening, in which case he'd just have to try again later, wouldn't he?

Tramping to the bus-stop across the coalyard surrounding Alfie's mum's—actually it was just churned-up black earth when you got close to it, where they had been on the verge of building more tower blocks until everyone had suddenly gone off the whole idea—it all seemed years ago rather than weeks ago. Ken, surprise, surprise, had never come looking for her and she wouldn't let herself go looking for him. She'd stayed in the Half Moon from opening time until closing time every night and then left messages where she'd be. That was as far as she would go.

Never say never, Mags. The situation had changed now, hadn't it?

A pity she hadn't put her act together and got the bad news from a doctor a few days earlier back in Notting Hill, when getting across to Islington wouldn't have involved her in a jolting, bilious-making bus journey taking the best part of two hours.

Maggie wouldn't have called herself slow-witted, but she had done that journey three times before the penny dropped. Her chances of accidentally bumping into Ken in the Duke of Clarence were about the same as her chances of bumping into Frank Sinatra. Bumping into Ken would need more than an accident, it would need a bloody miracle, because not only was he no longer in Islington, he was no longer in London.

She knew before anyone told her. Suddenly, she could tell. It was something about the feel of the pub. No, not the pub itself, you couldn't sense a change of atmosphere in a place that had never had any. It was the people in it, the regulars. They'd regrouped, that's what they'd done The adoring mob of student teachers who used to gather around Ken, the ones she'd noticed looking at him as if the new moon shone out of his arse when he and she had first clocked each other, had splintered. A bit like a family breaking up when the father dies.

The sub-school or outer ring of raffia instructors and drama lecturers that gravitated towards Ken for more professional reasons, that had broken up too. All the same odds and sods were still here—rather, all the same odds and sods but one sod were still here—but they were now spread out, dispersed among the random knots of punters who straggled all along the enormous bar. Several of them seemed to recognise Maggie, but no one bothered to nod or smile. They had seen her with Ken, yes, but Ken didn't come in here any more.

She finally got the story from one of the student teachers who infested the pub, a pert-looking chick she'd always thought of as Susan although it wasn't her name. Susan had had a thing going with Ken before Maggie arrived on the scene, so she had probably marked Maggie down as the one to blame for her being rowed out. At any rate, it seemed to afford her enormous chuffiness to be able to give Maggie the score.

Ken had taken some kind of desk job in Derbyshire, even cushier than the one he'd had down here. He'd applied for it, had the interview and been accepted while on his course, jacked the course in, come back to London to take up his standing redundancy offer, got shut of the flat down here while his wife negotiated for a flat up there, loaded his furniture into a removal van, had the electricity cut off, taken his library books back and pissed off. All within the space of a month and without so much as a kiss-my-arse.

'Surprised you weren't at his leaving party,' said Susan.

'I wasn't invited.' Might as well give the silly little cat her moneysworth. 'Where was it?'

'Here—where else?'

Ah, well, Mags, can't win them all, she told herself on the long bus-ride back to Alfie's mum's. And looking at it rationally she couldn't really say she'd lost very much.

Even if the bastard hadn't done a moonlight on her, what would he have done if it had been a case of, 'Hello, Ken, well well well, fancy meeting you, welcome back, how was Matlock, how's the wife, yes I'd love to have lunch with you on Tuesday week but I'd better warn you it'll cost you, because I'm eating for two now'? Maggie knew the answer, she didn't know why she'd wasted so much bus fare on looking for it. Bunged her a hundred and fifty to get shut of it, that's what he'd have done, and then given her the big E. With regrets, of course.

So all she had lost, on balance, was the satisfaction of chucking half a pint of real ale in his face.

Bubbles to him.

Back at Clem Attlee House, as the council called Alfie's mum's block of flats and who could blame them, she drank cup after cup of sweet tea while considering her position against a curiously comforting men-are-all-alike curtain of chuntering from Alfie's mum. (Maggie had partly confided in her, not because she needed to but because Alfie's mum did like a nice morsel of gossip, it put colour into her cheeks.)

It dawned on her at last that in a dream-sequence sort of way, while preoccupied with Ken—deliberately preoccupied, she now realised, so as to stop her dwelling too much on the messy, bleah-like business of giving birth—she had enormously complicated her life.

First, there was Alfie's mum's doctor in his ratty surgery among the boarded-up shops, with whom she was now registered as a patient. Alfie's mum, refusing to be persuaded that the council didn't have access to all documents filed on council property, had originally insisted on introducing Maggie as a niece who was staying with her for a few days. With a waiting room packed with grizzling kids and depressive-looking women scratching the skin off their hands as they waited for their fix of tranquillisers, the doctor wouldn't have cared if Maggie had been posing as Alfie's mum's granny. Not until the pee-test proved positive, when he wanted to give her a note to her own doctor and Maggie had to confess that he was the only doctor in her life, did he show any interest in taking down her particulars, smirk smirk. That meant embroidering the story a little. Maggie told the doctor that she had now decided to stay with her auntie until the baby was born so that her sister with whom she shared a flat in Parsons Green and who didn't go a bundle on unmarried mothers, wouldn't get to hear about it. He didn't believe a word of it but, like the casualty clerk at Charing Cross Hospital when Maggie had wheeled in Sean, he wanted a permanent address to write down on a nice white card, so she gave him Riggsy's.

Riggsy didn't know about this yet.

Knowing herself of old, Maggie was prepared to tell herself for nothing that now she'd got herself a doctor at last, there was no way she was ever going to transfer to another one, even after the babe was born. It was going to be bloody inconvenient trailing back to the wrong side of Shepherds Bush for her nerve tonic and elastic bandages in years to come. In fact it was going to be bloody inconvenient much sooner than that, because if Maggie had to go on living at Alfie's mum's much longer she would throw herself out of Alfie's mum's eighth-floor window. Definitely time to move on, morning upchuck or no morning upchuck.

The next complication was the hospital, North Pole General as Maggie called it, to whose maternity unit and ante-natal clinic her harassed doctor had unloaded her with all possible speed. More white cards to be filled in. This time, troubled by vague apprehensions that as Parsons

Green was probably way outside their area they wouldn't accept her if she gave them Riggsy's address, Maggie thought she'd better tell the women who sat behind the desks where she was really living. Without, of course, bothering to mention that she would soon be living somewhere else.

Who's a dum-dum, then? Maggie really had lumbered herself now. Every time they wanted to examine her tits or prod her belly it was going to mean setting off at cracko and writing the whole day off. If she moved any further away from Clem Attlee House than say Earl's Court, she was going to have to become an in-patient for her relaxation classes. Plus, seriously though, she had let herself in for a tedious series of milk round-type calls on Alfie's mum, because they were bound to start bombarding her with appointment cards, anti-smoking leaflets, vouchers for buckshee orange juice and Christ only knew what else. What a drag. Whereas if she'd given them Riggsy's address they'd probably have transferred her to Fulham or somewhere, to a proper sooty-looking hospital five floors high, instead of the North Pole General's single-storey straggle of orange-brick 'units' joined by glass corridors and surrounded by wet grass.

Yes, but there would still have been the problem of all that crap coming through the post. Riggsy wouldn't have taken too kindly to someone else's free orange juice vouchers whizzing through her letter-box, unless she happened to be on a Bucks Fizz kick at the time.

Come to that, Alfie's mum wasn't exactly best pleased when she heard that Maggie had given the North Pole General her address. Maggie managed to convince her that giving false information to a hospital was a criminal offence. Shitty thing to do, looking back.

The final complication was a bit scarey. When it got to zero hour, and Maggie felt her twinges coming on or the bloody waters breaking or whatever warning sign they would tell her to watch out for or so it was to be sincerely hoped, how the fuck was she supposed to get herself down the hospital? Easier said than done, matey. Once again she wished she were better informed on the citizens' rights of a person secretly living in one area while pretending to live in another: could an ambulance in Earl's Court refuse to take you beyond the Hammersmith border? The bastards would probably tip her off the stretcher at Shepherds Bush and make her hoof it. Of course, you did hear of chicks whose time had come while they were trolling merrily off to the maternity ward on the number nine bus, but then the number nine bus didn't take two hours to get from point bloody A to point bloody B, did it? And another thing: what about all those stories you heard about chicks who'd left things a bit late dropping it on the back seat, with the Paki conductor acting as midwife? Sod that.

For the first time, Maggie gave proper thought to the pros and cons of going through with it. But not for long. Abortion meant now. The other thing was months away, bunches of time away. Anything could happen before then. End of argument.

Alfie's mum would be shocked if she knew what a snap decision it basically was. She took it for granted that Maggie had sat down in her damp, distempered bedroom and thought the whole thing through, considering the alternatives most seriously before coming to her difficult decision. She admired Maggie for doing the right thing.

'There's not many'd do what you're doing, love, when you stop to think what you *could* do, this day and age,' said Alfie's mum, more than once. 'Not them what's in *the same position as what you're in*, anyway. 'Cause if there's no one'll take the responsibility they go for the easy way out, don't they? Invariable.'

Filling in the blanks occasioned by Alfie's mum's strong bias towards euphemism was a bit like trying to put the bones back into a kipper fillet, but since once she'd found something to say she tended to keep on repeating it until some other thought came along to replace it, you got what she was driving at in the end.

With this testimonial, Maggie felt encouraged to ask Alfie's mum a favour. Got some good news and some bad news. The bad news was she would have to be moving on soon, nothing personal, loved the flat, loved Alfie's mum, loved her cups of tea and fried slices, loved the view of the coalyard, but tell the truth, could do with being just a bit more central. Sorry about that. The good news was, how would Alfie's mum feel about her moving back for a couple of weeks when it got a bit nearer her time, she meant before the confinement (confinement! Christ! It sounded as if they were going to brick her up!)? Would be no trouble, quiet as an avocado-shaped flaming dormouse she'd be, just propped up on cushions watching telly and mixing her own Horlicks: but the thing was, it would take a load off her mind knowing she was handy for North Pole General and that the ambulance could be there within minutes if need be. Unless of course the room wouldn't be available on account of Alfie's mum having decided to run the risk of illegally sub-letting it to some other punter . . .

What a flaming cheek. But the poor old cow wore it. No, not poor old cow: because even if Maggie was out of order in taking such liberties, there was something in it for Alfie's mum too. It gave her something to look forward to. She lived a blank life in a blank domino block on a blank plateau of dried mud. She had a blank, pudding face: Alfie's Up-West-wise, split-apple-pudding face at least looked cracked and lived in, it had interesting, uneven features, but his mum had a suet-pudding-without-the-apple face. Blank. Her smile was blank, because she didn't understand what she was smiling at, her walls were blank, because of the condensation. Her mind was blank. If there had been an engagement calendar pinned to the blank flush door of her blank kitchen, its pages would have been blank. Well, then: now at least there was a date for her to put a big red circle round. She could knit matinée jackets and fill hot water-bottles and make Maggie put her feet up, and come with her to the hospital and then visit her with gifts of cut flowers and a Hallmark card, fetched personally because she wouldn't trust the post. Watch how her blank face would light up. 'Poor little mite,' she would say. It wasn't Alfie's mum doing Maggie any favours, it was Maggie doing her one.

Maggie made her move to Earl's Court and began her journeying backwards and forwards to North Pole General and Clem Attlee House. It went as smoothly as could be expected: that was to say, not very smoothly. She came to detest the wrong side of Shepherds Bush even more than she had detested Doncaster when, as an adolescent, she would wake up some mornings and weep tears of rage at Doncaster for not being Leeds or Manchester or London. The whole experience was disastersville: the only thing she had got out of it was that whenever she came across Alfie these days she got a free cab-ride, even when she didn't want to go anywhere.

Funny to think, though, that if only Mr. Veerekananda had chucked all that pegboard in the builders' skip, it might all have worked out differently. V. differently indeed, if Maggie hadn't had to move out of Notting Hill. Over on the wrong side of Shepherds Bush, looking for a place among all those dough-faced punters hunched up on rows of tip-up chairs in a doctor's waiting-room that still looked like the failed fruit shop it had once been, with tattered stickers advertising bananas and grapefruit on the steel-mesh guarded plate-glass windows, it just never occurred to you that there was anything to do about a babe except have it. Mention anything about getting rid to some of those clapped-out mums with their snotty hordes of 'kiddies' all blotched like raspberry yoghurt from crying, and they would bloody lynch you. Whereas if you'd minnied up West into one of those confidential, personalised, reliable, registered pregnancy advice centres, staffed by cool young chicks in seersucker dungarees who took it all as calmly as if they were running a temps bureau, it would all have been—well, more sophisticated, nudge nudge.

Just think: nearly no Dan. Thank Christ the poor little sod would never know he probably owed his life to a few sheets of pegboard.

Although Maggie should have turned left for Pegboard Manor she wandered right. But deliberately this time. By following the streets round in a rough, meandering square she could get where she wanted to be yet avoid going past the Gay Gordons which stood squatly in the middle of the more direct route. The Gay Gordons, or The Scotsman Garden Bar and Hawaiian Room as it was known to the brewers, was—had been: she had better start getting her tenses right—one of Sean's favourite pubs, although he had never taken her to it. It was a tarted-up brown-ale hangar whose striped black and orange canopies and fretwork palm trees would do nothing to disguise the uncompromising frontage of glazed biscuit tiles (Sean liked them—he always said that being treated to a drink in a public urinal was his idea of Utopia). It was nearly opening time by now and there were bound to be some of his little leather-boy friends hanging about outside. They would be talking about Sean, and if any of them recognised Maggie as they might from other pubs that she and Sean had used around here, they would want to talk about him with her too. Couldn't be doing with it.

Anyway, she might be tempted to go in for a drink, unless women were barred in there. That really would be curtainsville.

Maggie was surprised, now that he had slipped back into her mind, how little she had been thinking of Sean while wandering around the streets these last twenty minutes or so. That was down to Aliboo. She had made Maggie feel such a right nana that it had jolted her out of that zombified, sleep-walking state she had been in on the tube. Or had it? No, she was still feeling quite zombified, thanks ever so for asking, but being made a see-you-en-tee of, as Ken would have put it, had made her jump the points of that Circle Line in her head (Did he fall? No, he jumped. Why did he do it? Why did he do it to me? But *did* he do it to me? Did he jump? Or did he fall) that she had been travelling round and round on. It had given her something else to think about.

Herself, for a change. No one could ever accuse Maggie of being selfish.

Nearing the end of her roundabout route she turned into a rundown residential avenue which she had always called Dogshit Mile when she lived around here. Its piebald stuccoed villas behind their tumbling walls looked like seedy private hotels, but surprisingly they were mostly still family homes, with pianos instead of coin-operated pool tables in their drawing-rooms, and their stoved-in chequerboard-tile front paths twisting the ankles of schoolgirls with satchels rather than New Zealand students with rucksacks. But every so often along this avenue you saw the yellow builders' skip, the jangling heap of scaffolding clamps, and the semicircle of no-waiting cones around a tarpaulin-covered pile of new bricks, and you knew that one more tactical retreat had been made to Dulwich or Richmond, and that when the front-window shutters were tossed in the skip you would be able to peep into the divided drawing-room and see that where once a fireplace had been, there was now only a marble ledge sticking out of a smooth buff-painted wall, like a skeleton hand sticking out of a grave. Once, pissed, in the moonlight,

Maggie and Sean had scooped up armfuls of scaffolding clamps and clanked them like chains, moaning in ghostly voices from the top of a pile of builders' sand, 'We're coming! We're coming!' Rotten pigs that they were. A punter in a tweedy suit, who was taking his dog for a shit, asked them what they thought they were doing. The poor sod looked more anxious than angry: probably sensed that it was only a matter of time now before he found himself living next door to an abortion clinic. Maggie put her fingers to her lips and said owlishly, 'The scum also rises.' Boom boom.

Pisspots. She had come all this way round to avoid Sean's rough-trade chums and now look who was here, beaming at her like a human traffic light from the corner of Dogshit Mile and the crescent that would bring her round to Pegboard Manor. If Maggie had to name all the faces she didn't want to see this morning, Jimmy with his boiled beetroot head and his checky suit with the carnation buttonhole would have been high on the list. He was one of the Portobello dealers, not a pal of hers especially, but he had rowed himself into that Hagerty's drinking school that she and Sean had found themselves in—when was it now?

Yesterday lunchtime. Couldn't believe it.

The only way to avoid him was by turning back. But he had seen Maggie and was waiting for her. Double pisspots.

'Morning, Maggie, how's Maggie?'

The saloon-bar greeting was accompanied by an upward swivelling of the eyeballs and other facial contortions to suggest that as fellow members of a secret freemasonry of drinkers they knew what went on at some of those lodge meetings. Just in time, Maggie remembered the response required of her: the pained 'Don't ask' grimace, together with a sharp intake of breath and a vigorous waggling of the right hand like a schoolboy who has just been caned.

'What, went too far last night? Or even far too far? Which was it, too far or far too far?'

He hadn't heard about Sean. Couldn't have done. He was carrying under his arm an elaborate filigree brass fender which he would have bought as scrap and would be about to sell as antique to a specialist in such things, so he had reason enough for sounding chirpy. But at least he would have gone through the motions of looking tragic if he'd heard. In fact not just gone through the motions, he would have done the death of Little Nell in spades. Inside every dealer there was a ham actor trying to get out.

He went into the ritual inquest on yesterday's boozing activities. Where did you finish up then, could see it was going to be a night of magic right from the start, wouldn't have minded but only went in for a quickie, good job I'd just had my drinking boots soled and heeled—all that. All through the familiar exchanges Maggie was praying, don't let him mention Sean, don't let him mention Sean, don't let him mention Sean.

If Jimmy did mention him she would have to talk about Sean as if he were still alive, nothing else for it. Definitely feeling no pain last I saw of him, *reeled* off into the night with that Irish mate of his. She would feel like a Victorian poisoner entertaining friends to tea while the body lay under the rockery.

But Jimmy didn't mention Sean. He just took it for granted that whichever 'dens of iniquity' Maggie had 'graced by her presence' last night, Sean would not have left her side. The pronoun 'you', as in 'you had definitely had the one', implied 'you both'.

'You're not about to visit the scene of the crime, by any chance?' asked Jimmy, jerking his head towards a street that would lead down to the Portobello and Hagerty's.

'No I am bloody not, I've too much to do.' Who said Maggie never refused a drink?

If Jimmy had gone on at his usual length about hairs of dogs, twisting arms and merest tinctures of the juniper berry, she might have weakened, but luckily the brass fender he had bought seemed to have become a burden. He transferred it from one arm to the other and after only a perfunctory 'Sure I can't tempt you? Speak now or forever hold your peace', went on his way. Maggie headed for Pegboard Manor congratulating herself.

On what? On refusing a drink? No, on not having been cornered into talking about Sean.

Oh, yes, and what was there to be proud of in that? Anyone'd think that being dead was a guilty secret, and that in managing not to bring it to Jimmy's attention she'd skilfully avoided committing an unforgivable social gaffe.

And anyway, she wasn't out of the wood yet. Notting Hill was crawling with Sean's friends.

Pegboard Manor, like an old man growing older, had deteriorated noticeably to Maggie since her last milk round, but probably only imperceptibly to the occupiers of its neighbouring junk-antique shops and cheap restaurants. The two big bald patches where the stucco had fallen away to reveal raw brick had expanded, and looked as if they were only waiting for someone to give the front door a good slam for them to merge. The windowsills had crumbled a bit more and the roof gutter, which had always sagged, was now on the verge of falling away. It all made Maggie feel quite homesick. Mr. Veerekananda would wait until the council served a dangerous structure notice on him, then he would do the minimum of patching-up and the drip-drip-drip process of corrosion would continue under a coating of thinned-down paint. Maggie wouldn't have had it any other way. It was only because people like Mr. Veerekananda kept places like this in a condition like this that people like her could afford to live in them.

You entered Pegboard Manor along a narrow passageway that looked as if it ought to lead to a mini-cab office or bucket-shop travel agent's. The passage turned sharp left and then sharp right, following the pegboard contours of an expanded hall cupboard that was now known as Ground Floor Flat, and culminating at a surprisingly wide flight of uncarpeted wooden stairs. Criminal waste of space, and Mr. Veerekananda doubtless had plans for pegboarding the staircase down the middle and converting the side nearest the wall into split-level flatlets. For the present, though, and in the absence of anything like a hall table or shelf, there was room on the third and fourth stairs for Pegboard Manor's accumulation of mail. Letters were put there, or rather tossed there, by anyone who happened to pick them up out of the concrete doormat well by the front door.

Junk mail, mostly. Football coupons for tenants who had long ago moved on, special offers for those who were in prison or dead, sucker-list window envelopes addressed to punters who had probably never existed. THE CONTENTS OF THIS LETTER MAY BE WORTH £25,000. Sometimes there was a Sotheby's letter or Christie's catalogue for a Mrs. Fairfax-Freen who must have lived there in double-barrelled elegance when it was a classy three-floor maisonette. If there was, Maggie always snitched it and gave it to one of her mates down the Bello. Worth a drink, as Sid the Squirrel would say.

Sitting on the stairs, Maggie filleted the proper letters from the rubbish. There weren't very many of them and those that there were had heelmarks all over them so that even if they had been delivered only this morning they looked as if they had been lying around for months. Most of them had, of course. Maggie recognised several of them from her last milk round. Rayber, Paish, Bluett, Marynka: four ships that had pissed off in the night, probably owing Mr. Veerekananda rent. There was a whole list of such names that she had accumulated from the shelves and windowsills and hall tables and uncarpeted stairways of the places she had lived in. She could recite them and in the small hours sometimes did, instead of counting sheep. Berry, Sappe, Jonzen, Mackenzie, Garth, Meah, Tsentides, Freeman, Sarda, Gandish . . . She wondered about them all sometimes, who they were and where they were now and who was trying to get in touch with them and why. Maggie lived in hopes that she would meet one of them some day. 'Not Rastaph Meah?' she would say. 'I suppose you know there's a letter waiting for you at Chalk Farm?'

L. Ngobi: now there was a name from the past, if she could only place it. Ought to be able to, she didn't know all that many spades. Menzies: that was one of the hookers on the first floor. Miss Kane, her stage name was. McMahon, McSomething anyway: never heard of him.

There was a postcard for Miss M. Moon. Will you please call at this dental surgery at your earliest convenience, as your periodical examination is now due. No bloody fear. She dropped the card into her lap and looked at the remaining letters. Airmail. Ngobi again. Liberation Ngobi. Oh, him! Remembered: he was a cousin or something of those two spade chicks who lived in the next room to Sean's in Ladbroke Grove. Had been dossing down on their floor at the time Maggie left Pegboard Manor, and Sean had advised him to get his skates on and get round to see Mr. Veerekananda. Evidently he'd scored.

Nilsville. That was the lot, then. Nothing else for Mags, not that she was expecting anything. She was about to tip the letters off her lap when the one to McMahon or whoever caught her eye again. It had been walked over many times and the name and address were almost obliterated by footprints, but looking at it from a new angle she could see now that the scrawled name wasn't anything like McMahon, it was Moon. Ms. M. Moon.

Fancy. Billet-doux for Mags. A real live letter, with a real live stamp and everything. Posted, if she could make out the real live postmark, about two weeks ago. Bit puzzling, though. She hadn't stayed in Pegboard Manor long enough for anyone to know her address, except that flaming Aussie dentist and the Premium Bond people. And the Premium Bond people would have sent her £25,000 OHMS. It was probably a bloody mouthwash circular.

Maggie slit open the envelope with her thumbnail and tipped out a piece of white card about the size of a playing-card. An ordinary postcard cut in half. Printed across it in uneven ballpoint capitals were the words:

GO TO JAIL. GO DIRECTLY TO JAIL. DO NOT PASS GO. DO NOT COLLECT £200.

Sean. Who else but?

She could remember the exact spot where this Monopoly joke of his had started. They had been coming up past the Kentish Town public library on the way back to the tube station on the last lap but one of the milk round, and Sean, his little leggings beginning to give out, had complained that it was like traipsing round a bloody great Monopoly board. From then on, the milk round *was* a life-sized game of Monopoly, like one of those freaky games of chess played with human beings. Sean and Maggie had even decided which pieces they were: Sean was the top hat, Maggie the boot. 'Now the minute we land on the Angel, Islington, Boot,' instructed Sean, 'Boot can go and collect its rents or pick up its Community Chest card or do what it likes, but Top Hat is going to build a hotel and put its feet up in the leeounge for half an hour.'

And he'd been keeping this wheeze up his sleeve ever since. No wonder he'd kept on asking ever-so-casually when she meant to do her milk round again.

Maggie, still looking at the card, put it in her shoulder-bag and took out her hanky. Nice one, Sean. Worth a tiny sniffle, she reckoned.

She was screwing the handkerchief into a ball after dabbing her eyes when a high-pitched, highly-strung voice behind her on the stairs demanded: 'Hey, man, what you doing with my mail?'

Looking up she saw a young, gangling West African-looking face, with Mary Quant tribal marks on his thin cheeks, dressed all in black leather with a wickedly studded belt and cuffs. On his way to the Gay Gordons, at a guess. A corrupting influence. My goodness, Liberation Ngobi, how you've changed, man.

'Oh, is this yours? Sorry.' Pretending that she'd only been blowing her nose, Maggie stuffed the crumpled handkerchief into her bag and handed up the airmail letter from the top of the pile in her lap. 'There's another one here somewhere.'

'I *know* what's there, man. You don' answer the question, what you doing with my mail?'

This could turn ugly. Maggie held up both hands in the accepted pacifying gesture. 'Look. I used to live here, right? I came back to pick up my mail, right? I was just going through this heap of letters to see if there was anything for me, which there is. This dental card here, and this envelope here. M. Moon. That's me. OK? OK.'

'Them could be anybody mail, man. How I know you used to live here? *I* never see you before.'

'You *have* seen me before but you don't remember. You used to shack up with two chicks in Ladbroke Grove, and you've seen me going in and out of Sean's room next door. And the room you're in now—third floor back, right?—used to be mine, and it was Sean who put you on to it, right?'

'You a friend of Sean?'

'I'm a *very good friend* of Sean.'

'OK, if you a friend of Sean, that OK. That different. I not know you a friend of Sean. I am sorry. I apologise.'

Liberation bent over Maggie and held out his hand. Thinking he wanted her to give him his other letter she started riffling through the pile on her lap, then realised that what he was trying to do was to shake hands. The momentary confusion, plus her sense of relief at having talked her way out of what could have been a nasty one, kept Maggie from properly taking in that they had both been speaking about Sean in the present, living tense.

'I not seen Sean for oh, long time now. How he, I hope he well?'

She had got her tenses sorted out now, though. Slight error there'd been, just there. I'm a very good friend of Sean, she had claimed, as if their very good friendship were still flourishing, as if she'd be meeting him tonight or tomorrow for a drink or for a nosh at their Italian restaurant, when she'd tell him, because it would make him laugh, about this little misunderstanding with his mate Liberation Ngobi. What a scream of an act she could make of it, what a cruel imitation she could do of Liberation's accent, if she were ever to see Sean again to swop their embroidered stories.

'Didn't you know?' Maggie heard herself saying, far off. 'He went under a tube train, Fulham Broadway, midnight last night. Shocking. Pissed out of his skull, apparently.'

Mags. Mags. What a right little wanker you are.

6

Not Drowning but Waving

Maggie was careful never to indulge in dreams about what might have been, but if she were forced at gunpoint to have her time all over again, there was one thing she really would have liked to have done differently.

She would have liked to have used a different name at each of her different addresses. Then she could don her aliases as one dons a coat selected from a wardrobe, and flit unseen out of one life and into another.

She bet she could think up some good names for herself too. Queenie, she could have called herself back in the days when she was poncing around Camden Town and developing her hollow legs. Pamela Smith, when she was playing at mistresses in Islington. Jean Jenkins: that would have been a good round-shouldered name to have popped in her bag like a half-knitted cardie and dragged along to the wrong side of Shepherds Bush.

What a shame you couldn't change your name retroactively. How convenient and comforting it would be to backtrack to Pegboard Manor and persuade that spade she had just been rabbiting to that she wasn't Maggie at all, she was called Little Mary Bullshit.

Sorry, Sean. Never meant to spew it all out in technicolour like that. Feel really bad about it.

What had happened? She didn't quite know. She had suddenly felt that the event of Sean's death was locked up inside her body and was doing something in there, growing, developing, changing, as a tumour does. She had to let it out or terrible things would happen to her, she didn't know what.

But to let it out like that, as a titbit, a spicy dollop of

gossip? All that drooling? Really sorry, Sean, truly-ruly sorry. Only way it could be handled: by talking in coloured pictures. Talk in coloured pictures and it doesn't seem real. Only black and white is real. Ask Little Mary Bullshit.

Seriously, though: she really did wish she'd used a different name sometimes. The babe, stop calling him the babe, little Dan: he should have been born under a different name, he was going to have one soon enough in any case. Better all round. Wrap that bit of your life in a parcel, stick a label on it with the name of the person who lived that bit of your life, and put it on a shelf. Finish. All on to the next chapter.

She knew why she was thinking like this. Paddington. Not the happiest of bijou staylets for Maggie, Paddington hadn't been. And here she really had thought of using a different name, and had always wished she had.

Pity about Paddington, really, because she liked the area. Quite classy it was, in a ratty sort of way: far classier than a lot of faces gave it credit for when they said they would rather live in Neasden. You had the Great Western Royal Hotel for a start: that was so classy they wouldn't let Maggie through the door the last time she'd tried to use their lavs. Must have thought she was on the game. Then you had several cobbled mews with some quite nice drinking clubs, and leafy squares, all quiet and secluded, but still handy for the all-night Wimpy Bar and with plenty of room for the luxury-type coaches to park when they dropped their Cup Final punters at the private hotels. The main drag past the station, Praed Street, was almost like a little local high street with all kinds of old traditional shops. The Marital Aid Centre, established in 1901 so it said. Classy.

Always took the piss out of Paddington, did Maggie. Bit on the defensive, probably.

She'd liked her room there, though. Well, not so much the room as the house it was in, with its back windows overlooking the District and Circle Lines, where they neared the tube station. No. 1 Paddington, Maggie called that house. If she'd had a happier time there, she wouldn't have exchanged that address for No. 1 Piccadilly.

The District Line bit of the station was much of a muchness with Notting Hill Gate two stations down, except that the girders of its arched glass canopy were painted bright red, and v. jolly they looked too. What really made your heart take off and fly, though, was when your eye travelled up along the vaulted brickwork at either end of the platform approaches and came across unexpected vistas of tall sash windows, some curtained, some not, some half-open with men in shirtsleeves leaning out or bedsheets airing, one with a cat washing itself on the sill, one with a woman flitting across it carrying a saucepan, some with their roller-blinds so tightly down that you wondered what they were up to in there at this time of day, some with washing hanging up, two, no three, with birdcages, one with a geezer sitting at a table bent over his paper work, the light from a green-shaded lamp shining on his bald patch, one with a pale-faced chick in a dressing-gown holding a book, but not turning the pages.

Like Naples, Sean had said. Really must go to Italy one of these days. (But who with? Would have liked to have gone with Sean. Too late for that now, chucky-egg, you should have spoken up sooner.)

That window there, third one up, just by that drainpipe, that was Maggie's. Well, put it this way—it was the one she had always called hers: it was just a window on the stairs really, her room had been the first-floor front on the street side, worse luck. But when she was living there she would often put on her coat and lock up her room as if she were going for a walk, then climb to the third-floor landing and stand very still at that window, looking out over the District Line. It had to be the third floor because you got the best bird's-eye view of the station, better than the second which had hoardings in the way and the fourth and fifth which were too far up and overlooked only the arched roof. She wore her coat because it was winter and you could get very cold on the unheated landing if you stood there for long with the window open. Sometimes, especially late at night or very early in the morning when the other occupants of the house would not disturb her with their comings and goings, she would stand there for as long as two hours, counting the red trains as they pulled in or out of the station platforms below. She had watched the last train depart and the first one arrive, and in between, mesmerised by the glinting railway lines, she had watched until the mysterious dead-of-night engineering works wagons rumbled through with piles of rusted bolts and sleeper-clamps, then disappeared into the far black tunnel on muffled wheels, giving the illusion of going down into the earth, so that you could fancy they were clandestinely mining in reverse and depositing their iron load back where it had come from. The quiet afternoons were a good time for watching too, and the busy evenings. In her few weeks at Paddington Maggie had spent so many hours gazing down at the District Line that when, as she was doing now, she looked up at that third-floor window as the train pulled into the station, she half expected to see herself, waving.

Maggie turned out of the station forecourt, put her tongue out mentally at the Great Western Royal Hotel opposite, and shivered a little as she walked the few steps round to No. 1 Paddington. The sky was overcast now and the pavement was wet. They must have worked in a crafty April showerette between Notting Hill Gate and here. It was the first she had noticed of the weather since watching how the weak morning sunbeams pierced the slime-green threadbare curtain at whatever-the-guy's-name-was near Putney Bridge that morning.

She could remember how hopefully she had turned this corner when she had first come to look at No. 1 Paddington —what was it, four years ago, five years ago? Didn't keep a diary so couldn't say. Time for a change from the same old Camden Town—Kentish Town—Chalk Farm eternal bloody triangle, she had thought. (The Bermuda Triangle, she called it, on account of she had taken what was left of her innocence there and it had never been seen since.) And some face or other had said: 'I do know of one place going begging, but I don't suppose you fancy overlooking the tube?' Didn't she just!

She was disappointed that it was a front-facing room, but she got a promise that when one looking over the railway became vacant, she could have it, so long as she didn't mind paying front double-room rent for a back single. The Cypriot hunchback who looked after the place and collected the rents, who obviously looked forward to pocketing the difference, plainly thought she was bananas. Maggie didn't care. Paddington felt good and it would get her out of the just-that-little-bit-slaggy rut she had let herself drift into. Well, more of a jump than a drift really. But she'd had enough of all that. She meant to knock back a bit less of the sherbet and stop putting herself about with faces she didn't really know and didn't even really like. She would be handy for the Portobello where she could do some serious grafting instead of just playing at it. Hire a telly, stay in some evenings. Save a bit of bread. Do something, go somewhere. Read a book. Eat meals. Time for a touch of the tomorrow we'll get organiseds.

Could have worked out well, Paddington could, if things had been different. But things never were different, were they?

No. 1 Paddington hadn't changed a bit. Like Pegboard Manor, it was given over to commerce at ground-floor level —a hotel employment agency and an obscure Polish bookshop with a sideline in neglected-looking peasant dolls. In the recess formed by their curving windows was a narrow black door which, as Maggie had anticipated, was locked. Drawing-pinned to the inside of the door there would still be the time-ochred scrap of card advising, 'So as, to keep out undessirable, pleased to keep this door LOCKED at all hour.'

Meths drinkers pissing in the doorway, that referred to, not Maggie. She selected from her bunch of Yale keys the one with the identifying wisp of yellow thread—yellow for Paddington, as on the Underground direction lights: brown for Euston, red for Piccadilly, blue for Waterloo, yellow for Paddington—and opened the door. If the Cypriot hunchback was on the prowl, which was v. unlikely as he had four or five other places to look after and was also believed to be running a small sandwich bar on the side, she would say she was visiting Mrs. Kresakova on the third floor. Mrs. K. was the old mother, maybe even the old grandmother, of the drained-looking guy who mooned about the Polish bookshop, jangling his change and waiting for trade. She sat in her room all day long, talking to herself in Polish and sometimes weeping. Maggie, watching the trains go by, used to hear her crying sometimes. It was the kind of bleahness you had to take in your stride when you lived in rooms: bit like being a hospital nurse when you thought about it, you got what was the word, inured. Maggie had yet to find the place where, in the quiet night hours, there was never sobbing to be heard if you listened for it. Pigeons cooing, she would kid herself if it went on too long, unless the sound came from her own pillow.

No. 1 Paddington had no hall to speak of. The front door

opened almost directly on to the steep-rising staircase, shit-brown-painted with home-made diarrhoea-patterned lino treads. The overhead light-fitting, though lacking a bulb, had one of those globular Japanese paper shades that you often glimpsed in the basement kitchens of real houses. Altogether a classier establishment than Pegboard Manor.

There was no window on the first-floor landing, whose outer wall formed part of the brick embankment stretching up from the railway lines. Instead there was an alcove meant for a decorative bust or a vase of flowers, and used as a repository for mail.

When Maggie had put No. 1 Paddington on her milk round, it was in fear rather than expectation. There were usually one or two bits and pieces for her—she'd gone raving mad and sent off for some holiday brochures when she moved in here, and some of the poor optimistic buggers still kept her on their mailing lists—but it was the reassurance of two letters *not* being there that she was looking for. No, not two any more; only one really, these days. She no longer had sleepless nights wondering whether there'd be another discreet but official-looking envelope from—well, never mind who from; but she couldn't understand why the TV hire company had never bombarded her with threatening letters. Other faces who had pulled the same fast one assured her that the firm was notorious for its inefficient computer, but Maggie didn't trust people who didn't trust computers: she believed that those microchipped digital-chattering metal bastards got you in the end. The hire company had only itself to blame, of course, for parting with a set to someone who was plainly going to vanish into the night with it—Maggie had been aided and abetted by a randy but clueless salesman who had been so hellbent on pulling her that he had filled in his own name on the application form as a reference—but that didn't alter the fact that she *had* vanished into the night with it, finally abandoning it in that Maida Vale squat she'd once lived in. You could get your collar felt for that.

There was no fanlight over the street door, and what light there was on a darkening morning had to filter down the stairwell from the upper floors. Scooping up the dusty sprawl of letters, Maggie had to hold them close to her face to make out who they were for.

More familiar names. Funny that none of them ever

recurred, as her own did, on any other shabby stairway that she knew of. Maybe they'd all put that name-changing idea of hers into practice. Maybe Meah of Chalk Farm was the same person as Marynka of Pegboard Manor, and Marynka of Pegboard Manor was Mrs. Kresakova who was probably weeping in her third-floor room at this very moment because there was nothing for her in the post.

Nothing from the TV people, thank Christ: she really didn't know why she let herself get in such a tizzy about it, they must have written her off as a bad debt years ago. Nothing from the travel agents this time, either. Maybe they'd given up at last, or maybe the Cypriot hunchback had made enough out of his sandwich bar to think about taking a holiday in Benidorm.

But there was a white envelope, addressed in ballpoint to what looked, in the gloom of the stairway, like McMahon or McScrawl.

Oh, Sean, not again! Gone too far this time.

The crafty bugger must have jotted down the address, that time when he—

You know what this means, don't you, Mags? There's going to be one of these letters at every stop on the milk round.

What an odd feeling: a flitter-flutter of anticipation that was also a lurch of apprehension. Not often you got two opposite sensations for the price of one.

Maggie was climbing the stairs in search of more light, ripping open the envelope as she went. She tipped out a piece of card just like the other one, blank side up, and turned it over. All right, Sean, let's have it.

DEAR MADAM, IF YOU WILL KINDLY REPORT TO THE PRAED STREET POX CLINIC (BACK ENTRANCE) YOU MAY HEAR SOMETHING TO YOUR DISADVANTAGE.

Ho bloody ho. Not fucking funny, Sean. Not funny at all.

God, he could be a vicious sod when he wanted. And it was no use telling him, it only made him worse. 'I know, dear, I know,' he'd mock. 'It's what comes of having cruel lips.'

Don't take on, Mags. How was he to know? She'd never told him, she'd never told anybody. Couldn't think why: in the same boat, he would certainly have told her. And made it all sound a hoot. What Maggie should have done: made a story of it, with funny voices. The best way she knew of blotting out unpleasant memories.

It had been five days after she'd moved into the first-floor front. Got her telly, got her box of chocs, got her slip-slaps, got plenty of shillings for the gas, got a meat-safe full of scoff, got her fags, got her tea-bags, got a big thick library book to read, got a nice armchair, it was snowing, and she couldn't have been cosier if she'd been a kitten in a basket.

Own semi-private lav, too: that was nice. The two first-floor backs, not having windows, were used as store-rooms (the Cypriot hunchback's boss ought to put them in Henry's hands: he'd soon find them tenants) so she only had to share with the other first-floor front. Luxury, that was, the next best thing to having a sunken bath en suite. Maggie felt quite spoiled.

One night she had to get up to go to her own semi-private lav and it was like peeing prussic acid.

Oh, Christ.

Right: that was it, then, wasn't it? The dreaded lurgy. Couldn't be anything else, Mags, so no use fooling yourself. That flapping of tiny wings she heard wasn't her heart beating in panic, it was the sound of all her chickens coming home to roost.

She sat on the bed, angled the bedside lamp towards her, and examined first her discarded knickers then her own person. No stain, no discharge, no other symptoms. It was possible to be wrong. It didn't one hundred per cent *have* to be the dreaded lurgy. There must be a dozen bijou complaintettes that made peeing painful. Change of diet, even. Knocking vodka on the head, which she more or less had done in favour of white wine, and not even that until six in the evening and only if she went out which she hadn't done more than three times all week—that could make a difference. In fact of course it bloody did. Wine was acid. Generally known fact.

Maggie got dressed and went up to the third-floor landing and looked down at the shining railway lines for a long time. Three times she felt a burning in her crotch and tiptoed into Mrs. Kresakova's lav to inspect herself. Nothing. She had a pee and even though she was forcing herself it was less painful than it had been. Acid white wine, passing through the system. She watched the first train go through with a stripe of fresh snow along its carriage roofs and then went down to her room and dozed off fully-dressed. She woke, refreshed, relieved and hungry, at about ten. She felt ever so slightly damp, and resignedly tugged off her knickers, telling herself sternly that there was no way she was going to go through today like she'd gone through last night. There was a tiny smudge of wet, surrounded by the tidemark of a slightly wider stain. Bleah.

Maggie knew exactly what to do: nothing. A great walker-away from other people's troubles, she believed in trying whenever possible to walk away from her own. Sometimes she would do this literally, by packing her gear and moving on. If other faces were involved, that was always the best way: simply remove yourself from their sphere of influence. There was no human agency to be taken account of, as with an attack of toothache or the time Maggie thought she had cervical cancer after a chick had told her you could get it from screwing too young, her instinct was to take refuge in an all-enveloping inertia that would, fingers crossed, cocoon her from anything bleah until the bleahness had passed over.

The dreaded lurgy wouldn't go away.

Maggie spent the next two weeks in a muzzy torpor of anxiety, refusing to centre her thoughts except on fruitless hopes that her next self-examination under the bedside lamp would produce a more encouraging result than the last. She spent a lot of time at her third-floor window, watching the trains go in and out, or waiting through the dawn for the first train to arrive. She went out not at all except on quick, head-down expeditions into the slushy street to buy bread and milk and too many cigarettes. She ate practically nothing and lost weight. She saw no one and spoke to no one. She slept little, and only from exhaustion. She felt and looked terrible. When a sore appeared on her lip she dragged herself to the dreaded lurgy clinic.

Not the Praed Street one round the corner, so nyah nyah nyah to Sean: she would have been terrified ever afterwards of bumping into one of the nurses or orderlies or whoever in the all-night Wimpy Bar or somewhere. She shuffled off south of the river where nobody knew her.

She hadn't meant to give her proper name but she felt too wretched to think up a false one. The person who sat behind the desk wrote it down on a white card, then she was sent in to see the quack. A woman, thank Christ—lady doctor, as

Maggie thought of her, unthinkingly using the words her Mum would have used. It didn't take long.

Bloody virus infection, wasn't it? (With a cold sore thrown in just to scare the shit out of her.) Not even cystitis, which she would have happily settled for.

If she'd had her card marked by a few of the faces in the Half Moon instead of running up and down like a blue-arsed fly, she could have saved herself a lot of aggro. How many times had she heard that lot boring for England on the self-same subject ('Morning drip, the lot. I don't mind telling you, I was petrified')? And didn't it always turn out to be something other than the dreaded lurgy?

What nobody ever told, of course, was the story on similar lines where the punchline was that their nose was about to drop off from tertiary syphilis. So you didn't know. But three cheers, anyway, for all those who had bored for England on the topic of morning drip: without the tiny, secret hope that having heard from them so often allowed her to nurture, she would never have made it to the clinic and would have thought even more seriously than she already had done of jumping out of her third-floor window.

Cleanish bill of health, then. Maggie was indignant that the lady doctor wouldn't leave it at that. Writing out a prescription for antibiotics, the cow had the cheek to ask, without looking up: 'Why did you think it might be something else?'

There was no answer to that, was there? What the hell was Maggie supposed to say? Ah, well, you see, I've been putting myself about a bit too much lately, very naughty I know, slap wrist; but every time I got round to thinking that's it, Mags, gone too far, it's all got to stop, I had the great misfortune to get so roaring pissed I'd forget what my Mum always told me —never pick up a geezer when you don't know where he's been.

She said lamely: 'Well . . . it *could* have been something else. I mean I'm not a nun, am I?'

'You're saying you sleep around quite a lot?'

Cheeky cat. Maggie hated that phrase 'sleeping around', anyway. It always put her in mind of thin-lipped spinsters writing poison-pen letters. If the lady doctor meant screwing around, why couldn't she say so?

Shrug. 'Depends what you mean by sleeping around.'

'Let me put it this way. You don't have a regular boyfriend?'

Regular boyfriend? Thought you'd never ask, dear. Doesn't every nice girl have a regular boyfriend—a steady, as we say in the trade? Brian, his name is, would you like to see some snaps? This is Brian polishing his Ford Escort, this is Brian having a night out with the boys, this is Brian giving someone a fat lip for trying to grope me at the firm's dinner dance, and this is Brian saving up to get married.

'Not really.'

The lady doctor, taking longer than she needed over her prescription-writing and note-scribbling so as not to put her patient to the embarrassment of meeting her eye, delivered what Maggie supposed was her standard lecturette on the unwisdom of putting oneself about. It included a dire warning about gargling too much or 'getting woozy' as the lady doctor put it, which medical research had proved to be the prime cause of the dreaded lurgy.

Pull the other one. She'd be telling Maggie next that you could pick up cirrhosis of the liver from lavatory seats.

Maggie thanked the lady doctor kindly, took a swift cab to the Half Moon, and became instantly legless. The next morning she took her big thick book back to the public library and threw away the ticket.

She was supposed to report back to the lady doctor for a check-up when the infection cleared up but she never did. There was no way they were getting her inside that dreaded-lurgy clinic again, for all that the nurse who gave her the appointment card had routinely tried to convince her that as they dealt with every type of between-the-legs disorder there was no stigma in going there. After a couple of weeks they sent her a printed reminder in a plain buff envelope (so much for them trying to pass themselves off as being no more sinister than a flaming hair clinic). That worried her rather. If what she'd had was so minor, why were they pestering her? Had they taken another skeg at her smear-test and found that she'd got the dreaded lurgy after all?

If they really did want to see her again, they weren't going to let it rest there, they'd write to her again. She knew they didn't give a sod about you really, but they wouldn't leave it till you woke up one morning and found your nose lying on the pillow beside you, now would they?

Maggie had already arranged to leave No. 1 Paddington—pity, but it could never be bless-this-houseville for her now, not after all those stomach-lurching nights—for half a semi-basement (did that make it a quarter-basement?) around Lisson Grove not far away. For the next three months she was to be drawn back at weekly intervals, sometimes twice weekly when for a while peeing became painful again, to reassure herself that there was no plain buff envelope among the pile of letters in the alcove on the first-floor landing. Thereafter, No. 1 Paddington remained a priority call on her milk round. It was not until a good year later that her anxiety began to fade, and even then the nasty aftertaste of the whole grubby episode continued to linger. It affected her life in the sack, such as it was: if she had any reputation for frigidity over the next few months, it was all down to that particular experience.

So on the whole, Sean, taking it by and large, your pox-clinic joke was not exactly the big titter of the morning. Standing at the open third-floor window, looking down at two trains dawdling past one another as the signals changed, Maggie was about to rip the piece of card up, but couldn't bring herself to—it was still a memento of Sean, all the more so because it was in definitely dodgy taste. Instead, she symbolically tore up the envelope it had been posted in, then let the pieces flutter down like the big snowflakes that she used to watch from here, on those endless winter nights.

Stop being all bitter and twisted about it now, Mags. If you can't take a joke you shouldn't have joined.

She lit a cigarette, dropping the spent match on the windowsill then flicking it away with her fingernail. She remembered how last time she had stood at this window she had done just the same thing and Sean, because she had asked him to help her cut down her smoking, had said, 'Seven'.

'Six,' said Maggie. 'Anyway, who's counting?'

'I am, dear. Remember we're smoking for two now.'

'Piss off. You're getting a real little naggy-boots, Sean, do you know that?'

Touch of the raging humps, that particular remark caused. They stood at the third-floor window in moody silence—Sean moody with Maggie, Maggie moody with Sean for being moody with her—until, puffing furiously, she had finished her cigarette. Ostentatiously lighting another one from the stub, Maggie announced defiantly, as smoke curled out of her mouth, '*Seven*'.

Sean wouldn't reply. A train rumbled through, then it was quiet again. From Mrs. Kresakova's room along the landing could be heard the muffled sound of crying. Miserable old bat. Feeling sorry for herself because nobody felt sorry for her.

In a gust of anger Maggie tossed her newly-lighted cigarette out of the window she snapped: 'God, why doesn't she *fucking* drown herself?'

Sean, standing huffily with arms folded, one shoulder deliberately turned away from her, gave such a campish pout that he could have been sending himself up, as he often did. 'Why don't *you*, dear, and do us *all* a favour?'

He'd gone so far over the top in his pettiness that it was funny. Maggie's own fit of the grumps blew away. 'Oh, come on, grumpy-drawers! Come here. Kiss better.'

Later that week, when he heard what she had done—it was Riggsy who put it all round the West End, of course—he was horrified. 'But kitten, I was *joking*!' he couldn't stop saying between hugs and bouts of tears. He was so upset that Maggie hadn't the heart to remind him that even if he hadn't meant it for real, he hadn't meant it as a joke.

She was very patient with him, considering that she didn't want to talk about it. 'It was nothing to do with you, my love, and it was nothing you said. You didn't put the idea in my head and for the ten million zillionth time I *wasn't trying to drown myself*.'

'So what *were* you doing? Walking on the water, I suppose.'

'Oh, do go and fuck yourself, Sean.'

'The impossible we can do now, miracles have to be practised at home in front of a mirror. Meanwhile, tell Sean.'

So she did, even though, being Sean, he shouldn't have had to ask.

Sean's favourite poem, which he would recite in full when maudlin pissed, and which Maggie often swore she was going to get embroidered on a tea-towel for him one of these days, was Stevie Smith's 'Not Waving But Drowning'. Maggie had never read it herself but by now she knew it just about by heart:

> Nobody heard him, the dead man,
> But still he lay moaning:
> I was much further out than you thought
> And not waving but drowning.

'I wasn't drowning, I was waving,' said Maggie.

Sean nodded slowly and gravely, several times, as he sometimes did mockingly when she had said something incomprehensible. This time it meant he understood.

Maggie shivered at the third-floor window, not from cold but from looking down at the tube lines and thinking of Sean's body there, when he had stopped waving.

She clattered down the lino-capped stairs and out through the tall black door into the street. As she turned the corner for the tube station, rain hit her in the face: a thin, mean drizzle. Maggie looked around for a public clock. Must be nearly time to be making tracks for the wrong side of Shepherds Bush. It was certainly the weather for it.

7

Tough Cookie

A good quarter of an hour she must have waited so far. If one didn't come soon—or rather if six didn't roll up in convoy, knowing London Transport—she would be late.

Still, bugger them. Serve them right for sticking their socially-committed Portakabins at the dog-end of the worst bus route in London.

Maggie had already endured one bus journey too many: the one that had decanted her here from Shepherds Bush tube station, at a crossroads so desolate you expected a pigging mail coach to come rattling through.

It really was the arsehole of the Western world, where she was standing now. There must have been buildings here at one time, but of what kind—warehouses, shops, offices, terraces, mansion flats, white ferro-concrete razor-blade factories, art deco cinemas, condemned semis, Edwardian villas, an entire High Street perhaps, inclusive of municipal library and swimming baths with a big illuminated clock—it was utterly impossible to tell. All hints of the past had been removed or obliterated, including even the pavements in case anyone trudging by tried to reconstruct the past from manhole covers. Where the bus shelter was, in a muddy safety-first indentation of the corrugated iron wall which otherwise ran flush along the roadside in all four directions as far as the eye could see, one panel of the tin-ribbed fencing had had its ribs kicked in to make a short cut across the dead land, to some haphazardly-sited blocks of council flats that looked, in the otherwise featureless middle distance, like the last few cigarette packets on a glass display shelf.

Scoff on, Mags. Compared with Clem Attlee House and its surroundings, that was Park Lane out there.

The splinterproof glass bus shelter, tilted several degrees out of true either by subsidence of a filled-in basement or cellar beneath its concrete base or by nightly efforts to uproot it and toss it over the corrugated iron fence, was closely tattooed with marker-pen graffiti in primary colours. At first the ornately embellished hieroglyphics had looked to Maggie like Arabic, and then as if they might be the secret language of a secret cult; but now she had come to recognise them as English. Most of the lettering was so elaborately done that you couldn't read it at all, but here and there, by focussing one eye like a camera lens upon an intricate pattern of serifs and curlicues, you could make out a word or a small group of words. FRENZY. JUNK FOOD. MAGIC EARRING. HEAVY METAL. SCROTUM. PAIN.

Names of rock bands at a guess: Maggie wouldn't know, she wasn't into that stuff, play her the Rolling Stones and that was about it. Didn't see what else they could be, though, they made no other kind of sense. Except. Except that in a fruitcake sort of way, if you strung those unstrung words together, like popperbeads, they seemed to be saying something. ALLDAY GLUE. Z-LEVEL. HARD ROAD. HOT ROD. SHIT.

What you had there was a primitive mass autobiography, of the kind you could see in museums on ancient rolls of papyrus, but with words that represented pictographs instead of pictographs that represented words. It was a corporate life story, composed in the natural medium of those who were living it.

Not a lot going for it as life stories went, Maggie would have added to herself, had she not been reviewing her own life on and off. CIGARETTES. VODKA. ROOMS. POX CLINIC. BABY. TRAIN LINES. Who could talk?

On impulse she delved into her shoulder-bag for her felt-tip pen and scrawled on the wired glass screen in the little bit of space between SCROTUM and PAIN—now what was the name she wished she'd called herself for the wrong side of Shepherds Bush? Oh yes: JEAN JENKINS WAS HERE.

Childish bloody thing to do. Really, Mags!

Put it down to boredom: it had to be getting on for half an hour she'd been waiting here by now. Boredom and keeping things out of her mind: bringing little things to the foreground, so as to keep the big things in the background.

She had a passing urge to take her shoe off and see if she could smash the bus shelter's vandalproof glass. Go on, Mags, act your age: thirteen.

This corrugated iron junction was too quiet for her liking. There was hardly any traffic: the roads didn't lead to anywhere that had car-owners, and there was no activity within a square mile except for some ramshackle rag-and-bone yards and a car-crushing plant, where slow, evil-smelling fires burned all day and all night long, like smouldering ruins in a war.

The bunched-up-looking truncated cab section of an articulated lorry, as absurd and incomplete as the front legs of a pantomime horse, bounced along the pot-holed road on its way to some distant depot. The driver slowed down as he saw Maggie and called out something about getting them off.

On your way, short-arse.

He made a crude phallic gesture with his forearm and drove off. There was still no bus coming and nothing else in sight.

What's a nice girl like you doing in a dump like this, Mags? You could get into a lot of aggro standing here all on your lonesome. Skinheads, bovver boys, gang-bangers, they must be crawling about like lice over on that housing estate. Put the boot in as soon as look at you, those little buggers would.

Maggie had sometimes come across them on the bus as she went backwards and forwards to Alfie's mum's and the North Pole General. You kept very still and very quiet as they swaggered sheepishly past you along the aisle, and nobody would dream of, though they might have nightmares about, telling the ignorant little sods to take their feet off the seats.

Swaggered sheepishly: contradiction in terms, but it was what they did. It was the defiant, smirking gait of kids who have driven all the adults to the edge of a nervous breakdown, and know it, but don't know what to do next. 'YEW FACKING BARSTARD!' they would yell at one another across the bus, and cowering punters would lower their eyes, too frightened even to look disapproving. Maggie too: scared shitless, she was.

ALLDAY GLUE. Z-LEVEL. HARD ROAD. It wasn't only here at the arse-end of the universe that you saw them, either. Was at one time, but no longer. They were inching forward like slugs. FRENZY. SCROTUM. PAIN. You saw their pictographs everywhere. In the tube even, disgrace disgrace. Some day the tube was going to look like the New York subway that you saw in colour-supp photographs, all psychedelic scrawl and threatening. They were coming, they were inching forward.

'We're coming! We're coming!' was what Maggie and Sean had crowed from the top of a pile of builders' sand in a disintegrating residential avenue, one silly night. We're coming to get you. How long before these little swine came to get faces like Maggie?

Far off along the empty road a bus had come into view at last and stopped at a featureless junction, a replica of the one where Maggie was standing, which was the terminus of a meandering circular route through the wasteland. The conductor and driver were leaning against the bonnet, having a quick drag. Only a few minutes now. Thank God for that: saved from a fate worse than rape, most likely.

JEAN JENKINS WAS HERE. Wetting her finger, Maggie rubbed JEAN JENKINS into a blue smudge on the glass and wrote over it MAGGIE MUGGINS.

Wouldn't it be a hoot if by a zillion-to-one chance some face who knew her somehow landed up at this same bus shelter and saw her name? It would be like thinking you were the first man on Mars, then finding a matchstick.

The bus hadn't set off yet. She rubbed out MUGGINS and substituted her civilian name. MAGGIE MOON WAS HERE. It looked strange, as it always did when she saw it written down. Who was Maggie Moon? Did Maggie Muggins know her from somewhere?

She obliterated her little graffito altogether, even though the chances of anyone recognising it had increased to ten zillion to one with that alteration. Those faces who knew her civilian name could be counted on the fingers of one hand. Minus the thumb, now that Sean had gone.

Of course, that didn't include all the women who sat behind desks writing on white cards, or the Filth, or her various landlords over the years, or her Dad, or whoever might still remember her in Doncaster. Not that most of that lot had it more than half right: to them she was what it said on her birth certificate, Maggie Moon. Or, if they'd been at school with her, Margot, the name she had insisted on for a few terms. But her proper name, her civilian name, was Maggie Moon, shortened to Mags if you were one of three faces: Sean, Ken and herself. (Down to one face, now that one of them was dead and the other sod ought to be.) She had never changed it by deed poll or anything because she had always understood that you didn't have to, you just said it was your name and that was it, all legal, like a Moslem getting a divorce by clapping his hands. It made her livid when the women who sat behind desks insisted that Maggie had to be a contraction of Margaret. It didn't, it wasn't. Different name, different personality. She had been a Margaret in some other life, and had stopped being it in much the same way and for much the same reason as she had stopped believing in Father Christmas. Margaret Moon, Margot Moon, Maggie Moon, Maggie Muggins: that was the transition, if anyone was interested.

Maggie could hardly remember Margaret, except from photographs. Her Dad had had the front room plastered with them at one time: Margaret at the seaside, Margaret at the zoo, Margaret at the fair, Margaret's birthday party, Margaret in the park. In all of them she was a dumpy little thing with straight hair tied with a ribbon, her cheeks shiny with excitement and her tongue sticking out of the side of her mouth in the sheer concentration of being spoiled rotten. There were so many treats, all of them with her Dad while her Mum sat at home having migraines, that the cinema usherettes, icecream vendors and balloon sellers of Doncaster could well have taken Margaret for the product of a broken home whose guilt-ridden father had reasonable access at weekends. Saturday's child is full of chocolate. They would have been wrong: Margaret's home wasn't broken, you couldn't have broken it with a sledgehammer. Her Mum and Dad huddled under its roof like two frightened hermit crabs in the same shell. Maggie came to suspect that her Dad would have liked to have made a bolt for it but didn't have the guts, and that was why he made such a fuss of his only child—to kid himself that the reason he didn't bugger off was that he would be blighting her precious golden summers. Perhaps in her previous life as Margaret she had sensed that too. In some of those happy snapshots she seemed to be developing a lazy eye; what her Mum who whined and worried about it didn't know, and what her Dad who took her to the eye clinic and then on to the circus didn't know, was that she was squinting slyly off-camera, looking expectantly for her next treat.

The treats got fewer and fewer as she became less and less responsive to them and her Dad became more and more aware that he was getting a diminishing return on his selfless investment of affection and generosity. Instead of doing what Maggie would have done in his place and giving Margaret a good swift kick up the backside, he fell into a prolonged and almost permanent sulk, from which however he emerged intermittently to see if the happy-snapshot era couldn't be magically revived with a visit to the pantomime or some other tempting diversion. But Margaret, having discovered a gift for abrasiveness, was so objectionable on these occasions that eventually he gave up altogether. 'I simply don't understand you, Margaret,' he would sigh, when she had said something unusually wounding. No, he didn't. One thing he didn't understand was that she was no longer Margaret, she had become Margot, who was an even bigger little cow than Margaret if that were possible.

Margot belonged to Maggie's snob period. Like many girls of her age—she was about thirteen by now—she grew terribly ashamed of her parents, though not for the usual reason that they weren't rich enough. Almost the reverse.

To please her they had moved from a respectable end-terrace 'through house' near the town centre to a Dunroamin-type semi on the outskirts, thinking it would be nice for her to go to 'a good school' with playing fields and bring her friends home to a house that had french windows. She despised it. She despised her Dad's new Morris Minor and her Mum's finicky salad teas. She despised the lawnmower-pushers who were her Dad's friends—like him they were all local government 'executive officers' or jumped-up clerks—and the provincial moaning Minnies who were her Mum's. The new-wave northern films were all the rage at the time and their mockery of small-town suburban life struck a jubilant chord with Margot. She mocked the french windows, mocked her parents' genteel northern accents and the way they said 'pat' instead of 'put' ('Shall I pat some castard on the padding?' she would ask maliciously at 'lanch'), mocked their modest aspirations of a fitted carpet for the spare bedroom or a holiday abroad. Quite the Aliboo of Doncaster she was, in those days.

When they finally did drag themselves off to Majorca, with a flowered toilet bag bulging with Enterovioform and her Mum travel-sick before the taxi had even left the Crescent, Margot refused to go with them. She was sixteen and in her first term at a private secretarial college that despite her sneers her Dad had insisted on her trying out ('You'll always have those skills to fall back on'); much to her surprise she quite liked it. She threw a drunken cider party for her new classmates, gave her virginity away at last to an aspiring pop-group guitarist of her own age who had already had several unsuccessful cracks at taking it, and became the toast of the secretarial college. By the time her Mum and Dad came back, with a shell-encrusted trinket box for her which she accidentally-on-purpose dropped and broke, Margot had become the embryo Maggie.

It was the embryo Maggie—not Maggie Muggins yet, just Maggie Moon—who took herself off to live in Leeds, thirty miles up the A1, just after her seventeenth birthday. Although, until she quietly dropped the establishment from her curriculum vitae altogether, she always claimed to have been expelled from her secretarial college, in fact she was merely weeded out at the end of her first year for having failed all her proficiency tests. Without qualifications ('You see,' crowed her Dad, getting a bit of his own back for all her sneers and sniggers, 'you have no skills to fall back on') there were no interesting jobs to be found in Doncaster. There were no interesting jobs to be found in Leeds either, but going to stay with her Aunt May got her away from the french windows, the salad teas and the migraines, although she was expected to report back at weekends. She worked in a bookshop and didn't like it, in a travel agency and didn't like it, in a couple of dogsbody clerical jobs and didn't like them, as a department store cashier and didn't like it, as a hotel receptionist and didn't like it. 'I'm beginning to think you don't like work at all,' her Dad complained. He never spoke a truer word. After that she didn't bother to mention it when she changed jobs.

She liked living in a city, though, liked everything about it. She liked the blackened Gothic, the pointing statues, the striking clocks, the big glass domes and copper steeples, the viaducts, the civic fountains, the arcades, the wine lodges, the shouting news vendors selling buff finals. Pretending to look for congenial work she would amble around happily for hours. Yet sometimes on these wanderings she could turn a corner in happy anticipation of some favourite sight, and without warning her spirits would plunge into such depths that she felt cold, as if the sun had gone in on a chill day. These moments were the first intimation of the fits of depression, or glooms as Maggie preferred to call them, that were to seize her regularly as she got older.

Without consciously identifying the cause of her sudden waves of wretchedness as loneliness, she began to gravitate in the evenings towards the university district where she would be likely to meet people of her own age. She soon fell in with a crowd of, not students exactly—the students tended to keep themselves to themselves, toffee-nosed lot that they were—but of restless, rootless characters who like herself were attracted to the area because the pubs were 'artistic' and enlivened sometimes by a bit of jazz or the odd poetry reading. With their beards and cords and tartan shirts and sandals, they looked more studenty than the students themselves. They were all trying to get into the theatre or write books or become professional musicians or painters or photographers, anything that would be more creative than the 'boring nine-to-five jobs' which they were forced to do 'for the moment'.

Making two or three halves of lager last all evening, Maggie was very happy in this company. Most of them had paired themselves off in an easy-going sort of way, and it wasn't long before Maggie was paired off too, with a morose-looking red-bearded art-student dropout called Clive. He was the only one among them whose everyday work was remotely interesting: he sold secondhand books from a barrow. Maggie, having rashly told him that she used to work in a bookshop, soon found herself looking after the barrow on Saturday mornings while Clive was buying new stock. Selling old books in the street was far more to her taste than selling new ones from a shop, and surprisingly profitable. After a few weeks Maggie threw up her latest job in an estate agent's office and joined Clive full-time.

They were already sleeping partners, now they were working partners too: it seemed silly to spend practically every minute together and yet technically live apart. By this time Maggie was no longer lodging with her Aunt May, who had proved a bit too 'family' for her liking, always wanting to know if she'd had a cooked lunch and what time she intended coming home every night. Her brief career as a hotel receptionist, where you could 'live in' if you wanted to (Maggie claimed it was compulsory) had given her the opportunity to glide out of Aunt May's life with the minimum fuss. After that she lived in the YWCA, saying that it would be unfair to go back to imposing on her relatives. Now she moved in with Clive.

This was something else that Maggie didn't bother to tell her folks. It was very easy to deceive them, for she saw very little of them these days: she was going back to Doncaster only one weekend in three or four by now, and they never came to Leeds. Her Mum did occasionally ring her at the YWCA (her Dad never: he maintained, in that aggrieved way of his, that it was up to her to ring them) but then so did the mums of a lot of other girls who were less securely tucked up for the night than was fondly supposed back home; a fairly foolproof grapevine message system took care of that kind of situation. All that Maggie really needed to do to maintain the deception was to release as little information as possible about herself. That came naturally. Maggie, when she thought of how it would go down at home if they knew she was shacking up with an actual real live man and selling secondhand books from a barrow instead of zombifying in a girls' hostel and working in an office, began to see the advantages of making privacy a personal cult.

Life with Clive was a disaster. Maggie quickly discovered that behind the morose expression, which at medium range had seemed all very soulful and D. H. Lawrenceish, was a morose and sullen character. Like her Dad, he was a sulkpot. Worse than her Dad, he sulked not only if Maggie displeased him but if the world displeased him. It only needed rain coming through the ceiling and he would lapse into an injured, in fact just about mortally-wounded silence which Maggie found oppressive and claustrophobic. It also made her angry. She was buggered if she could see why she should put up with it.

Clive's trouble, she diagnosed from his martyred sighs when his breakfast bacon wasn't crisp enough for him, was that for all his bearded, bohemian front, his secret goal was to win back all the creature comforts he had lost by leaving home. Living in one room was only an interim step for him, whereas for Maggie it was so much the opposite of the uncut moquette orderliness she had grown up with that she didn't want anything else. She loved that room, with its rocking bamboo furniture and its popping gas-fire. She loved coming back to it up the shabby stairs; it was only when the light under the door told her that Clive was back before her that she felt depressed.

The secondhand book operation, after the initial lucky streak of brisk trade that had tempted Maggie into sinking her few pounds' savings into it, failed to prosper. One week, when it rained every day, they made no money at all. Clive's responsive sulk degenerated this time into a profound and dispiriting apathy. He took to staying in bed half the morning, staring at the damp patch on the ceiling and whining about the cold.

To tide them through a bad winter, Maggie took a part-time job as a coffee-bar waitress, mornings and lunch-times. She would come home and find Clive still in bed. She had been paying half the rent, now she paid all the rent. The part-time job became a full-time one. Clive did nothing except moon around and send laundry home to his mother: he developed a repertoire of excuses for not trying to sell books—waiting for the weather to change, waiting to find new stock, waiting for the next university term to begin. The lock-up garage over the road where they kept the barrow and their stock of books remained padlocked. One evening just before Easter Sunday, when there was to be a Spring fair in the streets, Maggie insisted on going across and loading up the barrow: she would be out selling over the holiday, even if Clive wasn't. She found that the roof of the asbestos panels had caved in under the winter snows, and all the books were ruined. 'Ah well, easy come, easy go,' sighed Maggie. Clive, whose neglect of their little business was the sole cause of the tragedy, was not to be consoled.

They went down to the pub where they still met the crowd at weekends. Lately Maggie had been slipping Clive a quid before they went in so that he could buy his round—the system was that each of the three or four small tables occupied by the crowd became its own school—but tonight, a bit upset by the sight of two thousand books lying in puddles, she had forgotten. No one minded Clive sitting there glooming all evening—quite a lot of glooming went on among the would-be poets and frustrated actors in their group—but he was expected to get his round in, even if he had to borrow to do it. Clive didn't. He sat there cracking his knuckles and staring into space while his companions very obviously toyed with their empty glasses, one of them finally going so far as to pretend to screw his half-pint tankard into his eye like a jeweller's eye-glass. Maggie was furious. It wasn't this sulking lump of deadweight not having any money that she minded, it was—no, she was wrong. It *was* the bugger not having any money. Why couldn't he pawn his watch, write home to his mummy, tap his friends, sell his records, steal, or even in quiet desperation do a day's bloody work?

Maggie rose and collected the empty glasses. Ostentatiously addressing thin air, she said heavily: 'Nothing else for it—it's all down to Maggie Muggins again, isn't it?'

There was no row later, and she didn't pick one. She didn't want a post-mortem. One day when Clive bestirred himself enough to go out for some cigarettes, she got as many of her things together as she could in the short time available, and left.

That was the end of her first and last experience of living with a man.

There was no point in staying on in Leeds: her own crowd were the only people she knew and he would be bound to go mooching after her friends like a lost dog until he found her again. Anyway, she had done Leeds. She went back to Doncaster, making it clear right from the first moment that she hadn't come back to stay.

Her Mum didn't like the change in her at all. 'You've become very hard,' she said. But of course, dear. She *was* hard. Tough cookie. Knew her way around. A few days later, Maggie Muggins was driven by Maggie Moon's Dad (who still thought of himself as Margaret Moon's Daddy though he knew she would prefer to be called Margot) down to the station in his Morris Minor, where she caught a train for King's Cross.

It was as Maggie Muggins that, from the start, she would invariably introduce herself when she began to make friends in London. Though she would pronounce the name in appropriately self-mocking tones, there was always a quality of inverted arrogance in her voice that made most people look twice. She quite liked that. But the device had a practical use too. With her developing passion for privacy, Maggie was wary about giving people her real name—her 'civilian name', as she had begun to call it—before she knew anything about them. Her Mum had relatives in Ealing or somewhere—she no longer thought of them as her own relatives—and she wouldn't want them filtering reports of her doings back to Doncaster, not that they'd be likely to hear about goings-on in Soho and such places, but you never knew.

The name stuck. There were few West End faces these days who had never heard of Maggie Muggins. Flattering in a way, for being known throughout Soho by a nickname really did separate you from the common-or-garden punters; but Maggie sincerely did hope and pray she wasn't thought of as a 'character'. She couldn't be doing with 'characters', had despised them ever since those days back up in Leeds when every bar-counter propped up a twinkling-eyed gaffer in a cloth cap who would cock his head to one side like a pigging budgerigar and ask you to guess how old he was. Maggie thought it was disgusting that there were people who would make mascots of themselves to get a little attention, who could bring themselves to hold out their hats for the small change of her passing interest, like beggars in the gutter. She felt so strongly about this that there were pubs she wouldn't go into because of the droll or whimsical personalities who lurked there, streets she avoided for fear of encountering their resident fruitcakes with parrots on their shoulders or carnations in their hair. She couldn't even stand hearing stories about them: to be trapped on a bar-stool while somebody recounted the latest exploits of one of Soho's repertory company of 'real nut-cases' or 'right lunatics' such as Wooden-leg Pete or Charlie Meths would have been as bum-numbing to Maggie as a night at the opera.

So what, or who, had brought this little outburst on, then? The bloody singing bus conductor, that was who. One of those oldstyle bloody cockneys he was, they were the worst. He hadn't stopped rabbiting since Maggie had got on the bus. 'Any more for any more? Any more fares now? Speak now or forever hold thy peace!' he would cry, pacing up and down the bus, and his captive audience of three or four daft old women, the only passengers besides Maggie, would bare their false teeth and titter dutifully. 'Masons Arms the very next stop. Any one-armed masons on board, this is your destination . . . Hold very tight now, as the bishop said to the actress.' In between the patter he would sing, over and over again, the phrase, 'We all live in a yellow submarine,' the only snatch of the song he seemed to know. Maggie would happily have pushed him off his own bus if she could have got away with it.

Mercifully, the stop for Clem Attlee House and the Portakabins was coming up. 'Clement Attlee Five-Star Hotel your very next stop. All you followers of the late Sir Winston Churchill, kindly keep your seats, I thank you.' Piss off. Maggie gave the preening conductor the filthiest look she could muster as she stood on the platform beside him. Any lip from him as she got off and he would get the V-sign. She might see the silly old bugger again on the journey back but she didn't care: after today she would never be setting foot in this rathole again.

Her heart lifted slightly at the prospect, then sank at once as she saw the Social Services day centre across the acres of rubble and remembered why she was here.

8

Giggle a Minute

There were five Portakabins now: there had been only four the last time she was here. Either they were breeding like rabbits or business was looking up for Miss Roberts and her pals. They stood in a cemented compound surrounded by breezeblock walls, which the community workers had got kids to daub with crude murals in an effort to make them look more cheerful. From this distance the murals looked like the camouflage you saw on army installations. The Portakabins themselves—located a good two hundred yards away from Clem Attlee House so that the customers could get nice and wet while traipsing across to whine about how living there was getting them down—put Maggie in mind of casualty stations for the walking wounded. Which, she supposed, was exactly what they were.

The thin, spiteful drizzle had started again as she hurried along the grass-sprouting pavement past the padlocked adventure playground and the boarded-up shops, vandalised communal laundry and other abandoned outbuildings around the forecourt of Clem Attlee House. A narrow concrete path ran across the churned-up no-man's-land to the Portakabin compound. Maggie caught up with, and passed, a straggle of suicidal-looking women shuffling along like refugees past the noticeboard that warned, DUMPING IS AN OFFENCE. THIS AREA IS UNDER SURVEILLANCE. The black earth was turning to mud and the drizzle was sticky-wet on her velvet jacket. Never mind: get this over with and then nip smartly back to Clem Attlee House for a nice cup of hot sweet tea with Alfie's mum. Maybe a biccy or two if there was anything going in that line, she'd had nothing to eat since that Chinese nosh last night and all this non-drinking she was doing was making her peckish.

One of the Portakabins was used as a general office and waiting area, and the others were where they interviewed you. The new one, she saw from a paint-streaked sign outside the door, was especially for teenagers. HEY KIDS! IF YOU HAVE ANY HASSLES WE'RE HERE TO HELP. Poor little sods, no wonder they were all so anti-social. Maggie too would have burned down a youth club or two if she'd had Miss Roberts to have nightmares about as well as her bloody puberty.

In Maggie's mind, nearly all the social workers were called Miss Roberts. The few who weren't Miss Robertses she thought of as Jenny. Miss Roberts dressed like a school-teacher and was thirtyish to middle-aged and bossy. Jenny dressed like a polytechnic student and was very young and bossy. Both Miss Roberts and Jenny had her name down as Margaret on their white cards, but addressed her as Maggie: Miss Roberts as if she were her probation officer, Jenny as if she were her best friend. Maggie disliked them equally.

She had dealt mainly with Miss Roberts, as often as not the same one, who after initially trying to discourage Maggie from doing what she had quite made her mind up to do, had briskly, though with increasing distaste for her client whose lifestyle seemed to offend her, arranged the various preliminary stages of the adoption process, on each occasion carefully explaining, as if to an idiot, how far they had got along in the procedure. While this Miss Roberts would never become her best friend and indeed had quickly made the short list for her worst enemy, Maggie could not fault her approach as such: it persuaded her that she was being remorsely carried along on a bureaucratic conveyor-belt and that decisions were being made for her whether she approved of them or not. But once or twice, when her regular Miss Roberts had been called away on a wife-battering case or some such emergency, she had been allocated a different Miss Roberts and on one occasion a Jenny, and they had jolted her into remembering angrily that the decision was hers and that she could stop the machine if she wanted to. Quite early on, one of these temporary Miss Robertses, who must have misread Maggie's dates, took her into one of the interview cubicles and began, 'I just want to explore with you the various ways in which a pragnancy situation might be resolved.' Then, when she was six months gone, another one tried to get her back to square one, or rather square two, by pressing on her some leaflets about schemes and benefits for one-parent families. As for Jenny: she turned up at the North Pole General post-natal ward to whisk the babe to the foster home and incidentally with some more forms to sign, or it might have been that she turned up with some forms to sign and incidentally to whisk the babe off to the foster home, but she made Maggie feel all weepy by telling her that she must expect to feel all weepy and then explaining why. So you could say that all in all, the Miss Robertses and the Jennys were not among Maggie's nominations for Best Mate Of The Year.

It was standing-room only in the waiting area, where Maggie recognised a cross-section of the same washed-out, worn-out, tranquilliser-forcefed punters she had first encountered at Alfie's mum's quack's surgery in the failed fruitshop across the mud, and whose case histories had become long-running sagas for the social workers. But they had an efficient battery-hen system here, so if you had an appointment card instead of just dropping in on spec to ask them how to get through the day, they reached you fairly quickly.

'You should have been here at a quarter-past,' said the woman who sat behind the desk, taking her card.

'Yes, I know, but I'm late,' said Maggie in tones of sweet reason. Living as she did on Muggins Mean Time, she had evolved that as the perfect excuse. She got away with it nine times out of ten, although she sometimes noted some highly comical double-takes as she trolled through to her appointment.

'All right—Tirlsneck, unit seven. Wait for the green light.'

All the Portakabins were named after illustrious local councillors who qualified for the honour by being dead. Councillor Tirlsneck, if Alfie's mum had it right, was the noted housing committee chairman who had got Clem Attlee House and similar semi-criminal developments off the drawing-board. Unit seven meant the seventh interview cubicle along.

A narrow corridor ran down the centre of Tirlsneck, so narrow that you had to flatten yourself against the wall to let the miserable punters clutching their bedding vouchers and maintenance dockets squeeze past. At two-yard intervals on either side of this division were the white-painted numbered doors of the interview cubicles, sixteen of them in all. Until the social workers had been required by the council to maximise their space with hardboard partitions, the sixteen interview cubicles had been eight interview rooms. A bulls-eye of red light shone above each door. The effect, to Maggie, was of a mobile knocking-shop.

She paced up and down the thin corridor, moving at a brisk outdoor walking speed so as not to be able to unscramble any individual urban lament among the low chorus of despondent voices. Presently the red light over door seven switched to green as a dumpling-faced woman dressed in jumble-sale oddments emerged, looking as if she'd just been told she'd got terminal cancer. Oh, dear, why didn't she get down the supermarket and do a spot of shoplifting, cheer herself up a bit? As Maggie flattened herself against the wall to let the poor old cow shamble sightlessly past, a chick of about twenty-five wearing a blue tracksuit appeared in the doorway and called along the corridor: 'And Betty!' She too then brushed past Maggie, who heard her saying as she caught up with the woman: 'If he *does* change the lock again, you come back *to* me and we'll sort something out, all right? Or you can ring the emergency number, now you *do have* the emergency number. . . ?'

Oh pisspots. A sodding, flaming Jenny. Not that it made much difference, because all Maggie had to do now was to sign on the dotted line and if any chick just off a three-year course wanted to spout sociology at her, she would just stick two fingers in the air and toe it. But she would have preferred her regular Miss Roberts with the thin lips and the chilly patter: 'Now I want you to be crystal-clear about what you're signing at this stage and what you're not signing . . .' Goodness, she wasn't going soft on Miss Roberts, was she? If Sean had been here she would have said, 'The second you hear me say, "She wasn't a bad old stick in many ways", just be a love and cut my tongue out at the roots, would you?'

Jenny was still nattering away at the end of the corridor, or rather being nattered at. She'd opened a real can of peas in telling the dumpling-faced punter to ring the emergency number, because the dumpling-faced punter was having to explain to her at length that there was no such thing as an unvandalised telephone box between here and Surrey. New to the game, Jenny must be.

Maggie edged herself into cubicle number seven just as a weeping black woman with a bruised face came out of cubicle number eight, accompanied by one of the Miss Robertses who was carrying a file of papers. They'd be going down the Legal Aid Centre to start a divorce. Good. It meant there would be no one to overhear Maggie through the hardboard partition. She hated having to mumble: made her sound sheepish when she was no such thing.

The tiny room was furnished like a prison cell for someone sentenced to clerical servitude: a trestle table serving as a desk, an olive-green metal filing cabinet, and two moulded stacking chairs in shiny red, one for Jenny and one for the client. If you were a couple, one of you had to stand. The personal touches consisted of a row of miniature cactuses along the window ledge, a collection of holiday postcards pinned to the hardboard wall, and a snapshot-size photograph frame facing Maggie's chair. Her eye caught it as she fished in her bag for cigarettes. Instead of a photograph it displayed a printed notice: 'WE'D SOONER YOU DIDN'T SMOKE BUT WE QUITE UNDERSTAND IF YOU MUST.' Jesus! A Jenny Plus. And there was no ashtray.

'Hello, I'm Libby,' said Jenny, as she entered the cubicle and closed the door. 'And you're—?'

'Miss Moon.'

'*That's* right! Maggie, isn't it?' Giving Maggie full points for knowing her own name, which she checked off on the bulldog-clip board she was carrying, Jenny crossed to the filing cabinet and unlocked it with a key that she wore round her neck like a games-mistress's whistle. 'Now Mrs. Trask *is* still on sick leave and we *don't* know when she'll return exactly, so your case *has* been passed to me. I *have* read all the notes so we *shan't* have to go over too much old ground.'

Mrs. Trask was Miss Roberts. Didn't even know she was ill. Must send her a hope-it's-terminal card.

As for droning bloody Jenny, who had now extracted Maggie's file and carried it to her desk, all Maggie would wish on her was permanent laryngitis. She had one of those fingernail-scraping, off-cockney, South Circular Road voices that sounded to Maggie like metal being cut, the kind that models, policewomen and commercial radio traffic reporters had, with the traffic reporter's trick of putting emphasis on unimportant words.

Hang about. What 'case'? What notes? What old ground? Maggie wasn't one of the walking wounded from Clem Attlee House, all she was here for was to sign the form, get the date when she had to go down the County Court and sign another form, and bugger off. Finish, apart from a bit more rigmarole in a few months' time. What case?

That file, in the puke-yellow folder that always made her shudder, was a hell of a lot thicker than when she had seen it last. And another thing: what was that batch of typed foolscap in aid of? A report of some kind, that looked like.

Feeling her throat drying up, Maggie ventured: 'I think there's just the blue form to be signed, isn't there?'

'There *is* the adoption memorandum form *to* be signed at this stage, Maggie, but if you *will* bear with me I *would* like just to get one or two details clear.'

As well as having a voicebox like a Black and Decker drill, Jenny was one of those aggravating little buggers who dump every sentence they speak into your lap and leave the next move to you, so that you find yourself in a game of conversational pass-the-parcel.

'I'm sorry, what details are those?' Maggie was made to say.

'Can we get one point cleared up right away, Maggie, and I *can* assure you that anything you want to tell me *is* confidential and won't go out of this day centre, all right?'

Maggie nodded guardedly. The young cow was on to something.

'All right. Now are you, or *have you been*, in any kind of trouble? And we're not talking about being an unmarried mum, all right?'

Then what are we talking about? Sound firm, Mags. 'No.'

'No trouble at all. No trouble with the police, for instance?'

Bit too casual, that question. Did Jenny know?

She was leafing through Maggie's file as if looking for something. Yes, of course Jenny knew. All these buggers were in cahoots with one another: Old Bill, the social workers, the social security investigators, the whole bloody boiling. They had you in a central computer, didn't they?

'Depends what you call trouble.' Maggie tried to sound as

if it wasn't a definition that would have occurred to her personally. 'If you're talking about the time I wandered into the river . . .'

'Yes? Go on.'

Too bloody cool by half, that sounded. And Jenny was trying her stupid best to look poker-faced. Pisspots and double pisspots, she didn't know after all. She was just fishing.

Too late now, Mags, you've blown it, mate.

She gave Jenny a brief and underplayed account of her drowning, stressing that she was very drunk at the time and that all she was doing was trying to draw attention to herself. Jenny made notes and asked questions.

'Now if this date you've given me *is* correct, you must have been quite pregnant by then.'

'Yes, about nine weeks, I think.'

'You think nine weeks. Now when you say you *were* trying to draw attention to yourself, you mean you were trying to hit back at the father. Probably hoping he'd hear about it and come rushing back to you?'

Piss off. 'No.'

'But there was someone *in* particular you hoped to impress. A *new chap*, probably?'

'No.'

'Not a *new chap* and nobody in particular. Would I be right in saying that *at* that time you were feeling very sorry for yourself?'

Maggie heard her inner voice answering sardonically, 'You're getting warmer.' Aloud, she said 'Yes.'

'And you were hoping that whoever *did* come along and pull you out of the water would feel sorry for you and make a fuss of you?'

Sorry, chucky-egg, now you're cold again.

What could Maggie say? 'I didn't want them to feel sorry and I didn't want a fuss made, I just wanted to bring myself to their attention. I wanted them to see something had to be done about me, and then do it'?

'I suppose so,' said Maggie.

The answer seemed to satisfy Jenny, and she scribbled something down. 'Cry for help', it looked like to Maggie, trying to read her notes upside down. How bloody humiliating.

'Now even though this *wasn't* a serious attempt, you *were* nine weeks gone. Couldn't that have been dangerous *for* the baby?'

'Yes,' said Maggie sullenly.

'Did you mean it to be?'

'Yes.'

'You were hoping for a miscarriage?'

'Yes.'

Another note. 'All right, Maggie, now I am going to leave that for the moment, although I wish you *had* told us all this when you first made contact. But then you haven't been very frank with us at all, now have you?'

Pass the parcel again. By now Maggie had a pretty good idea what it was that Jenny was driving at, but just in case the crafty little cow was fishing again she wasn't going to do any more jumping in feet first.

'I don't know what you mean.'

'You don't know what I mean. All right, Maggie, I *do* have a very heavy caseload today so let me save my time *and* your time and summarise what's in this report by Sue. You *do remember* Sue?'

Natch. Jenny, her name was.

'The one who came to see me in hospital?'

'That's *right*. She *did* make an in-ward visit and she *did* make a note that she *was* worried about you. Do you know why Sue should be worried about you, Maggie?'

Pass.

Because she's paid to.

'I've no idea.'

'What Sue *has* written about you, Maggie, is, "I formed the view that she *was* suffering from post-natal depression, aggravated *by* the ongoing adoption experience." And Sue *does* go on to say, and I'm afraid I *do* agree with her, that the particular hospital we're all talking about doesn't have a particularly forward-looking record in that regard. I expect they told you to snap out of it.'

Maggie irrelevantly and irreverently wondered if Jenny talked like this when she was getting laid. By her 'chap'. 'All right, that *is* fantastic, Dave (or Kev, or Ron), I *am* coming, I *am* coming, all right . . .'

'Maggie? Were you in fact suffering *from* post-natal depression? Baby blues, as it's called? More *to* the point, are you still?'

If Maggie really was one of the walking wounded from Clem Attlee House, she would know how you were expected to handle questions like that.

Post-natal depression, miss? Please miss, yes miss: but post-natal to meself, if you takes my meaning. See miss, I been depressed ever since the day I was born.

'No.'

'*You* say no, Maggie, but I'm not sure you *are* the best judge. However. All right. Now after consultation *with* her team-leader who *did* agree we should keep an eye on you, Sue tried *to* establish follow-up contact with you *at* number eight-one-six Clem Attlee House, where she spoke to a Mrs. Shoats.'

Here it comes, Mags. And did Alfie's mum spill the beans, the whole beans and nothing but the beans?

Better get her own tenpennorth in while she could. 'Yes, well, I wasn't living at Mrs. Shoats's by then, was I?'

'So far as this day centre *is* concerned, Maggie, you were never living *at* Mrs. Shoats's at all, apart from the few days prior to your confinement, all right?'

They couldn't do anything to you for this, could they? 'Yes. I was.'

'Maggie. We do *have* a statement from Mrs. Shoats. You stayed *with* her briefly *at* the commencement of your pregnancy, all right? You then *did* leave the area until you returned for that one or two days before your confinement, all right? Mrs. Shoats thinks you were living in Earl's Court. Yet when you came to seek adoption advice *at* this day centre several weeks after you'd left, you *did* give eight-one-six Clem Attlee House *as* your address, and that's the address you've put on *all* your adoption documents processed up to press, all right?'

What could they do to her, then? They couldn't make her take the babe back, nobody could do that, not even if she'd given her address as the Little House on the Prairie and signed all the adoption papers Laura Ingalls Parsons. They couldn't ever drag her back to the Portakabins again, she just wouldn't come. Perhaps they would take her to court, it might even be the kind of thing you got slung in jail for. What would the charge be? It wasn't forgery, it could be something like giving false information on an official document. They took a v. dim view of that, didn't they?

And Alfie's mum would have to give evidence, poor old trout. Maggie felt a gust of anger at Jenny—not this one, the one who'd gone round and harassed Alfie's mum, writing everything down in a big spiral notebook and scaring the shit out of her.

She might as well be angry at this Jenny too, who you could bet would have done the same thing in the other Jenny's place. And she was still boring on:

'Sue *then* goes on to report that *in* an effort to make contact with you, she made referral to Dr. Muley *at* Clem Attlee, but he hadn't set eyes on you for several months. He *did* recall that you'd come to him *from* an address in Parsons Green but unfortunately he *wasn't* able to make reference to it because your card *was* among those destroyed when the surgery was set on fire by youths, all right?'

Three cheers for vandalism. Riggsy wouldn't have been best pleased to have been dragged out of bed by a team of bloody social workers at eleven in the morning. She would probably have thought they'd come to take her off to the council hostel for inebriates. They probably would have done too, once they'd got her in their clutches.

'Now before we *do* go on, Maggie, is the Parsons Green address you gave Dr. Muley in fact where you're living now?'

'Yes.'

'Mrs. Shoats had the impression Earl's Court.'

The idea of telling Jenny where she really lived did not even enter Maggie's mind. It was unthinkable. She would sooner have given her address to a heavy breather on the telephone.

'No. Parsons Green.'

'All right, Maggie, and would you like to give me that address?'

Maggie recklessly dictated Riggsy's address. Sorry, Riggsy, but Mags's need is greater. Tiny touch of panicsville around here just at prez.

'What Dr. Muley *also* remembers, and this is why I *did* ask if you *were* in any kind of trouble, was that your motives for coming to Clem Attlee were far from satisfactory, and that there *was* some attempt to pass yourself off as Mrs. Shoats's niece. Can you explain that at all, Maggie?'

No. Yes. No.

Why the fuck should she, anyway? What did it have to do with all these Jennys and Miss Robertses and assorted prattfaces where she was living or wasn't living or why she was living there or not living there? Why was she being treated as a 'case'? If it was job-satisfaction that Jenny was looking for she could go and ask the walking wounded out there if *they* had any satisfactory motives for coming to Clem Attlee House. Go and ask *them* if they were in any kind of trouble.

'I think you're making a lot out of nothing,' said Maggie, in the low voice that she couldn't help using even though she knew there was no one to overhear in the next cubicle. 'In the first place, I came to Mrs. Shoats's because I'd nowhere else to live.'

'Then why didn't you come to us, or to the Social Services department in your own borough? You do know that if you *are* involuntarily homeless, the local authority *does* have a statutory obligation to find you accommodation?'

One end of the trestle table was given over to a selection of leaflets, all neatly displayed like magazines in a dentist's waiting-room. It was reflex action, now that a specific social problem had been touched on, for Jenny to reach out for the appropriate leaflet.

Stick it up your arse.

'It was only a temporary problem,' Maggie said. 'As for calling myself Mrs. Shoats's niece, she was worried about losing her tenancy if the council got to know she was taking in lodgers.'

'Well. *Yes.* Mrs. Shoats had every reason *to* be worried, the housing regulations are very clear *about* sub-tenancies. If Mrs. Shoats *had* financial difficulties, she should have come to us.'

Yes, 'You'd like that, wouldn't you, Jenny? You'd like the whole flaming world queueing up outside your Portakabins.

Jenny still wanted her pound of flesh: 'But this still *doesn't* explain why you gave Clem Attlee *as* your address when in fact you *were* no longer living there, or why in fact you came to this day centre *at all* for adoption advice, instead of going to the appropriate advisory service in your own borough.'

'To make life simpler,' explained Maggie.

At that, Jenny smiled. But to herself, not at Maggie. It was a private smile. She had just squirrelled Maggie's absurd reply away to tell her 'chap', just as Maggie had always squirrelled things away to tell Sean.

Succeeding in amusing Jenny seemed, anyway, to have had the effect of bringing the interrogation to an end. Hopefully Maggie asked: 'Can I sign the form now?'

'I'm afraid it's not as easy as that, Maggie.'

Yes it is. It's as easy as that and as difficult as that. So give me the pigging form.

Luckily the social worker in Jenny got the upper hand of the bureaucrat in Jenny. After she had listed the various stumbling-blocks such as all the letters that would have to be written and all the documents that would have to be re-processed by clerical staff already hard-pressed, she allowed Maggie to cross out Alfie's mum's address on the adoption memorandum, substitute Riggsy's address, initial it, and sign her name.

'All right, Maggie, now what you are signing *does* clear the way for the adoptive process proper to commence, but as your adoption counsellor *will* have explained, it's not yet legally binding . . .'

As Jenny went through the routine spiel, Maggie reflected that it had been less of an ordeal than she'd feared. Legally binding or not, this was the signature that delivered Dan into the hands of some awfully-nice middle-class professional Cortina-driving Ibiza-holidaying dinner-party-giving sherry-sipping double-glazed childless couple in a Span House in Blackheath or Dulwich or Twickenham, and Maggie had tensed herself up for a big emotional and probably tearful moment. She was surprised at registering nothing but relief. She supposed she ought to be grateful to Jenny, whose alarming cross-examination had preoccupied her to the exclusion of any mawkish introspection that might have sloshed to the surface.

Not that she had got Jenny off her back yet.

'All right, Maggie, now you do know there *is* a further signing procedure *at* the County Court in a few weeks' time?'

'Yes, Mrs. Trask has explained all that. I'll ring her office at the end of the month and get the date.'

'And in the meanwhile you can be contacted at this Parsons Green address?'

Ah.

'Why should anyone want to contact me?' asked Maggie warily.

'Well *for* one thing, Maggie, I'm sure Mrs. Trask *when* she returns from sick leave will want to tell you something about the adopting family, what kind of people they are, roughly where they live and so on.'

No. Don't want to know.

'I've already told Mrs. Trask I don't want to hear any of that stuff.'

'And you don't want to know *how* your baby's progressing? Whether he's settled in?'

I don't have a baby. I was just carrier.

'No, I don't want to know anything.'

Jenny shook her head in what could have been disparagement, disbelief or professionally simulated sorrow, Maggie couldn't judge which. 'All right, Maggie, that's for your adoption counsellor to sort out. But would you mind *if* I asked you a question?'

It was on a par with a wino asking if anyone minded if he took another sip. It was Maggie's turn to smile. It was the first time she had smiled all day and the contracting face muscles felt stiff, like her legs sometimes did after sitting too long. Several snide answers flashed through her head but she settled for, 'Go ahead.'

'All right, it might help me *as* your social worker if you *could* tell me briefly why you wanted to have the baby in the first place.'

Mind your own sodding business.

Because the alternative to having it was not having it, and the prospect of not having it had scared her—well, all right, not scared her but put her off, made her feel all bleah—even more than the prospect of having it. And because not having it would have been a decision, where having it was a process. And because.

Because in the end, after her drowning, she'd wanted to have a baby, even though she'd known she would never want to keep it unless it was a baby that didn't shit. She'd wanted to feel whatever it was you were supposed to feel, even to experience the wrenching pain and sadness you were supposed to experience when they came to take the baby away. She had wanted not to be numb any more; and she wouldn't have minded what that might have cost her in grief, any more than a man who has been paralysed all his life would mind if someone held a lighted match to his hand and he felt it burning. But she had felt nothing, nothing except physical discomfort and distaste for all the bedpan-type indignities attendant upon being a walking capsule when it is required to disgorge its contents.

Even had Maggie been able to explain all this, it was bugger-all to do with Jenny, because she wasn't one of Jenny's walking wounded.

'I don't know what you mean when you say it would help you as my social worker,' she said, her voice shaking a little. 'It's news to me that I *have* a social worker. I mean the only reason I come out to the day centre is that Mrs. Trask doesn't have anywhere else to see people.'

'All right, fair enough, and now that you *have* cleared matters up about where you're living I suppose *strictly* speaking you're not my Department's responsibility.' In aggrieved tones, as if she had caught Maggie out trying to freeload on the Social Services, Jenny added, 'We *are* hard-pressed enough, you know, *without* having to cope with clients not residing in-borough.'

Ingratiatingly, Maggie suggested, 'Shall we leave it at that, then?'

'Promise you'll do something, Maggie. When you get *back* to Parsons Green, will you make an appointment *to* see my opposite number at your local Social Services day centre?'

'Why should I want to do that?'

'Maggie, you must know we *are* all very worried about you.'

What, lie awake thinking about me, do you? Pace up and down the streets wondering what can be done about poor Maggie Muggins? Piss off.

She gave the reply she always gave to her Dad when he said the selfsame thing. 'I don't see why you should be.'

'I think you know as well as I do, Maggie. You *don't* have the happiest of lives, now do you?'

'I wouldn't say that. Giggle a minute, mostly.'

'Yes, well you *don't* look very giggly to me, I'm sorry to say. In fact I'd say you look terrible.'

'I don't feel terrible.' Don't feel anything.

Jenny, having consulted her digital watch, began stacking the papers in Maggie's file. 'All right, as I said, Maggie, I *do* have a heavy caseload at the moment. *Do* make referral to your Social Services office in Parsons Green, and I *will* make contact with them to say we'll make your file available if they need background.'

A silly, childish idea came into Maggie's head: 'I could take the file with me if you liked.'

Jenny shook her head slowly and sardonically. Ah well, worth a try, Mags.

Jenny got up and went over to the filing cabinet to put Maggie's file away. It was the signal for Maggie to get up too, but she didn't. Although she had been looking for any excuse to put the Portakabins behind her from the moment she'd arrived, now that the time had come she was curiously reluctant to move. There was, it had to be faced, a soothing quality, like Nivea cream applied to a cracked lip, about Jenny's droning concern.

'All right, Maggie?' Jenny opened the door to encourage her to leave. Out in the corridor a shabbily-dressed, heavily-pregnant punter was resignedly pushing a coffee-coloured kid backwards and forwards in its stroller. She looked too old and tired for any more child-bearing and the kid was too old for the dummy that had been rammed into its mouth. '*Shan't* keep you a sec, June.'

Jenny half-closed the door again and turned back to Maggie, who had not yet risen. For the first time her voice sounded as if it belonged to her personally, rather than as if it had been issued to her by the Department along with her notebooks and pens: 'Come on, love. You've just let yourself get a bit disorganised, that's all.'

Oh, sure. File under M for Muggins.

9

Saving it for Teddy

Lunch.

Three-thirtyish in the afternoon by now, Muggins Mean Time, and drink hadn't passed her lips all day. It went to show: she could knock it on the head any time she pleased.

Maggie had just had a bijou time-capsule experience. Meaning to look up and down Camden High Street for a Joe's-caff-style eating place, she had found herself following her nose like a Bisto kid to the Lyons teashop that had years ago closed down and was now an Oxfam shop. She knew that: yet even as she approached it her saliva glands were anticipating beans on toast, slab cake and hot sweet tea, her favourite nosh-up when she'd first come to live in the Bermuda Triangle eight years ago.

She crossed on the zebra to the Oxfam shop and stared through the window past the forlorn clutter of imitation-bone salad-servers, Third World basketware and obsolescent electrical gadgets that looked pretty Third World themselves in their dear old chromium-plated way, to the teashop she remembered: the long counter with its little glass-covered pigeonholes that held still-life snacks of an apple on a plate or a cheese-wedge and crackers; and the table for four in the corner formed by the L-shaped aluminium runners that you slid your tray along, where no four people ever sat, nor even three or two, because it was always occupied by one of those crazy old men that you used to find in Lyons's, taking a tea-break from directing traffic. Now a crazy old woman sat there, scooping the beans off her toast with a teaspoon, then spooning up the soggy toast, then sucking the crusts, and all the time chuntering to a companion who, like herself, didn't exist.

Maggie watched herself sitting there at the teashop table. Her hair was white, shorter even than she customarily wore it, but now sticking out in tufts for want of washing. The creases in her caved-in cheeks held a residue of grime, as hillside crevices retain traces of gritty snow long after the Spring had come. She wore a greasy, buttonless mackintosh over the one good coat she'd ever owned, the navy Fenwick's number she'd abandoned in that Maida Vale squat when the lining was in shreds. Now streamers of shot satin trailed unheeded down to her mud-caked tennis shoes. Around her feet were all her bits and pieces and little newspaper parcels in four or five plastic bin-liners, and near at hand was the Tesco trolley she used to wheel her possessions from one warm grating to the next.

Maggie realised that she was at once looking backwards into a time when there were teashops but no bag-ladies and forward into a time when there would be many bag-ladies but no teashops. Did the paradox cancel itself out, then? It was to be sincerely bloody hoped so, touch wood. Becoming raddled like Riggsy and trailing back each dawn to a family of nightclub teddy bears and a suicide's gas fire was about as low as she ever planned to sink. Making the grade as a bag-lady had never entered her thinking before. A touch theatrical, was she being? Self-pity was it, again? A case of lachrymatory masturbation or jerking off of the eye-ducts as she'd once stingingly called it when Sean had been indulging himself in a weeping fit? Cruel, she was. Did the trick, though. 'Ooh, get Miss Whiplash! You've missed your vocation, dear!' Sean sniffed, then dabbed his eyes on the back of his wrist, so delicately that it was as if he didn't want to smudge his mascara.

Tears were welling into her own eyes now. Perhaps all the Jennys were right and there was such a thing as post-natal depression after all. Or perhaps the tears were for Sean. Post-fatal depression, in that case. Joke. Get it, Sean? Post-fatal? Never mind. She blinked the tears back fiercely, and the white-haired bag-lady at the teashop table dissolved into the Oxfam cash-desk woman reflected obliquely in the mirror of a second-hand wardrobe.

All right, sunshine, so much for the Ghost Of Christmas Yet To Come, now how about something to eat?

She found a cramped, corridor-like high-street snack-bar,

another of London's half-rooms, carved out of an old shop that still had QUALITY PORK BUTCHER picked out in black-and-white tiles across its set-back frontage. On the other side of the strawboard-faced wall that divided the double doors like an East-West European frontier, another half-shop was selling video tapes. You would have thought, mused Maggie as she transported her coffee and doughnut almost a full turn of her body from the serving counter to the narrow ledge opposite where customers were supposed to stand in a row and eat like picnickers in a public urinal, that there was enough pigging trade in video cassettes and junk food in this capital pigging city to entitle them to a whole shop each. Seemingly not. The chocolate mini-logs and specimen pizzas on exhibition were separated by such blank expanses of refrigerated glass shelf as to suggest a food shortage, while the video centre's window display was as sparse and desolate as the Oxfam shop's. It looked like flaming Poland or somewhere.

QUALITY PORK BUTCHER. The shopfront mosaic took Maggie back to the Edwardian arcades of Leeds with their purveyors of fine potted meats and sheet music stores and the curved brass nameplates worn like parish church tombstones. She would have liked to have seen the high streets of London before the quality pork butchers were sliced off in segments like quality pork chops, and when there were gentlemen's outfitters and provision merchants, and the sign HOVIS on a wall in gilt wooden letters (thirty quid that'd fetch, down the Bello) directed you to a bakery, not to a hole-in-the-wall gallery of electronic space-invaders machines giving out a sound like a chorus of farting robots.

Do leave off, Mags: you'll be wanting the trams back next.

What was it she was trying to keep out of her mind, then? Why was she building up this barricade of aimless thoughts?

It wasn't the big things: not the babe, and not Sean.

The time was rapidly approaching when Maggie would be counting her footsteps up and down the length of platform one at King's Cross Station as she waited the arrival of her Dad with his annual lecturette on the theme of her wasted life and what she had done to her hair. It wasn't that either. That was just something to be swallowed at a given hour, like nasty medicine.

It was something trivial, but embarrassing, one of those

oh-Christ moments that bring you out in a sweat at four in the morning.

Leave it till four in the morning, then. Why was she trying to remember something she was trying to forget, for crying out—?

Alfie's mum. Oh Christ.

Coming out of the Portakabins into the unhappy drizzle, and crossing the napalmed-looking acre of black mud towards Clem Attlee House, the only route it was possible to take, Maggie had seen Alfie's mum approaching along the concrete path, her already rounded shoulders drooping under a new check coat of sad bright colours that Alfie must have treated her to on a shopping expedition up West.

Both faltered—Maggie guiltily, Alfie's mum evasively—to put off having to face trouble. Then both screwing up courage, they advanced on one another through the thin rain.

Like flaming High Noon, it was.

There were no preambles. 'You dropped me *right* in it this time, didn't you, gel?' was Alfie's mum's opening shot. There was a tremble in her voice. Unused to standing up for herself, she sounded more defiant than angry.

She looked ill and old, swaying there on her bad feet. Her suet-pudding face had crumpled in—more like a dumpling now.

'So I've just gathered, love, I was horrified. I was on my way to see you, try and explain,' Maggie lied.

May God strike you down deadikins, Mags.

Could still be doing with that sweet tea and biccy though, Alfie's mum. Can't we go back to your place and drain the big brown teapot between us, while you suck in your cheeks and tell and re-tell what all the Jennys and Miss Robertses said to you and what you said to them, crocheting the tale together line by line and then unpicking it to catch the dropped stitches—what you said to them before what they said to you, what they said to you after what you said back to them? Wouldn't you like that, ducks? Come on, Mrs. S., you could spin it out for hours. Make your day, it would.

'I'm very sorry, but I don't want you coming round to that flat ever again,' said Alfie's mum, with what sounded horrifyingly like dignity to Maggie. 'Because you've done enough damage already.'

'You mean because the social worker came round and asked you questions?' (*'We do have a statement from Mrs. Shoats.'* The shits.) 'You didn't have to let her in, you know, love.'

'*It's you* what I shouldn't have let in, Maggie. If I hadn't been so soft in the head. You was told and *told* I didn't want nobody to know you'd been living here. Alfie told you and I told you. But you wouldn't *be* told, would you? And now see what you've done.'

Oh Christ. 'They've not—?' Not what? What was it Alfie had said would happen if the council heard his mum was entertaining sub-tenants? It would affect her rent rebate, whatever that might mean. 'But I was only here for the blink of an eyelid! Don't say it's affected your rent rebate?'

'They say they *can't reduce the rent no more,* what with Alfie partly supporting me,' said Alfie's mum obscurely.

Maggie, out of her depth, looked blank. Alfie's mum wagged her dumpling head in the direction of the Portakabins.

'Miss Deraniyagali.' Miss Roberts, she meant—the one who ponced around in a sari. 'She said if I couldn't manage on what I had coming in, never mind taking matters into your own hands she says, you should have come to us. But then she took down all the details and said I didn't qualify for nothing, so it was no use making application.'

The ease with which Alfie's mum was able to get her drained lips round this Deraniyagali chick's name, as well as her use of the foreign phrase 'making application', suggested that she'd been spending a lot of her time in the Portakabins since last seen by Maggie. But why? What had they got on her? And if her rent rebate hadn't been affected—one way or the other, as it now turned out—what was she moaning about? What was this damage that Maggie was supposed to have caused?

'So the council aren't involved after all?' she ventured.

'What are *that lot* if not council?' demanded Alfie's mum, again jabbing her head towards the Portakabins. 'And now they've been given notification of my case, I've got to report once a week till it's all been straightened out.'

What case, for Christ's sake? All *what* straightened out?

Her case. Yes, of course. Obvious, when you thought about it: come in, Mags. They were all cases in Clem Attlee

House, weren't they, with their depressions and their nerves and their rent arrears and their migraines and their delinquent kids and the condensation running down the walls and the piss-saturated lifts not working and the long pointless days ahead of them, and not enough spirit left in them to go out and get roaring legless, then destroy with axes and hammers what wasn't already vandalised; but some cases liked to keep out of the Social Services net where others were only too grateful to be trawled in—and Alfie's mum had always prided herself on looking after herself and keeping a clean home and managing and not being a burden or a bother to anyone.

The bastards hadn't netted her, they'd hooked her and reeled her in. And Maggie had provided the bait.

Sorry, love.

'I'm sorry, love.'

'*And* they've got me under Dr. Muley. Meprobam, he's put me on—two every morning I've got to take, and two last thing at night.'

For the control of unfocussed anxieties. Yes: Sean used to take them, she happened to know. But then he'd knock back any prescription he could lay his tiny fists on, as if it were a tube of Smarties, and he alone knew what else he took. Alfie's mum had probably never taken anything more insidious than Disprin in all her born days—now Meprobam tripped off her tongue as readily as the name of Miss Deraniyaglai.

Sorry, love. Truly-ruly.

Tiny bubbles of fine rain had settled like morning dew on Alfie's mum's new coat and Maggie's velvet jacket. A raindrop ran like a tear down Alfie's mum's cheek. She brushed it away and snuffled gustily. The poor old bag would probably take to her bed with imaginary pneumonia, now they'd turned her into a state-registered hypochondriac.

'I really am sorry, love. I hate to think of you being put to all that trouble.'

Mollified somewhat, Alfie's mum said that what was done couldn't be undone. Maggie, to change the subject, asked if Alfie had been round lately. Alfie's mum divulged that like everyone else from these parts at some time or another he had been laid up with a bad back, so he hadn't been able to get over as much as she would have liked him to. There was a whine creeping into her voice—a suggestion that Alfie was neglecting her. Clinging to Miss Deranibloodygali with one arm, she wanted him as her other crutch. Mags, Mags, what have you done?

'Oh, and he's got a letter for you, what come about two weeks ago. He said he didn't know when he'd be seeing you again but *I made him take it*. Because I don't want it on these premises, I said. I said we've had enough trouble already.'

'Thanks, love,' cut in Maggie, before Alfie's mum could embark on the whole saga afresh. 'I expect he'll drop it in at the Half Moon when he's round that way.' From Sean. Had to be: apart from North Pole General and all the Jennys and Miss Robertses, who'd already blown her cover so no point in writing to her at an address they knew she didn't live at, he was the only one with knowledge of her bijou fling as an unofficial council-flat sub-tenantette. She'd dragged him all the way over to the wrong side of Shepherds Bush just to pick up a breast-feeding circular as it turned out, and he'd joked feebly, as they played paper aeroplanes with it while waiting hours at the bus stop, 'At least we know now why you call this your milk round.' Not one of your better mots, Sean. Never mind, it was lovely to have his company. The only occasion she'd gone into Clem Attlee House smiling.

She was glad Alfie's mum had mentioned Sean's letter off her own bat. Saved her the embarrassment of blurting out, 'Oh, by the way, Mrs. S., any messages?'

Alfie's mum pulled up the three-inches-too-long sleeve of her new check coat to make a great show of consulting a tiny rhinestone-encrusted watch with its strap cutting into her wrist like a rubber band—more to flash it, Maggie guessed, than to tell the time. Another there-there prezzie from her ever-loving son, evidently. One of the Portakabin walking wounded Alfie's mum may have become, but she wasn't doing too badly on compensation.

With an ostentatious, sympathy-inviting sigh, Alfie's mum said: 'I'll have to be making tracks. Because if you're not there at the time what it says on your card, they make you wait and wait till it suits their convenience.'

Maggie's anger with the Jennys and Miss Robertses mingled with impatience at Alfie's mum's spinelessness. On impulse she offered: 'Look, love, would you like me to come with you and—?' And what? Give Miss Deraniyagali Roberts a punch up the bracket? Get hold of Alfie's mum's file and flush it down the lav? Tell the whole boiling-pot of them what to do with their Portakabins? They're not bloody probation officers you know, sweetheart. They can't *make* you report to them, you know.

Yes. They can. They've got you, haven't they? Sorry, love.

Alfie's mum was shaking her head, rejecting Maggie's offer for the irrelevant absurdity it was. She made to move on towards the Portakabins, then unexpectedly she asked: 'And how's my little darling?'

The babe, she meant. Dan. She'd only seen the poor little bugger once, when she'd turned up at North Pole General with bales of knitted booties and bibs, but he'd been her little darling from the age of minus eight months on.

What was Maggie supposed to say? Did Alfie's mum know about the adoption? No, couldn't: they kept very schtum about things like that, didn't they? Noted for it.

Dan? Oh, fine.

'Dan? He's at home with—

Sleeps like a—

Bless him, he's no trouble at—

'He—' and Maggie to her own surprise broke down. She didn't cry at once but she couldn't speak for the lump that was lodged in her throat like a fishbone. How silly, how out of place: if she was going to carry on like this at all, why hadn't she carried on like it back in the Portakabins when Jenny had at last poured her out a measured teaspoonful of understanding?

Tears blistered her eyes and she began to shake her head from side to side in angry apology at the exhibition she was making of herself. 'I'm sorry, sorry, sorry!'

Alfie's mum, so self-obsessed had she become since the Jennys and Miss Robertses had worked her over, was beyond even contemplating that the tears might not be for her. Maggie would have smiled, had she been able to: the silly old ratbag thought she was was still apologising for landing her in the shit with the Portakabin Gestapo.

Alfie's mum touched Maggie's arm, trying but failing to draw her into a clumsy embrace. As Maggie pulled away she made crooning sounds, as to a child that has grazed its knee: 'Ooh, ah, dear me, there, now, my, oh, tush, we can't have that!'

'I am sorry. I was just being stupid.'

'You're to think no more about it,' Alfie's mum counselled, still wildly misunderstanding. She repeated, but without the martyred inflection, the words she had used earlier: 'What's done is done and can't be undone. It's *all right*, my love, it's *quite all right*.'

Maggie nodded vigorously with a smiling-through-tears smile.

'So I'll tell you what we'll do, my love,' went on Alfie's mum. 'You go over to the flats and get yourself in that hallway out of the rain till Miss Deraniyagali's got done with me, then we'll have a nice cup of tea and you can tell me all about how my little darling's getting on. My young man. My little cherub. Eh? Eh?'

'If I can,' babbled Maggie, and fled along the wet concrete path, so much in a hurry that she slipped on a mud-slick and nearly fell.

Yes, good material for a four-in-la-matin sweat. Any time she felt like a turkish bath without getting out of bed, she would only have to remember those humiliating five mins with Alfie's mum.

She finished her coffee but left most of the doughnut—mean to say, no point in stuffing her face when she wasn't hungry—and having moved out of the snack-bar stood irresolutely in front of QUALITY PORK BUTCHER mosaic.

Which way now? She'd already done Kentish Town—another bijou notelet from Sean among the trade cards and bright red-and-yellow film-development envelopes all slowly turning to compost beneath the leaking cold-water radiator in the hall of the Hotel Rat-trap, as she had dubbed this particular resting place in tribute to the many four-footed friends she had made there. IF YOU CAN'T TAKE A JOKE YOU SHOULDN'T HAVE JOINED, Sean had written—one of their catchphrases. Smiling, she'd slotted the card in between the other two in her bag. What happens when I've collected the full set, Sean? Do I send them off with only fifty pee to receive six magnificent Waterford glasses?

She could go up Camden Road and do Château Despair East next, or along Camden Parkway and do Château Despair West first. Either way it made no difference, because she'd still have to double back on her tracks to get the tube up to Chalk Farm. And after that she'd better knock the milk round on the head for a bit and get down to King's Cross.

Maggie tossed a mental coin, decided that it had come down heads, and set off for Château Despair East. The rain had just about stopped now, the sun was struggling through the drifting clouds, and the Irish drunks were picking up their bottles and rising from the doorways. After that trudge through the mud on the wrong side of Shepherds Bush, a strollette along Camden Road would be like taking the air on the Champs Elysées.

She had always been fond of the rattier end of NW1. If you included Kentish Town—technically NW5 but Maggie always insisted it was spiritually NW1½—she had had ten homes around here over a period of—what, four years, getting on five years? Four of them were still standing: Châteaux Despair East and West, the Hotel Rat-trap, and White Slave Towers over at Chalk Farm, named after the suspected activities of the Lebanese landlord. The other six, in no worse nick and in some cases in better nick than the surviving four, were now holes in the ground, traffic roundabouts or car parks. Shame. There'd been some really nice pads in NW1 at one time.

Maggie realised that even though it took her out of her way, she had crossed the road and was now proceeding along the gutter on the opposite side, looking for a gap in the long stretch of railings that separated the roaring traffic from the roaring drunks. Now why on earth had she done that? Instinct, clearly: but which instinct?

Self-preservation. She was dodging the turning that led to the Unemployment Benefit Office—years ago the scene of Maggie's brief life of crime when she had taken advice from a drop-out social security clerk on how to beat the system. Having fiddled two or three weeks' benefits by a process of vigorous and elaborate lying, she reached the conclusion that grafting for a living would be far less trouble and definitely easier on the nerves. She took the precaution of switching addresses to cover her tracks, then began to look for a job. Didn't matter what or where, so long as it wasn't within a quarter-mile radius of the Unemployment Office where one of the people who sat behind desks might spot her and take her in for questioning. She could, true, have cleared out of

NW1-NW1½ altogether, but the address they had on file —to which the dreaded buff envelope would be sent should her presence be required in some Ministerial interview booth—was obviously about to become the number one call on her milk round, and would remain so until it was boarded-up for demolition. Remaining near at hand saved on tube fares.

Where was it she'd gone to work now, in that mad panic? Couldn't remember. Didn't matter. It was only one of a series of casual jobs that Maggie had drifted in and out of, on and off, since arriving in London, usually part-time and never for very long—if you were going to tie yourself down you might as well go and work in the cocoa factory. They were studenty jobs mainly: washer-up, bistro waitress, cleaning lady, bit of barmaiding, street-sweeper even once, when she'd needed bread for Christmas. Pushed her little cartload of dog-turds round the borough, she did, and a ratepayer ticked her off for having a quick drag in a side street. Still, better than working in the cocoa factory.

The cocoa factory, as one of the Chums of St. Hilda's had once acidly observed when she was rather overdoing this particular catchphrase during a glum spell, loomed almost as large in Maggie's life as the blacking factory in Dickens's. 'I know,' countered Maggie, self-mocking, self-defensive: 'When I die they'll find "Cadbury's" engraved on my heart.' The same Chum, who knew a little about her home background, went on to point out cattily that there was no cocoa factory in Doncaster and that even if there had been it was doubtful if Maggie's destiny would have been to spend all her days there stamping out tin lids. But Maggie knew what Maggie meant. It was your actual symbolism, wasn't it? When she said, 'Better than the cocoa factory' or 'Beats stamping out tin lids', it meant that however rough metropolitan life sometimes was, it could only be an improvement on the bum-numbing provincial existence that most of the faces she knew congratulated themselves on having escaped from.

She'd certainly never claimed to know anything about factory life first-hand. On the other hand, she didn't care to admit to the string of weedy little jobs she'd had after leaving secretarial college. If asked directly what she'd done with herself before coming to London—and it was seldom that she was asked, for in the circles she had taken to moving in it was regarded as a breach of etiquette, on a par with asking a reformed criminal why he had been in prison—she would reply vaguely that she'd bummed around. Maggie was rather flattered to realise that the self-proclaimed artists, unemployed poets and other layabouts she was beginning to pick up with seemed to assume that like most of them she was not long out of some provincial art school or university—that must have been the residual influence of the Leeds student-type gang she'd mixed with. Someone even asked her if she had a degree. 'A first in fucking,' Maggie replied, with no other object than to be flippantly evasive. Amazing how talked-about she began to be after that, even though she made it plain it was only her little joke. It seemed that one audacious remark around here and they had you marked down as the Dorothy Parker of Camden Town.

Couldn't grumble, she had to admit. Maggie didn't mind being noticed, within limits. Looking back now, down all the shabby streets of time, it wasn't a bad old life on the Bermuda Triangle for the first couple of years. Bit like the Leeds days, only more so. Same type faces, only a wider choice, same kind of pubs, only over a wider area. More noshing in Chinese, Indian, Italian cheapo restaurants. More clubs. More parties. Studenty jobs in the afternoons, if grafting couldn't be avoided: long studenty evenings sitting on somebody's floorboards and drinking cider. Pig-snoring mornings.

Again like the Leeds days, there was a lot of pairing-off, but fewer long-term relationships and more casual shacking-up. 'This house,' spiritedly observed Maggie as the sounds of energetic coupling filtered into her current half-room from all directions, 'is the only one I've ever lived in with stereo bedsprings.' Good one, Maggie, you can use that: but meanwhile, she was talking to herself. None of the NW1-NW1½ crowd shared Maggie's bed, surprise surprise. Nor, for the present, she theirs. Since walking out on Clive up in Leeds there'd been nobody, absolute astonishment absolute astonishment. All right, then—hardly anybody. Back in the North Gower Street cellar days there'd been a brief fling with the character who lived upstairs, Mr. Nobody in person, mainly because he owned an electric fire and Maggie didn't. The affair died a natural death with the arrival of summer. Then there was a radio reporter she met at a publicity party that some face had rowed her into. That had lasted just over a fortnight, fizzling out due to her apathy and his inability to get it up before a broadcast because of tension, or afterwards because of nervous exhaustion.

She didn't bother much after that. Wasn't all that interested, tell the truth. It was like boozing, something else she could either take or leave alone if she wanted—only with the accent just the weeniest bit on leaving it alone.

Was that why she had boasted a first in fucking?

She wasn't short of partners, though, even after she had at last got it more or less firmly established, following on from that particular bijou japette, that far from being anybody's she was more inclined to be nobody's. Unlike some of the chicks she knew, she had always found it quite easy to hold the attention of the male gender for quite long periods without lying on her back with her drawers round her ankles.

Mostly, they were faces drawn from the crowd she hung around with. They generally lasted a couple of months and then, by mutual and amiable consent, were relegated to the reserves—the growing pool of casual mates to be dipped into only when time hung heavy or if she needed a sub for the rent. Few of them made the transition without first trying, with varying degrees of persistence, to get Maggie into bed. Couldn't blame them, all things considered. Since they nearly all knew one another, Maggie suspected that they compared notes, and that she was probably even being passed down the line as one after the other of them tried his luck, with probably a kitty to be won by the successful contender.

She didn't mind, found it quite amusing really. And if there was any collusion going on, it did mean there could be no complaints that they didn't know in advance what they were getting, or rather not getting. Those trying to soften her up with what the agony aunties termed mild petting, or a quick grope as Maggie called it with the bluntness that was making her world-famous all over NW1, were told: 'Sorry. Don't go in for cockteasing.' If they supplemented physical advances with verbal pleading, Maggie fell back on the standard response that had always worked so well when she was pestered, as a child, to eat up her rice pudding: 'I'm saving it for Teddy.' Bit twee—worked, though.

Life slid by pleasantly enough. Not a lot of time for

depression these days: kept on the go too much. Went to bed late, usually the teeniest bit smashed on cider or plonk, got up late and was kept busy-busy all day just catching up. Like a bloody Kilkenny cat she was, then. Kilkenny kitten, rather. Where did youth go?

Maggie got as near as she ever would to aspiring towards a vocation. Through one or two faces who were selling junk jewellery from blankets on the ground on the fringes of the antique markets, she began to meet some of the dealers who operated there. She liked them, liked their style: they were either street-market hucksters passing themselves off as scholars or they were genuine connoisseurs with the mentality of con artists. She liked the closed-circuit stab-in-the-back way they operated, always preferring to pull strokes on one another in cash rather than on the mug punters with their cheque-books and plastic. Comradeship, that was. Maggie was drawn to this world, then drawn in by it. She became what was known in the trade as a runner, buying odds and ends cheap from barrows and then running them from one dealer to the next until she found a good price. Or someone would give her a commission to keep an eye open for collectors' items—old mourning rings or glass walking-sticks or whatever—that they had a customer for. She got to be quite good at it: her book-barrow stint up in Leeds must have given her some flair for buying and selling. As she went on, she picked up scraps of specialist knowledge and learned about silver marks and such things. Soon she could have been making not a bad living if she'd chose to. Some of the dealers told her that she should set up on her own but it was all too much hassle.

And anyway, why spoil it? She was as close as she had ever been to having it made. Laughing and giggling, she was —well, smirking, anyway. She had found a congenial way of earning bread when she needed it—a doddle compared with barmaiding or waitressing, and definitely better than working in the cocoa factory. Had a roof over her head—most of a roof anyway: her latest half-room boxed out of a top landing, wasn't what she'd call watertight, but she could always move on if it got past a joke. Busy-busy days, pissy evenings, plenty of mates, lot of good laughs. And as for the other, she was still saving it for Teddy, wasn't she?

Then God help her, she had gone and blown it by meeting Teddy.

Maggie turned in through the hole in a dead privet hedge that was the gateway of Château Despair East—a tall, set-back, Georgian-she-supposed near-ruin in what had been a leafy avenue when she'd last lived in this neighbourhood. Perhaps leafy avenue was overdoing it. Street with trees, anyway, which had begun to lurch over the roadway at such an angle that they were forcing up the surrounding paving stones like cork tiles in a damp basement. Now they had all been lopped, danger to traffic wardens presumably, and the stumps of their amputated branches sealed with tar.

As for the front garden of Château Despair East, it really had been a garden when Maggie was living there. Crocuses, would you believe, lengths of string tied to bamboo canes, the full bit. There was a harmless old pratt living in the basement who used to potter about all day long. Dead now, she supposed, or thrown out on his ear: rock music blared from the basement these days, and among the garden's weeds and rubble and in the dead privet there were broken plastic syringes.

Sean, she'd noticed when he came with her on the milk round, had clocked them with interest but without comment—unusual, for someone who had a waspish remark for everything. 'Odd, that,' she'd said as they walked back down the ragged tarmac path that was crumbling away at the edges like stale cake.

'What, petal?'

'The dog that didn't bitch in the night.'

'And bollocks to you too, madam,' he'd said curtly, and so she'd changed the subject.

Maggie had often wondered about Sean and the drugs scene, but had never liked to ask. For herself, though a lot of the faces who knew her would find it hard to believe, she couldn't be doing with all that. She had smoked once or twice to be sociable but that was it, finish. Not prudishness—fastidiousness. Shoving shit up your nostrils, sticking things in your arms—bleah.

She hadn't started calling the house Château Despair East until long after leaving it, upon learning that it had been turned into an unofficial hostel for junkies who were supposed to be weaning themselves off the stuff. (Château Despair West, a couple of miles away, was now a refuge for ex-winos. 'Why don't we start a halfway-house for people who've got nothing wrong with them?' she had suggested to Sean. 'Who'd come?' he asked.) The hallway smelled of piss and she was not disposed to linger.

Someone, one of the denimed volunteer-task-force Jennys who ran the place, most probably, had actually got round to sorting what few letters there were and slotting them in a kind of latticed noticeboard affair. Maggie picked out the by-now familiar envelope from Sean and her heart thudded in alarm turning at once to relief, then indignation. Some interfering sod had scrawled 'Gone Away' all over it. Thank Christ they must all have been too stoned out of their brains to go out and re-post it.

Fearful of being accosted by one of the white-faced junkies who drifted about the landings like ghosts in a haunted manor house, she was already half-way down the crumbling path as she tore open the envelope. He'd written, IS THIS WHERE YOU PICK UP YOUR JUNK MAIL?

Fun-nee. And not only a joke, it was an apology for saying 'Bollocks' when she'd gently ribbed him for keeping schtum about the syringes in the garden. Had the subject really made him feel ill at ease, or was it just that he couldn't think of anything fun-nee at the time? She'd never know now, would she?

Oh, Sean. Why are you Gone Away?

All right, Mags, don't start snivelling again or you'll go like it. Putting the card away in her bag with the others, she set off briskly for Château Despair West.

Yes: Teddy. Not his real name, of course, it was her pet name for him—bearing in mind that some people kept snakes as pets. Come to that, his real name wasn't his real name either: it was his stage name. Quite a household one too, these days, but when Maggie knew him he was lucky to get the odd bit-part in the kind of earthy sitcom he now starred in. The rest of the time he spent in pubs. One of them was the Half Moon in Soho to which he was to introduce her, and which so suited Maggie that thereafter it became her base: so at least she could say she had got something out of the wreckage. Another pub was her then local in Kentish Town Road, a dump that everyone used at the time simply because everyone used it. It was there that she met him or not to piss about the bush was picked up by him.

Teddy was, to continue being frank about it, rough trade—at least by Maggie's yardstick of the time. He was one of your upstart kitchen-sink heavies who boasted that they'd always thought RADA was a detergent and that they'd learned all they knew at the Drama School of Life. Big, burly bugger he was. Sunglasses, sideburns, butch leather jacket, white cotton strides very tight around the bum.

Sipping draught cider in an alcove with her mates, while he sloshed back pints at the bar with his mates, she noticed him clocking her and was ever so fairly intrigued to note that she had trouble keeping her eyes off him. The faces he was drinking with mostly knew Maggie, slightly too well, and she rather hoped that they might moon across and row him into her company. No chance: it would make too big a school. But at the death he rowed himself in. Just ambled over to the alcove with his pint of catpiss, stood listening to Maggie finish the story she was telling—quite flustered she was, nearly blew the punchline—then suppressing a belch said, in reference to her flat northern accent that hadn't yet been mongrelised into Basement English: 'Ah bet *you* don't come from Yorkshire!' Then, in the same cloth-cap-with-bells-on voice: 'All reet if a Lancashire lad sits down?' Then, draining his pint and securing the table's clutter of empty glasses with five navvy thumbs like a mechanical crane in a funfair: 'Ah'm gerring 'em in. Wharra y'all 'aving?'

Hardly scintillating stuff: he'd be asking, 'Are there any more at home like you?' next. Yet Maggie, to the surprise and amusement of her mates, was visibly flattered. They weren't to know that he wasn't just an ugly face so far as she was concerned. Years ago, in Doncaster, she'd seen him playing a factory lout in one of those new-wave northern films that had made such an impression on her during her Margot period. Being chatted up by him now wasn't perhaps in the same class as being invited to dinner by Richard Burton, but it was a bijou experience for her all the same.

They engaged in some banter about the rival merits of Yorkshire and Lancashire. Maggie, sensing that any unseemly display of intelligence would scare him off, was careful not to be too abrasive or to say anything that might sound like wit. Not that it seemed to matter what she said, since he clearly looked on conversation only as a tiresome preliminary. From the rather maniacal way he was staring at her—perhaps he should have gone to RADA after all, if that was his idea of expressing lust—it was obvious where all this was leading.

If Maggie had any objections to the scheme, she couldn't bring them to mind. She was just rather surprised that she wasn't more excited. Taking another reading of her emotional temperature, though, she found it registering anxiety in case she had got him wrong and he was just whiling away half an hour with a game of mental footsy-footsy and would soon be gone. Her anxiety, she decided, was excitement in disguise.

Pity she didn't bugger off herself, as things turned out. Still, no use crying over spilt water under the bridge.

Finishing his second pint he refused the offer of another, lumbered to his feet, wiped his mouth with the back of his hand, and said to Maggie to the blunt exclusion of the others: 'Ah fancy a curry. Are your coming or not?'

As she put her coat on—he didn't help her on with it but was already making for the door, ever so take-me-or-leave-me he was—one of the faces she'd been drinking with, a good mate she'd been out a lot with at one time, said: 'Now remember you're saving it for Teddy!'

'I know,' said Maggie. 'I thought I might go down to the woods and see if he's got a big surprise.'

They went back to his place, a one-room-k-and-b in Primrose Hill, quite a nice pad compared with some of the ratholes she was to wake up in subsequently, and she stayed the night. She couldn't claim the experience was world-shattering but at least it was regular: they did it five times, in a variety of positions which he worked through (as she now wished she'd told him) as if auditioning for an X-certificate rep company. The next morning they did it again, then he went off to see his agent in Soho, giving her the address of the Half Moon and telling her to meet him there at lunchtime. They drank until three and then came back and did it some more. By now Maggie was getting the taste for it. She still hadn't felt the earth move but she was getting some interesting tremors. She went out and fetched some wine and a Chinese takeaway, and they picnicked in front of the two-bar electric fire then did it again on the floor. This time

Maggie took the initiative and found that she was beginning to enjoy herself hugely. They went to bed and she continued to develop a sexual repertoire that given time would probably match his. She woke him up in the morning and surprised both him and herself with her vigour. She turned up at the Half Moon by arrangement at lunchtime, and he wasn't there.

Well then, something must have turned up. He'd been living in hopes of doing a voice-over in a beer commercial so maybe they'd suddenly taken the plunge and decided that his attractive common-as-muck accent was just what they were looking for. Any road up, as Big Teddy would have said had he been there, the Half Moon was a nice enough boozer to hang around in—round mahogany bar, engraved mirrors, red plush, quite the gin palace it was. Friendly, mixed bunch of regulars: market traders, porn merchants, film technicians, stagehands, hookers, wheeler-dealers. Heavy night they must have had of it last night, from the way they all made a great production number of recoiling from the sight of one another as they came into the pub. The guvnor, Sid the Squirrel as she was to christen him, was a bit of a pain, endlessly prowling around the bar and earwigging everyone's conversation, but at least he didn't mind serving single ladies. Hinted, though, that she'd be happier sitting down. She didn't fancy the worn plush booths where the old flower-sellers and news vendors sat sipping Guinness and talking about their kidneys. Riggsy, then as now, was a gin-swilling fixture on her high stool by the frosted-glass partition. Maggie took the next stool, and soon they were rabbiting away and chain-smoking one another's ciggies turn and turn about.

Big Teddy didn't turn up that lunchtime or the next lunchtime either. She thought of going round to his flat and dropping a note through the letter-box, but couldn't think what to write—'Where did I go wrong?' or what? Instead she went back to her dumpsville local in Kentish Town Road and sought out the company of some of the faces who might know his movements.

It was the old mate she'd been drinking with on the evening they'd met, the one who'd said, 'Now remember you're saving it for Teddy,' who finally drew her on one side and marked her card for her. Tried to sound as if he thought it was something she ought to know for her own good, but Maggie wasn't so sure he hadn't been promising himself this moment as a bijou treatette. Couldn't blame him: when she'd trolled off out of his company the other night, it must have been blazingly obvious that Big Teddy was about to score where Little Non-teddy had never got to first base. Could have rankled, that.

'I did have the feeling something like that was going on,' said Maggie when he'd finished. 'Thanks for telling me.' She bought him a beer and herself—what to have? Wasn't a big spirit drinker but she thought she'd try a vodka for a change. She lit a cigarette, hoping that she seemed outwardly calm. It would be too sodding bad if she didn't, considering that she certainly felt inwardly calm. Not surprised, not shocked, no hurt pride. She just wanted to see Big Teddy again.

She had a couple more drinks for the sake of appearances and then toed it down to Soho, where she had the luck to catch him just as he was slipping out of the Leather Bottle opposite the Half Moon.

'Nah then, darlin'.' You'd think the bastard would have the grace to look sheepish.

'What happened? I waited two hours yesterday.'

'Sorry about that, kid. Ah got 'eld up.'

'And another two hours today.'

'Burrah di'n't say ah'd meet you today, did ah?'

'No, you didn't, but you could have put your head round the door to see if I was there,' said Maggie. 'Or would that have been against the club rules?'

'What club?'

'The one you and some of your mates in Camden Town are supposed to have started up. Someone nominates a chick with a reputation for playing hard to get, and you have to score with her or buy everyone a Chinese nosh.'

'The Fuck-of-the-month Club.' He grinned loutishly, but without embarrassment. ''Oo told you about that?'

'A lapsed member, I think.'

Mistakenly, he thought she was being bitter. He tried clumsy conciliation: 'It's only a standing blurry joke, luv. Any road, it's not as if you were a blurry nun, is it?'

'I'm not complaining,' said Maggie.

'Worrer you bring it up for, then?'

She didn't reply. She didn't know why she'd brought it up,

that was the size of it. Yes she did: to give him the chance to say it was all true but he'd finished up genuinely fancying her like mad.

Pathetic.

He shifted from one foot to the other, wanting to be off. 'Any road . . .' No one's stopping you, sunshine. On your bicycle.

But as he began a shuffling turn of his great gorilla-like body to move off, Maggie sidestepped smartly in front of him and to her own astonishment heard herself saying: 'Look, I'm not proud. Why don't we go into the Half Moon and I'll buy you that drink we didn't have yesterday?'

'Ah've stopped going in there, the beer tastes like piss,' he said doltishly.

'Somewhere else then. This pub you've just come out of.'

'That's even worse. Any road, what's the point?'

'I don't know. I thought we had something going for us.'

Jesus Christ, Mags, why don't you get down on your knees and beg?

She didn't even like him. What did she think she was doing? Aren't we a mite downmarket to be playing Lady Chatterley, ducky?

'Look, kid,' he was saying, 'you're making summat out of nowt. We 'ad a few laughs, it wor fun while it lasted—why don't we leave it at that?'

Very original. Who writes your scripts?

'Because I want to go on seeing you, stupid!' Maggie forced herself to say, recklessly and wretchedly. 'All right—if you don't want a drink, why don't we go back to your place?'

Gone too far, Mags. Blown it. He was angry.

'If you really wanner know, chuck, ah'll tell you. Only you won't like it. It's cos you're no blurry good at it, that's why. Ah'm sorry, but you've asked an' ah've told you.'

'Oh, I see,' said Maggie. Not a first in fucking after all.

She ran across to the Half Moon where she bought herself a large-type vodka and joined Riggsy and some other new-found friends, including a piss-artist of a Wardour Street sound-recordist who'd been giving her the eye at lunchtime.

A notable first Maggie chalked up next morning: the first time she ever woke up not knowing where the hell she was. It went on from there.

10

Pleasant Nightmares

Mainline stations didn't do a lot for her. Paddington, Euston, Victoria, Charing Cross, King's Cross were tube stations first and last to Maggie. Euston for Camden Town, Victoria for Earl's Court, Paddington for Notting Hill. From King's Cross you could go Inter-City to the Angel.

Underground, that was where the action was. The Orpheus Line. The first time she'd come to London she could have hung around all day in King's Cross tube station if they'd let her, watching the punters stream off the escalators and ferret down the tiled corridors, only to emerge seconds later like so many demon kings, so she would imagine, through the neon-shimmering wet pavements of Piccadilly Circus and Leicester Square. Up in those great half-empty parcel depots that the mainline trains departed from, you got a different class of punter altogether, the type who would open a carriage door for you as soon as look at you instead of elbowing you out of the way like any normal human being. Commuters and worse. A timid, anxious lot they seemed to Maggie, with their folded mackintoshes and string gloves, their two separate, leather-framed, plastic-faced luggage tags for each matching suitcase, their armfuls of glossy what they called 'reading matter', their packets of mints, and shiny, sterilised apples in clingfilm-sealed expanded-polystyrene four-packs. Everything but a pigging cleft stick, and to go where? Peterborough, Grantham, Retford, Doncaster and Leeds according to the milky flickering telescreen printouts with which some British Rail fantasist hoped to kid the travelling punter that this run-down inner-city aircraft hangar was Terminal 5, Heathrow. Why should anyone wish to go to poxy Grantham? Not to mention, it went without mentioning, poxy Doncaster.

The train her Dad should be on was going to be twelve minutes late. Either late take-off or stacking over Peterborough. Maggie found a perch on a porter's trolley near the big W.H. Smith's and began riffling through the little pile of mail she had assembled in her bag during the day's milk round.

Quite a haul she'd picked up at her last two stops: letter from the Inland Revenue acknowledging a letter from her which she couldn't remember writing—the matter was being looked into, whatever it was; miffy official card instructing her to exchange her national insurance contribution card forthwith—will do, sweethearts, as soon as it's got a few more stamps on it; v. useful Boozers' Diary from a theatrical agent she knew—got one every year, good case for either giving him her latest address or making a point of doing her milk round on Jan one; dusty Christmas card or two from faces who'd moved on from NW1 and NW1½ to SW19PQ4Z and similar planets, and hadn't heard that Maggie had moved on too; and, of course, two jokey notes from Sean, bless him.

One was supposed to be from the Camden Town Unemployment Office (she'd told Sean the saga of her benefits fiddle there): DEAR MADAM, IT HAS COME TO OUR NOTICE THAT SOME YEARS AGO YOU HAD A JOB. BEFORE STEPS ARE TAKEN IN THIS MATTER, CAN YOU OFFER ANY EXPLANATION? And the other, waiting for her at White Slave Towers where Sean had fancied he'd seen a ghostly hand beckoning from an attic window (probably had, too: it had become the kind of place where neglected old women die but aren't discovered until six months later), said simply: BOO!

Nice to get letters. Made you feel wanted—even if you were only wanted by the Department of Health and Social Security. Quite a cosy feeling it gave you, particularly since you knew that those who wanted you had no idea where to find you.

Would Maggie ever do the milk round again, though? Begged leave to doubt it. Wouldn't be the same after today. That's another thing you've buggered up by dying, Sean. How could she bear to go back to Pegboard Manor and No. 1 Paddington and all those places and not find one of those crazy, heartbeat-stopping notes?

She could start a new milk round altogether, that's what she could do. It would be something to occupy her mind, if she got off her arse and got on with it. Pass on the Balmoral Gardens address to everyone who really needed to know where to get in touch with her, such as the national insurance stamp lot and the tax inspector and her Dad and the face who sent her the Boozers' Diary every year—then give Balmoral Gardens the elbow. Have a good look round, sus out a different place each day, give herself something to do. An object in life, that's what it would be: nothing like having an object in life for two or three weeks.

Might give Notting Hill another whirl. Or perhaps not: too close to Sean's old patch, though handy for the Bello. All round to the Bermuda Triangle again, then? No. Never go back—well-known old saying. Fulham? Possible. Pimlico? She'd see. Or not. Too tired. She'd stay where she was in Balmoral Gardens, lying on her bed and staring up at the chipboard-lowered ceiling, or at the infinite variety of footwear hoofing it past the area railings.

Funny how she'd never given Balmoral Gardens one of her nicknames. Sean had suggested one: Dunscrewin, he'd wanted her to call the seedy mansion block when she took up residence in her front-basement half-room. That was because most of the other tenants—bald-headed old women and dribbling old men who were living out the fag-end of their leases—were long ago past it, while Maggie herself at the time was nearly three months gone.

'Speak for youself, ducky,' Maggie had said. But though Dunscrewin never caught her fancy as a nice name for a bijou residence, she had to admit it was apt enough. Lived like a pigging nun she did, until she dropped the babe. Kept out of the Half Moon, knocked boozing on the head except for the odd glass of watered vino, gave ciggies the big E, more or less. Never went anywhere, except on her periodic traipses to North Pole General or the Portakabins and for the odd nosh with Sean at their Italian joint. Otherwise the only excitement was dodging her Iranian landlord on his sporadic swoops to see if any more of his geriatric leaseholders had kicked the bucket so he could move in with the plasterboard. If ever he sussed that the front-basement New Zealand teacher-training student (as he thought she was: he didn't let rooms to the English) was up the stick, she would be as welcome on his premises as the borough planning inspector.

A lot of afternoons she'd spent round at Sean's place, leafing through magazines while he tarted himself up for an evening of unbridled lust with his latest mystery. The rest of the time she'd just mooched around. Amazing how you could spend six months of your life doing crosswords and listening to your tranny and not get bored.

Bollocks: of course she'd been bored. Bored out of her tiny Chinese. Better lying awake bored, though, than lying awake scared shitless, as she'd talked herself into believing she'd be once she began to feel the babe move. Wasn't scared at all, when it came to it. Wasn't anything. Touch of the gloomsvilles, perhaps, but there was nothing out of the ordinary in that. Nothing else. There'd certainly been no stirring of your actual primeval maternal instincts as promised—or did she mean threatened?—by Miss Roberts. The only emotion she could bring to mind was of feeling like a walking bloody cucumber-frame, in which a process of growth and cultivation was going on that had nothing to do with her personally whatsoever. If you could call that an emotion.

Actually, if anyone really wanted to know, the one thing that really, truly-ruly bothered her, thinking back to that period, was so bloody silly it was unbelievable.

She'd wanted Sean to come over and do a jigsaw puzzle with her, but hadn't liked to ask.

It was such an intense and wistful longing that it had etched a picture into her mind that had remained there ever since, of the two of them sitting opposite one another, she on the bed, he perched on the arm of the shredded-wheat-type basket chair, with her rickety folding card-table between them, and the jigsaw, its edges already completed, spread out on the piebald green baize. She even knew what puzzle they were doing: a thirty-six-inches-by-eighteen of some Tudory-looking buildings by a pond that she'd seen in the newsagent's near the Earl's Court piazza, and nearly bought. She was filling in the roof outlines and Sean was sorting all the timbered bits into a little heap. They joked a lot and accused one another of hiding pieces they were looking for. The image was so vivid that when she looked at it with her mind's eye, she had to remind herself that she was remembering something that had never happened.

She did so wish they had done that jigsaw. And on evenings when they tired of it, or become exasperated because all the mullioned window pieces looked the same, they could have played Scrabble. He would have enjoyed that. They both would. But she could never ask him for fear of—well, for fear of him giving her the same kind of blistering answer she herself would have given if he'd asked *her* to do a poxy jigsaw puzzle and play pigging Scrabble. 'Ooh, goodikins! Bags you make the Horlicks.' That, and it would have been breaking her stupid rule that she had somehow allowed to become an obsession, of never letting anyone through the door. Private life and all that. But for Christ's sake, it was never meant to apply to Sean, was it? Everyone else in the world, yes, they could all go and fuck themselves, but why keep Sean out? It was like having a gas fire and not lighting it on cold nights.

Maggie shivered. Association of ideas, that must be, reflex action: she wasn't really cold. Bit tired, perhaps, after all that tramping about she'd been doing.

She became aware that some of the punters scurrying backwards and forwards through the station were giving her odd glances. They must be thinking what a miserable bitch she looked, squatting all hunched-up on that not-very-clean porter's trolley like a garden bloody gnome waiting to be put in the guard's van.

Bit tired was the understatement of the year. She was shagged out, if the truth be known. But she dreaded sleep, with the prospect of her jumbled recollections of the day's events tumbling and twirling about in the distorting kaleido-scope of her dreams.

Couldn't put it off forever. She would have to get her head down sooner or later, somewhere or other.

Anyway, you never knew your luck, it might be nice, dreaming about Sean. She could dream that he was still alive and that they were scoffing Italian nosh together, getting pissed together, doing jigsaw puzzles together. And then, bleah, she'd push him under a train.

She wasn't shivering, she was shuddering.

She hoped the bugger wouldn't come back to haunt her. He couldn't, could he, if he'd never set foot in her room? Not that she believed in any of that spiritualist shit—but wasn't it right that your authentic chain-clanking troubled spirits only haunted the places they'd been associated with in life?

She would have to ask. Someone in the Half Moon would know. They were all great authorities on the psychic phenomena bit down there, there was hardly one of them who hadn't at some time or another stayed in a house where they'd been aware of what, swear to God they weren't making it up, they could only describe as an evil presence; or who didn't know a face who knew a face who had had a hairy encounter with a poltergeist. Like a convention of bloody mediums it was in that pub, some nights. Even Sid the Squirrel, who had about as much imagination as a cervical smear, claimed that when he'd once stayed in an old inn where a young punter was supposed to have been bricked up in the fireplace in the year dot, he had been woken up by moaning.

Tiny pact, Sean. No fucking moaning, all right?

Maggie wondered what it was like, being dead. Just nothing, she supposed. Weird sensation it must be, not existing. Something approximating to all those blank patches in her life that were getting more and more frequent: a state of higher leglessness. Against that theory, though, you did get punters coming back from the dead, punters whose hearts had certifiably stopped and who had medically snuffed it for five or ten mins, and they always reported being swept down long velvety tunnels and hearing funny-sounding music and feelings of great peace and all that shit. That was another topic that got tossed around a great deal in the Half Moon. Maggie herself refused to believe that these punters could remember being dead, what they remembered was dying.

'She should know, if anyone does,' she'd overheard some cow murmur. It went a bit quiet after that. Only Maggie was allowed to make jokes about her drowning, at any rate in her own presence. 'That's all water under Battersea Bridge by now,' she thought of cracking, but decided not to in case her voice came out all shrill.

All Maggie could tell anyone about drowning, insofar as she had tried the experience, was that it wasn't your life that flashed before your eyes as you went down, it was a procession of Jennys and Miss Robertses and probation officers and district nurses, and a swirl of white appointment cards from the psychiatric clinic which for the benefit of prying neighbours called itself something non-committal like St. Mary's or the Broadmoor Cottage Hospital; and it was the vicar coming round (she was new to the parish—did they have a vicar in Earl's Court, or was it a New Zealand missionary?) and pretending that he was just doorknocking like a double-glazing cowboy, but in reality he would have been tipped off by the welfare chick in charge of her case. 'She's very belligerent with us but she might respond to you. Ring us at once if you smell gas.'

Maggie couldn't be doing with all that. That was why she had given the Filth Riggsy's address. The Garden Flat, 14A Gaspar Road, Parsons Green, London SW6PZ7D. The address was fresh in her mind because she'd only just recently given it to Alfie's mum's doctor when he'd insisted on knowing where she lived permanently. She'd remembered it —a walking *Kelly's Directory*, Maggie was, never needed to keep an address book—from picking Riggsy up in a minicab one New Year's Eve when they were invited to a thrash in Hampstead. Most of it, anyway. The postal code she'd made up. Thought it gave a nice touch of authenticity to a story that might otherwise have sounded dodgy.

She'd fleetingly thought of giving them one of her own old addresses—she had enough of them, God only knew—but then she realised that once the police quack had done with shining his torch up every conceivable orifice, and she'd signed on a dotted line for her dried-out clobber, they were hardly likely to turf her out into the street, were they? The nice lady-and-gentleman patrol team who'd fished her out of the drink would insist on driving her home, wouldn't they?

Riggsy's flat was quite near so it would be convenient for all concerned, except possibly Riggsy.

Mistake, that. Bijou boob. Maggie was banking on them just dropping her there, making sure there was someone to let her in—Riggsy would go bananas if she was already in kip, but that couldn't be helped—and then buggering off. What she hadn't reckoned on was that the Amazing Albert and Pam, as she'd already christened her two rescuers (put them in sequined leotards and they'd look like a circus act) would want to come in with her.

Obvious, if she'd thought about it for two seconds. For one thing, they wanted their blanket back.

At least they didn't have to knock Riggsy up. She was slummocking about in a tattered silk kimono with her flash-blond hair looking like straw where it fell about her shoulders, half-pissed, chain-smoking and playing patience. She wasn't best pleased, though. Nor would Maggie have been, if she'd been disturbed at two in the morning by Old Bill thumping on the door and a revolving blue lamp flashing through the window, and they'd asked her to sign for a boozing companion parcelled up in a blanket.

'I know we said goodnight hours ago but I couldn't sleep,' murmured Maggie wanly as the Amazing Albert carted her past the gaping Riggsy and dumped her in a creaking wicker-work sofa affair which, since Riggsy didn't have a spare bedroom so far as she could remember noticing, the Filth would have to be persuaded was Maggie's bed.

Pam, clomping behind with Maggie's sodden shoulder-bag and shoes, flourished them at Riggsy like a juggler's assistant displaying Indian clubs. 'Nothing to worry about, we've had a little accident,' she confided in tones as soothing as a station announcer's.

Riggsy remained speechless. Hopefully she would keep it that way until she had clued herself in. Though come to think of it, she probably wasn't on speaking terms with Maggie in the first place. If she was, she must be in a minority of one.

An absolute cow, Maggie had been in the Half Moon earlier. Maudlin and bitchy in turn, she'd practically cleared the bar. She was only amazed that Sid the Squirrel hadn't bounced her, especially after she'd retorted, having first called him a mean bugger for never buying her a drink, 'Never mind, Sid, I expect your heart's in the right place. Where d'you keep it—in your pigging strong-box?'

And she'd started out with the best of intentions, too, meaning only to have one last loon-up before walling herself up in her new pad like a condemned Vestal virgin and spending the next few months knitting matinée jackets and having morning sickness. It was all down to Sean, her going off her trolley like that. Admittedly she'd been a bit of a cow to him too lately, in fact since taking him on the milk round a few days earlier she'd barely said a civil word to him, ungrateful bitch that she was, considering that apart from that little barney at No. 1 Paddington he'd made it such a marvellous day. But he really was overdoing the sulkpots:

there was, after all, such a thing as showing a bit of pigging understanding for her condition. So when they met for a lunchtime bev in one of the Earl's Court pubs Maggie was trying out for size, she put the knife in from the start, with the result that within minutes he had pouted, 'If that's what being preggers does to you, Maggie Muggins, it's the best advert yet for Durex!' and flounced out in one of his poufy huffs.

After that it was downhillsville all the way. She went up to the bar to order herself a drink and the guvnor told her he didn't like the language she'd been using and anyway he didn't serve unescorted ladies. She went back to Balmoral Gardens and stood at the barred basement window watching the feet go past, deliberately inducing in herself the sensation of being in prison. She hated her room and wished she hadn't taken it. She hated Earl's Court. She hated Sean. She hated herself. At opening time she went down to the Half Moon and hated everyone in it until closing time. She went on to one of her drinking-clubs for a last self-pitying brandy but word of her mood had gone ahead of her and they wouldn't even let her in. She set off for Leicester Square tube station, meaning to go to Gloucester Road and make some trouble at the Waiters' Club before knocking it on the head for the night. But Tony might not let her in either, or having let her in might throw her out, and then she'd have to go home. She didn't want to go home. Reaching Leicester Square she kept on walking, and went on walking until she reached the Chelsea Embankment, where she turned left along one of the landing stages.

Pam was ploddingly enquiring of Riggsy if she could ask her if it would be putting her to too much trouble to prepare a hot beverage. Not hot drink, hot beverage. Maggie supposed there was a police manual with all this stuff written down, step by step. It was probably illustrated with line drawings, like the Girl Guide Handbook she'd browsed through at school before deciding not to join. Snuggling up in her blanket with her hands round a steaming beaker, she was going to look like fig 8: *Before taking further statements, ensure that the patient is warm and comfortable and has a hot beverage*.

Further statements. Oh, Christ, they weren't going to

start asking Riggsy questions, were they? No chance of giving Maggie five mins to mark her card first, was there?

As Riggsy slip-slapped off into the kitchen alcove to boil the kettle and have a quick gargle, if Maggie knew her, Pam made something of a ritual out of producing her notebook, folding it back at a clean page and placing it neatly on a little side-table as if preparing the Amazing Albert's next trick. He, meanwhile, was pacing with simulated casualness around Riggsy's flat, presumably on the lookout for sharp knives, drunken husbands, battered babies, or anything else that ought to be taken into consideration before signing Maggie over to a civilian.

Trying to look tired and weepy—she felt neither, just a bit on edge in case Riggsy took it into her head to come out of her alcoholic trance and ask why a face she hardly knew was being dumped on her like a kitten in a shoebox—Maggie said in her best whimpering voice; 'Look, I've given Mrs. Riggs enough trouble for one night, can't we leave the inquest for another time?'

'We can count ourselves fortunate there's no necessity for a *real* inquest,' countered Pam with heavy joviality. She had been calling Maggie 'we' all night. There, we're in good hands now, we'll soon be dry. And where are we living at present? That was probably in the manual too: talk to the patient as if she were mentally backward.

When it came to it, the only real ordeal was trying to keep down the revolting lukewarm sweet tea that was Riggsy's idea of a hot beverage. The questions were a doddle, Pam obligingly giving Maggie all the right cues to feed Riggsy her lines.

'And how long have we been living here, Maggie?'

'Oh, let me see. About six months, isn't it, Riggsy?'

'Something like that,' slurred Riggsy curtly. To slur curtly: difficult-to-impossible feat. Livid, she was. Couldn't blame her. Still, so long as she didn't give the game away.

'So you've been living here six months. And which of you is the actual tenant?'

Riggsy looked daggers at Maggie. 'Mrs. Riggs is,' said Maggie generously.

'So Mrs. Riggs is the actual tenant.' Repeating everything that was said to her was another little trick that Pam could have got from her manual. *The patient may be confused when answering questions. Every opportunity should be afforded for the correction of misleading or conflicting statements.* 'And I expect you go out to business, Mrs. Riggs?'

Riggsy, acknowledging the courtesy of the wooden-legged euphemism with a smeared-lipstick half-smile, confessed to helping out a friend in his West End tobacco and confectionery kiosk for a few hours daily, adding glucosely: 'Why should that concern you people?'

Why indeed? Not doddlesville after all, maybe.

'Because *I don't think* it would be beneficial for Maggie to be left alone at this stage, Mrs. Riggs,' said Pam with nose-tapping significance, stopping short only at jerking her head towards the gas-tap.

Oh, shit. 'Yes, but I go to work too,' put in Maggie quickly. 'I'm out all day.'

'In an office, would that be, Maggie, or—?'

Shop? Christmas-pudding warehouse? Cocoa factory? 'Moving about. Buying and selling antiques.' And throwing myself into rivers, she might as well have added.

'I *don't think* we should resume employment until after consultation with a welfare counsellor. They're properly qualified to advise you where the Metropolitan police aren't, do you see, Maggie? Now when would be a suitable time for the Social Services Department to establish contact?'

Double shit. Shit by the steaming po-full.

Before Riggsy could drawl out, 'I'm terribly sorry, but I'm afraid that won't be conveninent at all,' which she plainly had every intention of doing as soon as she had chain-lit her next ciggie from the lipstick-dunked butt she had been agitatedly dragging away at, Maggie blurted: 'Oh, but you see I shan't be here. I'm going straight up to Derbyshire first thing in the morning.' She had already spun the Amazing Albert and Pam a yarn about her bloke having pissed off up there after she'd told him she was in the club. They'd seemed to think she owed them some kind of general explanation as to what she was doing up to her neck in river. Anyway, it was true, more or less. It would serve bloody Ken bloody-well right if they got his name out of her and the Derbyshire Filth hauled him and bloody Helen out of bloody bed to corroborate her story.

'There's a chance of effecting a reconciliation up there, you believe, Maggie?'

'I think so. And my father lives not all that far away so I thought I might go and stay with him for a while.'

'That could *very well be* the best thing all round. Is there an address where you'll be contactable at all?'

She was going to get away with it. Pam, probably thinking of all the time she would have to use up chatting up social workers when she could be out nicking black women, seemed glad to be getting Maggie off her hands. The Amazing Albert, having cased Riggsy's flat to his satisfaction, had started to look as if what he could do with was a plate of sausage, beans and chips in the station canteen. And Riggsy seemed mollified. Well, comparatively mollified. About as mollified as a mangy Siamese cat that's been woken up with a prod from a broom-handle and then told it's all right, it can go back to sleep.

She could either give Pam her Dad's real address or make one up. Fifteen Snotrag Terrace, Scumthorpe. She decided on the real address. If Pam's manual required her to forward a report on the evening's excitements to the filth up there, Maggie would rather have to handle a puzzled letter from her Dad after the local Miss Roberts had turned up on his doorstep, than cope with a furious Riggsy after the Amazing Albert and Pam descended once again on hers upon learning that Maggie had not been entirely truthful.

There was just one more knicker-wetting moment, when Pam, in a murmur like an echo in a swimming-bath, asked Riggsy as she put her notebook away, '*Could* we just have a—?' and shanghaied her into the bedroom. Nothing to sweat about: she could be heard quite clearly briefing Riggsy on what had to be done should Maggie suffer a miscarriage during the night. The Amazing Albert, either from embarrassment or because he fancied his chances as a lay psychiatrist, ventured: 'Still, ne'er mind, eh? All the same in a hundred years' time.' Maggie liked the Amazing Albert but wondered if he knocked people about.

Twinkling podgily, Pam re-emerged with a queasy-looking Riggsy. Retrieving and folding up the police blanket in regulation *fold fig 1 to fig 2* style while Riggsy cocooned Maggie in a tea-blanched eiderdown, she delivered her curtain lines. 'We've been *just a wee bit silly* but we're not going to do it again, are we?' and so on. Then she and the Amazing Albert took their bows and went.

Riggsy got out the near-empty gin bottle and they drained it. She didn't carry on nearly as alarmingly as she might have done. Still, on balance, considering the interlude had given her a bit of gossip and the promise of a whole new bottle of gin tomorrow, she hadn't done so badly.

Maggie's only explanation for walking into the river was 'Pissed, wasn't I?' Riggsy didn't press her. She didn't want to know. That was one of the things Maggie liked about her—if Riggsy had come across her waving-not-drowning, she would have waved back and walked on. A true Samaritan.

'Now you will be out of here before I leave in the morning?' was the only question that concerned Riggsy.

'First thing, firm promise. Nighty-night, Riggsy. Pleasant nightmares.'

Yawnesville. Riggsy had kindly donated her something in the Valium line with her gin. She was going to sleep well for a change.

'Margaret? Margaret?

Must have zizzed off for a sec. Pull self together, Mags, a luggage trolley in the middle of King's Cross station is no place for a lady to take her afternoon Z.

11

Spoof

She focussed on the man who was touching her shoulder, taking in his blue mackintosh. The railway Filth? No. Looking up at his face she noted that it was a punter's face, not a face's face. He looked older and thinner than he had any right to be, but his hair seemed less grey than it ought to be. His new spectacles didn't suit him. His false teeth were far too white and even. In the course of making these observations she recognised him.

'Hello, Dad. You must be early, aren't you—I thought you were going to be late?'

'We were running thirteen minutes late, but we made it up after Peterborough.'

'Sorry. They didn't announce it or I'd have been on the platform.'

'I was beginning to wonder if you'd been to meet the earlier train and thought I wasn't coming.'

'No, I got the message all right. It's a good job you looked for me, though.' She was effortless at this civilian chat: could speak it fluently and keep it up as long as he could.

'I was just about to see if you were killing time in Smith's,' her Dad said. 'Do you always fall asleep on parcel trolleys?'

Why was he always asking her if she was 'always' doing this or that? Well, always when he saw her, anyway, it was only once a year thank Christ. And if it wasn't 'always' it was 'usually'. Do you always blow smoke through your nostrils, Margaret? Do you usually wear that colour nail varnish?

Once a year was enough and more. It was always towards the back end of April, when he passed through London on his way to Eastbourne. Annual conference of rating evaluation officers or some such crap, he never missed it. Whatever turns you on, baby. They'd drift into the Sore Bum Bistro or some other tarted-up railway buffet and have a cuppa and a cellophane-and-tomato-pip roll, or maybe go stark raving mad and stand one another a half of lager, then he'd belch genteely and be on his way. It he wasn't being too much of a pain in the arse she might take the tube to Victoria with him, it was only four stops after all. And that was it for another year. He'd given up hinting that there was an eight something-or-other he could catch if she had time for a meal, she was happy to say. They tried it once or twice but it had always got rather sticky once the half carafe of wine ran out, usually before her Dad had finished his melon and ginger. He didn't bother now.

'What time do you have to leave from Victoria?' asked Maggie in her normal-human-being voice.

'There's an 8.55 I could catch, gets me in at 10.18. It leaves me plenty of time for a meal, unless you have to dash off.'

Bugger. You couldn't trust anybody these days.

She wasn't taking him into Soho, that was for openers. In any case, the option didn't arise. At still only five to six it wasn't a question of where they went but who would have them. There was a kebab joint off the Euston Road that used to open for dinner straight after lunch, so desperate was it to drum up trade. With any luck, if the health inspector hadn't got to hear about the rats in the kitchen going down with food poisoning, it might still be in business.

'You like lamb, I know,' suggested Maggie, frankly hardly remembering even whether he ate meat.

'Just lead me to it,' her Dad responded with simulated heartiness.

She hadn't bargained for all this. What was this meal-buying kick he was suddenly on? She was far too virginally sober to be going out to dinner with an almost total stranger. What did he want? As they edged forward in the taxi queue, Margaret felt, much to her annoyance, shy—a word so foreign to her she could barely spell it.

The kebab house occupied a front room in a terrace of private hotels that had enjoyed earlier careers as town houses, and now, with red Vacancy signs glowing in their porticos and their stucco pillars encrusted with mirror-glass mosaic, looked like legalised knocking-shops. Its original tall sash windows and high ceiling had somehow survived the transition into seediness, so that despite the travel posters plastering the walls, the harsh fluorescent strips that had replaced the chandelier, and the damage done to its proportions by one corner having been boxed-in to make a cloakroom and lavatories, the restaurant still faintly retained the feel of having been someone's drawing-room. The sense of spaciousness was enhanced by the fact of it being completely empty, except for the two Cypriot waiters and the chef who were sitting smoking by the far wall. Maggie, on her occasional visits back in her North Gower Street days, had never seen it otherwise. She doubted if it had ever been occupied by more than six people at any one time. The scent of long years of failure hung in the air like a cooking smell. Just the place for a family reunion.

Both waiters put out their cigarettes and drifted towards them, one gesturing expansively to indicate the wide choice of tables available, most of them more suitable for small office parties than for a tête-à-tête dinner. As the second waiter took possession of Maggie's Dad's raincoat and suitcase, they selected the table for eight between the windows and sat opposite each other beneath a poster advertising Greek wine, which Maggie was able to use to her advantage by asking the waiter if it was that very nice house wine that they used to have, thus hint-hinting her Dad into ordering a carafe of it before he had even consulted the menu. Cheers. First today.

The second waiter returned with echoing footsteps across the big room and, absurdly, placed a cloakroom ticket on the table. Her Dad, only half-jokingly—he never made whole jokes—said: 'You may laugh, Margaret, but this is my proof of ownership. That's a new suitcase, I'll have you know.'

Yes, it was. New suitcase, new spectacle-frames, newish suit. They made Maggie vaguely uneasy. She knew what it was, she had once thought it out, but she had put the thought away for seeming callous. It was that she had been anticipating his death for so long now that she had come to believe that his life had just about run its course, and new possessions jerked her into the realisation that he proposed to go on living well beyond her expectations. It was not, Maggie told herself, that she wished him dead: it was that she had made herself ready for his being dead and wanted to get the experience over with. On their rare meetings, she was always on the lookout for signs of failing health, and was faintly anxious when there were none to be detected. A hypochondriac by proxy, that's what she was.

They ordered their food and painfully excavated a thin seam of facetious smalltalk turning on the restaurant's emptiness: how only Maggie's influence with the management had secured them a table when they hadn't booked, how Maggie's Dad was hard put to tell whether the meal came under the heading of a very late lunch or a very early dinner, and suchlike pleasantries.

He looked and sounded like a provincial schoolteacher pedantically relaxing in a museum cafeteria on a class visit to London. Piss off, Mr. Chips.

Not kind, Mags. Anyway, what do you think he's thinking about you?

She'd know soon enough, she expected.

The two waiters had started shuttling interminably backwards and forwards with wine, bread, olives and plates of Greek salad, as well as replacements for items of cutlery, napkins and glasses which they had over-efficiently removed when clearing the table's other six places. Prevented from driving the empty-restaurant joke any further into the ground, Maggie's Dad began to talk about Doncaster and the changes in the town since her last visit (must be getting on for seven years since they dug her Mum in). Some woods where she used to pick blackberries were now part of a housing estate. Serve the buggers right, those pigging blackberry thorns had once nearly put her eye out.

He was probably working up to suggesting that she went up for Christmas. Sorry, Dad. We only do funerals.

No he wasn't, he was just waiting for the waiters to stop buzzing round the table like wasps at a picnic, wasn't he? Pas devant les how's-your-father.

It was going to be personal, then. Really personal personal, not his usual snide run-of-the-mill 'I'm sure that's not a smoker's cough I hear, Margaret!' or 'Well, I suppose you keep warm in those corduroy trousers, that's one thing to be said for never wearing a frock.' Teeth gritted, she would give him the same bantering response year after year: 'Oh, Dad, I'm *twenty*-seven, not seven!' 'Oh, Dad, I'm *twenty*-eight, not eight!'

Coming up thirty now, Mags. Need a new line of patter.

Their kebabs arrived. The two waiters fetched, respectively, salt and a little jar of toothpicks from an adjoining table. Unable to find further small errands to occupy themselves, they repaired to the far end of the room and re-lit their stubbed-out cigarettes.

Maggie's Dad isolated a slice of cooked green pepper from a cube of lamb and forked it to the side of his plate. Carefully cutting into the meat as if performing quite an important operation he said: 'Well, Margaret, I can't say you're looking well, because you're not.'

Blast-off. He went on: 'In fact I'd go so far as to say you're looking *un*well. You're not ill, are you?' All this without looking up from his plate.

'No.' Maggie inflected her answer almost into a question. Might as well sound as if she didn't know what he was rabbiting on about and see how far it got her.

'Do you *know* you're not ill, have you seen a doctor lately?'

'I'm not ill, Dad. Bit tired, that's all.'

He had sliced the chunk of lamb almost in two and now, prising it apart with his fork, was peering into the gristly cross-section as if searching for a malignant growth. Trying but failing to put a light touch into his voice he said: 'You're not getting enough sleep, that's for sure, but I believe there's more to it than that, Margaret. Is anything troubling you, that you think I should know about?'

How would world peace grab you? The poor of India? No?

'I've had a bit of a shock, that's all,' said Maggie. 'A friend of mine threw himself under a tube train last night.'

Sorry, Sean, but it's helping-hand time.

'Good—God!'

That ought to keep him off the topic of her health and strength for a while. Thanks, Sean. Do the same for you sometime.

Inevitably, her Dad would be going on to ask who this friend was and why he had done himself in. The first part was simple: just a friend. The second part Maggie had given a lot of thought to during the day, and while she could be wrong, she'd reached the conclusion that the answer to that one was simple too. Not easy simple—just straightforward simple.

Some time after splitting from Maggie and what was his name again, Peter called Simon, and heading with his Irish mate for the faggots' pub last night, Sean would have found himself in the grip of one of his black depressions. His monster moods, as he called them. No particular reason, nothing anyone had done or said: like Maggie's own monster moods, they came and went like headaches.

He got so bitchy when one of these moods was on him that his Irish mate would unquestionably have taken the hump and left him to it. Only Maggie had ever been known to sit one of Sean's monster moods out.

So he was alone, smashed out of his brains, and depressed. An unusual combination, for Sean. Depressed and alone he might often have been—no one would ever know how often—but being pissed and alone wasn't his style. That was because being pissed at all wasn't really his style unless he was out with Maggie, and she would never leave him on a downer. Unconscious yes, on a downer no. Last night was a fluke.

He would have stayed in the faggots' pub until chucking-out time, rubbishing everyone within earshot and being generally unlovable. Rather like Maggie in the Half Moon on the night of her drowning, in fact. Failing, not surprisingly, to pull himself a little friend, he'd set off home by himself for once. District Line, Fulham Broadway to Notting Hill Gate.

His monster moods always began to pass after an hour or two, when his spirits would rise again rapidly. It was, Sean had said, like being lowered into a pit very slowly on the end of a rope, and then yanked up again. But before the ascent, he had to touch bottom. Just for a few seconds, that was all, so that he would know he had nowhere to go now but up.

Had he been on the Chelsea Embankment when that fleeting moment of despair came he would have walked into the river like Maggie, and been pulled out like Maggie. But he wasn't on the Embankment, he was in a tube station. He had meandered to the very end of the platform so as to be in position for the last carriage where the guard was—it was always wise for gays to have some protection in the tube, late at night. He stood on the platform's edge, and the black moment came just as the train hissed into the station. He was pissed enough to let himself fall forward, and too pissed to pull himself back. If he had been at the other end of the platform the moment would have flashed by before the train reached him. He had to be alone, pissed and depressed, and in that precise place at that precise second. It was a big bundle of events and circumstances coinciding, like the jackpot coming up on a fruit machine.

You got three lemons that time, Sean, didn't you, ducks?

'I think he was depressed,' said Maggie.

'What did he have to be depressed about?' her Dad asked in a vinegary voice. He didn't approve of depression, it was something you snapped out of.

'I don't know. Probably felt he wasn't getting anywhere.'

'What—in his career? Did he have ambitions?'

Yes. He wanted to live in a flat by the sea and have his gold cuff-links and ivory hairbrushes stolen by rough sailormen. But he couldn't get it together.

Maggie shrugged.

'What did he do for a living?' her Dad pursued.

Good question. Rent-boy, basically, but not full-time and not professionally. Didn't have his certificate, he always used to say. Failed me orals, dear.

'This and that, like a lot of people. I don't know, really. I didn't know him all that well.'

'But it was a shock for you. I should think it was.'

They ate on in silence, or rather Maggie's Dad ate on while Maggie poked at her food. The kebab was terrible, it was probably boiled rat. Even though she'd had nothing but half a doughnut all day she couldn't possibly eat it, she'd be sick. But if she didn't eat, he'd start going on about her sickly appetite as he called it. He could really get worked up on that one. Anorexia nervosa, he'd threatened her with last year. Got her so worried that she'd gone straight off and bought a Mars Bar.

'So there's nothing else troubling you, Margaret?' her Dad gave her one more shot at confirming or denying, after he had chewed on his boiled rat for a while.

'I don't think so.'

'You don't think so.'

No, Rastus, I don't think so.

What she could do, on the not-eating front, was to start craftily shovelling her bits of boiled rat away under the rice. She could tell him she didn't eat rice because it was too starchy, ten zillion calories or whatever in every grain. Another thing she could do, she could ask him if she could have some of his green pepper if he didn't like it. What with that and the piece of bread she was nibbling at, it would look as if she was scoffing her little head off, but intelligently because of her figure.

'. . . may be the case but I must say that's an extraordinary business I hear from your Aunt Clare, if what she has to tell me is true.'

Come again?

For starters: Aunt who?

Responding to Maggie's blank expression, her Dad supplemented: 'Your mother's sister living in Ealing. *And who's still patiently awaiting* that visit you promised us all you would make when you first came to live down here, but *which apparently* still doesn't suit your convenience.' Sarky sod.

V. sorry, but the name still didn't ring bells with Maggie. She'd given all her relatives up for Lent one year and never thought of them since.

Anyway, what about this Aunt Pigface?

'You're probably not aware that Sandra works in the registry at Lacey Memorial these days. She used to be at St. James's, you may remember my telling you, but she found it a long way to be travelling each day, and of course there were the fares.'

'Sandra,' protested Maggie politely, trying not to make it sound like a question.

'Your cousin Sandra.'

'Yes.'

'Clare's daughter.'

'I've got it, yes.'

St. James's. Hospital somewhere. Up west. Yes, he'd talked about her. Asked why Maggie didn't meet her for lunch one day. Probably crossed fingers and hoped she'd awaken a sense of vocation in his wayward daughter. Maggie Muggins, Probationer Nurse. It would make a good paperback.

Lacey Memorial. That was a hospital too, named after a long-dead local bigwig and re-christened by Maggie the North Pole General because of its inaccessible location.

Oh, no. Oh, Jesus.

Bluff it out. They had nothing more to go on than a name on a file-card. There must be more than one Margaret Moon in the world.

'Now I know there must be more than one Margaret Moon

in the world,' her Dad said. 'But it would be quite a coincidence, wouldn't it? The address wasn't a familiar one —something Clem Attlee House, wasn't it? Sounds almost like council accommodation!—but as I said to your Aunt Clare when she rang up to tell me what she thought I ought to know, you move around so much that I never know where you are from one month to the next.'

What a clown Maggie was. What an absolute bloody stupid, silly, simpering clown. To have imagined all these years that she could curtain off her life like windows and nobody would ever, ever be able to see in. And so cocksure confident had she been, that the question of telling her Dad about the babe had not even arisen in her mind. The only possible point in him knowing would have been if there were any chance of him finding out, and there wasn't. No one ever found out anything about Maggie Muggins. She was the original closed book.

Some closed book. A ten-year diary with the lock broken.

'I *think* I'm entitled to ask if what your Aunt Clare had to tell me is true,' her Dad said, quietly so as not to be overheard by the waiters. Or perhaps gently, so as not to upset Maggie. It was difficult to tell.

'Yes, it's true. I had a baby boy. His name's Dan.'

At least she wouldn't have to eat the boiled rat now.

He asked her all the questions she would have expected him to ask, had it ever occurred to her that he might find out. They were surprisingly easy to answer. She could be straightforward enough about Ken: the father being a louse who was already married was a Doncaster-type situation that her Dad could readily grasp. Having the babe and then giving it away was well within his range of comprehension too, or to put it another way he thought it was: he didn't believe in abortion. He found it harder to understand, speaking as a lifelong owner-occupier, how even she could have sunk so low as to become a council-flat dweller on the wrong side of Shepherds Bush, but he nodded his head slowly and sagely when she was inspired to explain, reaching for the obvious and heaven-sent Doncaster-tailored excuse, that she didn't want anyone to know she was an unmarried Mum. The concept of shame was one that he found eminently acceptable.

Maggie's Dad had stopped eating and she had stopped pretending to eat. As they spoke, both of them taking care to keep their voices down, he kept looking across his shoulder towards the two waiters to satisfy himself that they weren't eavesdropping. Perhaps, Maggie hoped, one of the waiters would interpret her Dad's frowning glances as a signal to come and take the boiled rat away and start trundling in and out of earshot with plates of Turkish delight on sticks, little cups of coffee, the bill, the change, and so on and so on until it was time for her Dad to catch his train to Eastbourne.

The waiters were lighting fresh cigarettes. They wouldn't come to her rescue unless she waved. Or drowned.

The question she knew was coming up came up.

'What I can't understand, Margaret, is why you didn't come to me.'

What, liked to have had a bash at a spot of midwifery, would you?'

Because you're not a pigging miracle worker, that's why I didn't come to you, honey-child. Your intelligence isn't superior to mine, I don't go much on your judgement, your insight is non-existent, your powers of observation are somewhere around the level of Alfie's mum's, your maturity is suspect, your knowledge of the world is slight, in short you lack the necessary qualifications.

'I don't see what you could have done,' said Maggie.

'Probably nothing at all, apart from offering you a roof over your head which I'm sure you would have rejected. But wouldn't it have helped to have talked about it?'

Oh definitely. Would have liked nothing better.

She meant it, in a way. While her Dad unhappily crumpled a piece off his bread roll and buttered it, she indulged in a fleeting, wistful fantasy of the pair of them tramping across the moors, she in Gor-ray skirt and flatties, he in something tweedy, with a dog at heel. They would toy with halves of bitter at a wayside inn and he would draw judiciously on his pipe while she told him what an absolute shit Ken was.

Didn't ring true, did it?

The trouble with her father was that he wasn't cut out to be a father figure. He was Mr. Zero, that was about the size of it. He wasn't even a Dad you could be decently ashamed of. Why couldn't he humiliate his daughter in public like everybody else's father up from the sticks? Why couldn't he cut his bread roll in two with his fish-knife instead of breaking bits off it in that lordly manner as if eating out came as naturally to him as boring holes with his Black and Decker drill?

Maybe it did. He was certainly caning the vino tonight, she'd noticed: maybe he'd developed a taste for wining and dining. Maybe he ate out five evenings a week. Maybe he had a mistress. Maybe he was the Doncaster rapist. She didn't know anything about him. He didn't know anything about her. 'Two ships that get pissed in the night,' she would have said if he'd been anyone but her Dad, as he poured what was left of the bottle into their emptied glasses.

He seemed to be expecting a reply of some kind. How about: 'I'm sorry if it caused you any worry but it was something I had to work out for myself. It's all over now'?

'Water under the bridge,' Maggie's Dad agreed, a shade owlishly it seemed to her. Could be he was just that teeniest bit smashed, he'd had the best part of half a bottle of wine after all. Even Maggie didn't feel entirely one hundred per cent sober. Never drink rough Greek wine on an empty stomach with your father.

Draining his glass he turned his chair to signal a waiter. No chance of another bottle, she supposed?

'Coffee, would you like?' her Dad asked.

The two waiters were putting out their cigarettes and in a moment would be resuming their shuttle-service double-act as they cleared the table. The worst must be over, then. He wouldn't have called them across if he'd wanted to go on with the inquest. He'd announce the verdict with the coffee.

'This friend you were talking about,' pursued Maggie's Dad in that musing, nagging way of his. 'The one who had the unfortunate accident.' The euphemism was for the benefit, or rather the non-benefit, of the waiters who were now hovering. He waited until they had moved off with a plate and a glass apiece before continuing. 'Do you go around with many people like that?'

Well no, Dad, it stands to reason, doesn't it? If the faces I go around with were like Sean they'd all be fucking dead, wouldn't they? If you mean did I go around with, past tense, many people like that: funny you should ask, I was totting them up only this morning and I made it eighteen.

'I don't know what "people like that" are,' Maggie said. Rewarding her Dad with what she hoped was an indulgent-looking smile for the quality of endearing unworldliness, she explained: 'They're not a social class, you know, people who throw themselves under trains.'

'Aren't they? I thought it was generally acknowledged by authorities more informed than either you or I that that particular tendency was characteristic of a particular type of personality.'

Pompous old fart. 'That may be so, Dad, but what I'm trying to say is that you simply can't tell. A lot of people talk about suicide who wouldn't dream of doing it. Others just quietly put an end to it all when you would have thought they had everything to live for. Then you get the ones who swallow a handful of pills or cut themselves or whatever, just to draw attention to themselves. You can't tell.'

'What an extraordinary world you do seem to live in, Margaret. *I* certainly don't know a single person who falls into *any* of those categories.'

No, you wouldn't, love. Hardly your scene. That's why daughters leave Doncaster.

The coffee came. As one of the waiters put down the tiny cups, while the other removed the salt and pepper in readiness for a future customer reminding him that the table lacked salt and pepper, Maggie's Dad astonished her by asking: 'Should we have a brandy, do you think?'

It was like hearing the Pope say, 'Get them off.' In all the time she'd known her Dad—call it about fourteen days over the last ten years—Maggie had never seen him touch anything stronger than Guinness. It was the half-bot of vino that had done for him: she'd be pushing him to Victoria in a wheelbarrow at this rate. Still: Cheers, Dad. Must do this more often.

Maggie's Dad offered a rambling apologia on how brandy and Turkish coffee, or Greek coffee as he imagined he should describe it in this particular establishment, were two acquired tastes which perfectly complemented one another. Whatever turns you on, buster. Maggie wondered mildly where he'd been doing this exotic taste-acquiring. His annual knees-up in Eastbourne, probably.

His drinking problem accounted for, her Dad was looking for a coffee-spoon to toy with. Failing to find one, he toyed with the coffee-cup itself, swilling its contents about in a ruminative manner. That meant he was coming to the moment when he would be saying, 'You know, I can't help worrying about you sometimes, Margaret.'

Maggie lit a cigarette, inhaled, and blew smoke vampishly through her nostrils. 'You know, Margaret, I can't help worrying about you sometimes,' her Dad said.

'I don't know why you should. You don't need to.' From his lackadaisical nod it seemed to be the reply he was expecting. Should be: he'd heard it often enough. Or maybe he was sitting there knowing all the time what she was going to say next just as she was sitting there knowing what he was about to say next.

No, he wasn't clever enough. Not in her league. She knew what he was going to say next but he didn't know what she was going to say next. He was going to say something very much on the lines of: 'When I look at the way things have turned out for you, Margaret, I can't help but think that your mother and I must have failed you in some way.' He dragged that one out about every three years and it must surely be due for another outing in the present context.

She knew he was going to say that but he didn't know she was going to reply, 'Oh, piss off, Dad.'

No, she wouldn't when it came down to it but it would be what she was thinking. He made Maggie so mad when he talked about failing her 'in some way'. It was always 'in some way', never in any specific way such as that he had failed to have the faintest pigging idea what she was all about or that he had failed to keep his nose out of her business or that he had failed to appreciate that you are not supposed to measure the aspirations, capabilities and achievements of your loved ones (if indeed she was a loved one) as if they were flaming fish that would have to be chucked back in the river if they didn't reach the regulation minimum size. That wasn't an admission of failure he was about to deliver: it was an accusation. 'I think what you mean is that you've failed at making me a success, isn't it?' Maggie had once thrown at him when he'd pushed his luck just that little bit too far on this particular theme. He had no idea what she was going on about and she had to spell it out: 'You say you're a failure, Dad, but what you mean is that I'm a failure.' He'd muttered, 'Well, let's say it's six of one and half a dozen of the other,' and moved on to the next item on his agenda.

Speak for yourself, ducky. What, Maggie would like to

know, was she a failure *at*? She hadn't set out to cover herself in glory as an actress or a writer or a brain surgeon, so no one could accuse her of not fulfilling an ambition she'd never had. Was not having a job being a failure? How about if you didn't like work? If you clocked in every day at the Ministry of Sludge but would rather be lying on a beach in Tenerife, did that make you a successful penpusher or a failed pools-winner? Did not having a hubby and 2.9 kiddies make Maggie a failure? If she'd married the punter next door and served ten years in a bungalow before crawling back to Doncaster because he'd taken to wearing a suspender-belt, would she be more of a failure or less of a failure than she was now? Having had her babe adopted instead of sleeping it in a dressing-table drawer until the Jennys and Miss Robertses closed in and took it away from her, was she a failed mother? Having not drowned herself, was she a failed suicide?

Go on, Dad. You were about to say?

'I don't suppose you remember Mrs. Beevers?' he asked abruptly, unexpectedly and inexplicably.

Never heard of her. Maggie's pigging godmother, she would probably turn out to be. Works in the slide-laboratory at the pox hospital these days. Now it may have been a different Margaret Moon going down there with morning drip, but it would be quite a coincidence, wouldn't it?

'Name rings a bell,' Maggie said cautiously.

'Vaseline,' her Dad announced, even more cryptically. The explanation could only be that he was bombed out of his head.

The entrance of a stray and solitary customer, a diffident-looking Japanese tourist, had deflected the attention of the two waiters. It took the services of only one of them to bring the two brandies, then he hurried back across the room to help his colleague. Maggie and her Dad would not be disturbed again, which was just as well if he was going to knock back his brandy in one go and then slide under the table.

'Cheers, Dad. I didn't catch what you just said. It sounded like Vaseline.'

'Jacqueline Wilson,' said her Dad, smiling strangely. Gone, totally. Had to be. 'She used to come to the house sometimes when you were a little girl. Usually she brought you a bar of Aero chocolate—never any other kind, always

Aero. You couldn't say Jacqueline, so you used to say Vaseline. 'Fank you, Vaseline,' you always used to say.'

Oh, *that* Vaseline!

'Yes, I remember now,' said Maggie, speaking truthfully for once. The Aero Fairy. Dark-haired chick, in her twenties she must have been, who worked in Dad's office and lived just down the street. She used to arrive with an armful of files and papers, and Dad would disappear with her into the front room. Some office social or welfare business, Maggie believed: like Ken, her Dad was into all that committee crap. Her Mum didn't seem to go much on these visits, she seemed to recall. Jealous because Vaseline didn't fetch her a bar of Aero too, was what Maggie had reckoned.

Then Vaseline got married—presumably to Mr. Beevers, if she was now Mrs. Beevers, the supply of Aero dried up, and she ceased to exist.

'Then you'll remember she married Ned Beevers who like Jacqueline was a colleague of mine at that time,' Maggie's Dad went on. (Oh, yes? Jacqueline was it now, nudge, nudge, say no more?) 'He took a post with the Yorkshire Electricity Board up in Leeds, where they bought a house, so we lost touch for a while.'

The crafty bugger's getting married again. This Beevers has popped his clogs, Dad and the Aero Fairy have met up again and he has been comforting her in her sorrow, not to mention getting his leg across. You little rascal, Dad. So that's what the new schmutter's in aid of, is it? Didn't know you had it in you.

He must have been giving young Vaseline one back in the Middle Ages when she used to come to the house. It would explain a lot, that would. It would certainly go a long way towards explaining why he was so disappointed in Maggie. It was on her account he'd never packed his suitcase and buggered off out of it, or so he would have convinced himself rather than admit to simple cowardice; and look how she'd turned out after all that sacrifice. A right scrubber.

Maggie's Dad, in much the same discursive manner as he had explained his new-found liking for brandy—the two rambling narratives no doubt had a linking point in the unexpurgated version—told Maggie at length what she had already summarised to herself in a sentence. '. . . and so considering that we seem to have been practically living in one another's pockets since she came back to Doncaster, yet have kept separate households going with all the duplicated cost of fuel and so forth, we've seriously begun to contemplate marriage. Registry office, naturally. In September, most probably.'

Maggie raised her brandy glass. 'Congratulations.'

'You're not violently opposed to the notion?'

'Why should I be? You're over twenty-one now, Dad. I hope you'll be very happy, as they say.'

She ought to lean over the table and kiss the bugger, she supposed. Couldn't bring herself to do it. Wasn't in kissing mood.

'Well, I hope so too. I'm sure we shall be. We do have very similar tastes, so we should be. Touch wood. Well. I suppose one can't toast oneself, but do wish me luck, Margaret.'

'I wish you all the luck in the world, Dad,' said Maggie, reaching across and squeezing his hand. Funnily enough, she half meant it.

He finished his brandy. No chance of an encore: he'd already asked for the bill and had started taking sly glances at his watch.

'It'll be a very quiet affair, very very few guests and we thought a small lunch rather than a reception proper, so we'd have to know exactly how many will be coming in order to make table arrangements. Jacqueline's two boys will be there and of course if you'd like to join us we'd be delighted.'

Keep away, that meant. He'd probably given Vaseline the impression that the little monster she used to ply with Aero chocolate was doing very well for herself in the Smoke with a Span maisonette in Wimbledon and a wardrobe full of Jaeger schmutter.

If she laid Vaseline's 'two boys', would that be incest?

'How old are they?' asked Maggie.

'Thirteen and fifteen,' her Dad said sheepishly.

'So they'll be living with you?'

'Well, they do have to live somewhere. Fortunately they're very nice boys, very well mannered.'

Ahhh! Be like the sons you never had, will they?

'If you come to the wedding,' her Dad added, but without making a gilt-edged invitation of it, 'you'll be able to meet them.'

'September,' said Maggie, making a pantomime of frowning. 'It could be difficult.'

At least he had the grace not to look relieved. 'Well, we'll have to see. I'll drop you a line when we have the date firmly arranged, by which time you'll probably know what your own plans are. Otherwise I'm not sure quite when we'll be meeting again, Margaret. You know I retire at the end of this year?'

Yes, he'd mentioned it last year and she'd been looking forward to it no end. She probably wouldn't have to see him again until he was lying in a box with pennies over his eyes. 'I shall have very little reason for coming south in future,' he said after she'd nodded. 'And Jacqueline's even less enthusiastic about travel for the sake of it than I am. So unless you can bring yourself to make the after-all-not-very-arduous journey to Doncaster occasionally, I'm afraid we'll be seeing each other even more infrequently or do I mean less frequently than at present, if that were possible.'

'We'll work something out,' lied Maggie.

'I'm sure we will,' lied Maggie's Dad. He picked up and stared hard at the scrawled bill. 'Is service included, would you think?'

'I shouldn't think so. It would say.'

Maggie watched her Dad as he messed about with notes and coins, counting them on to the plate and then subtracting some of them as he calculated what was plainly going to end up an embarrassingly stingy tip.

She brought to mind another of those words, like raddled, that you found only in books. Doleful. She was feeling doleful. Didn't know why she should be. Look at it this way, Mags: you're not gaining a stepmother, you're losing a father. Such as he is. And for his side of the bargain, he's gaining two stepsons.

'There's one matter I ought to mention to you, Margaret.' He pretended to be re-checking the bill against the amount he had put down, but she could see that he was just avoiding her eye. What other bijou surprisettes did he have in store, then? About to confess he'd poisoned her Mum with weedkiller? 'I don't know how clear your memory of Jacqueline is, but you'll probably recall that she was quite a young woman when you knew her. In fact I can give her a good fifteen years, and in actuarial terms there's no reason to suppose she won't survive me by a good twenty- or twenty-five. On top of which she does have her own responsibilities and commitments. I'm mentioning that now in case of any expectations you might have entertained as regards the property.'

Maggie was chagrined to feel herself blushing scarlet, a thing she hadn't done since she was about ten years old. Good heavens, it couldn't be more shaming if she'd just wet her knickers. And the worst of it was, the cheeky sod was taking one look at her flaming cheeks and thinking he'd uncovered her secret bloody avarice.

She was going to be very angry about this when she'd stopped being embarrassed by it.

'I didn't know I had any expectations, I've never given it a moment's thought,' said Maggie, trying for iciness but hitting lukewarmness at best, in other words sounding as if she was lying. Which, fair enough, she was. She'd thought about it a lot, to the extent that she didn't want to think about it. Terrified her, it did. His pad would be worth what at today's prices? Thirty grand? Forty grand? Got to be. She'd piss it all against the wall in twelve months flat and end up in a straitjacket in the drying-out ward. She didn't want to know. She could only live in hopes that he'd get so choked at her general slaggishness that he'd leave it all to the cats' home.

Then why, instead of relief, was she now beginning to feel the anger she'd been anticipating? And what, exactly, was she feeling angry at?

'Of course, there would be *something*,' her Dad elaborated with restrained thin-uncle heartiness. 'I just had to make it clear that if anything happens, the bulk of the estate, such as it is, would go to Jacqueline.'

'I really wasn't expecting anything, Dad,' Maggie felt obliged to say. And obliged to add, although she didn't: 'I mean it.'

Was she angry because he was spelling it out in words of one syllable with all the i's dotted and all the t's crossed, that he thought she was only living as she did because she saw a cut-off date in the not-too-far-off future when having got her fists on his loot she would 'settle down', as he would put it, in a little long-leasehold flat with a fitted carpet and a fridge and a deep-freeze and a pigging cat? Was it because not only did he not understand what she was doing in the world, which was scarcely to be wondered at since she was bloody sure she didn't understand herself, but he couldn't or wouldn't even give her credit for being wholeheartedly and passionately and permanently what and who she was, wouldn't even allow her shallow little life the one nugget it could really lay claim to?

It was partly that, and partly that he'd pulled a fast one.

There was a game called Spoof that Maggie often played with some of the faces in the Half Moon for small sums. The thinking man's pitch-and-toss, she called it. The players stood in a circle with fists outstretched. Concealed in each fist would be one, two or three coins, or perhaps no coins at all. Going clockwise, you had to make an educated guess at the total of coins held. It usually took several rounds to produce a winner, because an element of the game was bluffing. In order to throw your opponents you would pretend to have no coins in your hand when you had three, or three when you had none, deliberately making your call too low or too high until you could establish a behaviour pattern among the other players, some of whom would be bluffers like yourself, others not.

You had to be quite the amateur psychologist to be good at Spoof. Maggie was good at Spoof.

She felt as if she had been playing a prolonged game of Spoof with her Dad over a period that stretched back to her childhood, and that he'd at last unclenched his fist to reveal not the three coins she'd confidently judged and all along expected he would have, but none. Or was it three coins where she'd expected none? Whichever way round it was, it was egg-on-face time again for Maggie the Mug.

12

Getting Her Act Together

So what was she doing in Islington?

There would be nothing from Sean because true to his word he had deserted the milk round at the door of the Camden Head pub. 'Top Hat will be getting them in, Boot,' he'd said, pursuing their Monopoly joke. 'And Boot may join Top Hat for refreshments in Top Hat's hotel as soon as Boot's thrown a six.' Not knowing where she used to live up here, he couldn't possibly have written, could he? Unless the clever bugger had somehow found out the address for himself—she wouldn't put it past him. Was that what she was doing in Islington?

There would be an accumulation of political junk. Although she didn't give a sod about politics—middle-of-the-gutter was how Maggie would describe such political leanings as she had—she had once, to ingratiate herself with Ken who did give a sod about politics, briefly joined some grotty action group he was involved in; at once the leaflets, petitions, appeals, newsletters, invitations to protest meetings and suchlike garbage had come flooding in from all directions. Worse than the bloody *Reader's Digest* those bearded weirdos were, once they got you on their do-gooding mailing-list.

If she could ever be bothered to take a sack with her up to Islington on her milk round, she could have made a few bob flogging waste paper. But that was all there would be. There'd been a letter from Ken once, but she didn't expect he was going to make a habit of it.

That was the evening she learned from that Susan chick in the Duke of Clarence that he wasn't coming back. The pig might at least have written a thank-you-Maggie-and-goodbye note, she'd thought; then it occurred to her that even though she'd done the Islington branch of her milk round only a few days earlier, there might just be something waiting for her down at St. Luke's Terrace. There was. She read it three times—once under the street lamp, once on the tube from the Angel to King's Cross, and once on the long bus-ride from King's Cross to the wrong side of Shepherds Bush, when she tore it into little pieces and threw it under the seat —but that night as she sipped sweet tea with Alfie's mum she could recite that letter to herself from memory.

Now she could remember only fragments. *Best for both of us . . . not fair on Helen . . . clean break . . . I know I've been nine different kinds of shit . . .*

Goodness, what a perceptive fellow he was.

Maggie saw no point in coming back to Islington, yet here she was in the grotty lift at the Angel tube station where she'd broken down and cried that night in front of all those punters, and here was St. grotty Luke's grotty Terrace, and there was the grotty house.

She'd been bloody sleepwalking, that was about the size of it. Or sleep-tubetravelling. Said goodbye to her Dad at King's Cross, then taken a tube this way for no other reason than that he'd taken a tube the other way. Rather a sad, strained goodbye it had been, full of implied finalities like take care of yourself and don't forget to write. Toodle-pip, Dad: see you at the funeral. And next thing she knew the gates were clanking open as the Angel's grotty lift touched grotty pavement level.

'The People's Goods-hoist' was what Maggie used to call that lift. Very community-oriented they were in these parts. As it trundled her up or down she would always try to guess the socially-committed occupations of the other passengers; even through her stupid tears she'd caught herself doing it: tinker, tailor, social worker, therapist, community relations officer, polytechnic lecturer, playgroup surpervisor, project leader, attendance scheme organiser—and that bastard Ken. All tarred with the same caring brush.

When she left Islington for the wilder shores of Notting Hill she gave it out that she was sick of living in a borough where everyone you met was looking after No. 2.

Strange to wake up at the Angel and find herself playing her lift game again. She never played it anywhere else on her milk round: the Bermuda Triangle was so polyglot that you couldn't guess what anyone was doing there, and as for Earl's Court, Notting Hill and Paddington, you didn't care to. Much as she despised Islington, Maggie had to admit that the Angel lift offered a better class of riff-raff.

Actually there were two Angel lifts, as indeed there were two Earl's Court lifts and two lifts in nearly every other tube station that didn't run to an escalator; but never in all her ten years in London had Maggie ever seen any two lifts operating at the same time. That struck her as absolutely bloody typical. Everything running at half-capacity, everything going off at half-cock, everyone living half-lives, waking up half-dead, getting half-pissed and going back to their half-rooms.

It was when she'd said something on these lines in Ken's company, because one of the Duke of Clarence's two cigarette machines was always empty, that he'd shown an interest. That was her not-just-a-pretty-face ploy, that was.

The Duke of Clarence was a pub she'd quickly got into the habit of avoiding, partly because of its barn-like proportions but mainly because it was full of L-plate teachers from the training college opposite. Maggie, her judgement coloured by a non-experience with a non-starter, from that secretarial college she'd gone to in Doncaster, had ever since equated the vocation of teaching with wetness and impotence. 'He who teaches, can't,' was all she would say to support the prejudice, and she was so pleased with the quip that she refused thereafter to reconsider any evidence for the defence, until Ken came along as the exception that broke the rule. They were at it like knives from the start and unlike Teddy and a good few others she could name (or rather couldn't: she remembered them all generically as Dick), he thought she was rather good at it.

Not that he was a proper teacher. He had been, but now he had found his true vocation—getting pissed on the rates. He was supposed to consolidate or co-ordinate or co-something-ate a kind of flying squad of raffia-work instructors and sociology lecturers who stood in for regular teachers when they were off with the curse or having nervous breakdowns. A desk job, in other words, but he spent as little time as he could in his office and always briefed his task force in the pub.

Meeting for a jar, as he called it. Real ale, he drank: held it up to the light to inspect its purity, sent it back if it didn't have a good head, the full boring bit. Furthermore he wore tweed jackets and furthermore still, he smoked a pipe. Definitely Brianish, was Maggie's first impression.

Not that being on the Brianish side ruled him out. The reverse, in fact. Maggie was rather in the market for something in the Brian line, these days. Following her saving-it-for-Teddy period and her anybody's-for-a-bag-of-crisps period, she was now thinking seriously of entering a looking-for-Brian period. It would either have to be that or hieing her to a nunnery for a while, the way she'd started carrying on again once she'd finally recovered from giving herself that nasty fright at No. 1 Paddington. She couldn't honestly say she had any rooted objection in principle to being on the skids, but it did cross her mind some mornings as she lay in one more broken-backed bed looking up at one more buckling ceiling, that it would be nice to wake up to a touch more class one of these days. Brian would have his own Brianish flat with a glass coffee-table and a tiled kitchen, and it wouldn't matter about him living in Norwood because he'd drive her backwards and forwards in his Cortina 2000. He would take her out to steakhouses and on package holidays, and buy her bottles of scent. Dear Aunty Agony, I have met this very nice punter, do you think I should tell him about my past?

Having given the Duke of Clarence the Big E, Maggie would more than likely never have met Ken if she hadn't had to set foot in the dump again when looking for Lynne. She had had to find Lynne to tell her that their bog ceiling had fallen in. So all in all, the Ken disaster was down to some cowboy making a botch-job of sticking up a few composition ceiling tiles. No wonder British workmanship had such a bad name.

Lynne was one of Maggie's rare flat-sharing experiences. They had a room on the top floor of a grotty house off the New North grotty Road, plus so-called kitchenette and usual offices with detachable ceiling tiles. Maggie wasn't much of a one for sharing pads but it was better than the Maida Vale squat she'd been living in, and since the building was under sentence of death to make way for a stretch of corrugated iron fencing, she would be moving on again soon enough.

Anyway, she only used it as a place not to hang her clothes up in. Just so long as she had somewhere to go back to in the mornings.

Lynne scrubbed the Duke of Clarence's floors twice a week, but just as Ken wasn't a real teacher, so she wasn't a real cleaning lady. Maggie occasionally reflected that she knew very few faces who were a real anything: her own fault, perhaps, since when she did occasionally meet real anybodies she would belittle their qualifications and affect to believe that, say, an airline pilot was only flying the Atlantic until he got his novel published, or that inside every accountant was a pop singer who had left it too late to get out. No wonder she never woke up in a Brianish flat in Norwood.

An actress, Lynne was supposed to be in real life. She never got any jobs but it did vocationally entitle her, when she had squeezed out her mop for the day, to attach herself to the real-ale school of emergency raffia instructors and mainly female student teachers presided over by Ken. She wasn't quite lunchtime theatre but they did seem to think she added a little cultural tone to the place.

It was Lynne's reluctance to introduce Ken when tracked down in the pub that focussed Maggie's attention upon him. If only Lynne had said something a bit less begrudging than, 'Oh, this is my flatmate', she would probably have delivered the bad news about the bog ceiling falling down and then toed it down to the Half Moon to be among her own sort.

'Future ex-flatmate,' amended Maggie, 'unless you can prove we can't get cancer of the bum from asbestos dust.' While she issued her bulletin on the collapsed ceiling tiles she gave Ken what she called her twiceover.

Maggie's twiceover was what faces sometimes qualified for if a superficial onceover hadn't lost them maximum points for wearing signet rings or having hair growing out of their nostrils. Ken's leather elbow-patches would instantly have disqualified him but for Maggie's new Brian rules which entitled him to the benefit of the doubt. He had wrinkles—Maggie refused to call them crinkles, although that was what they were—around the eyes. The eyes were blue: well, they would be, wouldn't they? Thatch of iron-grey hair. Pipe. Forty-sevenish, maybe even a young fifty. Christ, thought Maggie, he looked like an illustration out of

Women's Own. Looking Brianish was one thing but this one laid it on with a trowel.

The redeeming factor was what Maggie, if she hadn't been Maggie, would have had to describe as his charisma. There was no doubt about it, he had bloody something, these student teacher chicks were round him like wasps round a toffee apple, and Lynne's eyes were only one off from barnacles. It certainly wasn't that he was a spellbinder, in fact what he was saying—something about a report on teachers' pay—sounded pretty heavy going to Maggie. Yet while he was talking, he somehow managed to radiate the idea that he was listening. As he probably was, she was to realise very much later: to the sound of his own bloody voice. But it seemed quite a knack at the time, and good listeners were always off to a flying start in Maggie's book.

The only one not hanging on his every word was this little Susan-type of about nineteen, wearing crisp-looking schmutter including a straight denim skirt that a man of the stocking-tops generation would enjoy putting his hand up. Susans looked as if butter wouldn't melt up their crotches, but were noted for putting themselves about as rattlesnakes.

It came to Maggie in a flash of intuition, or perhaps it was just plain observation, that he was a wolf in Brian's clothing. Nothing wrong with that: best of both worlds you'd get there, v. likely.

He was having Susan rotten, that was for sure. That was why she was standing slightly apart from the others, letting them make their saucer eyes and pick cotton threads from his jacket while they had the chance. Her turn would come later. She could wait.

So could Maggie, but not for ever. She made a mental note to fish out her damson corduroy skirt. If it hadn't started moulting by now it could give denim odds any day of the week.

She hadn't felt like this for any face since Big Teddy, and that was going back a bit. And even then, she recalled, she had reminded herself of a car engine warming up on a cold day: it had taken her a while to get going. Whereas with this bugger, if she was going to keep up the motoring metaphor, she was in full throttle from the start. Maybe he'd slipped Spanish Fly into her vino.

'If they're the usual composition tiles, you don't have to

worry about asbestos. What are they—white?' This was one of the emergency squad of raffia instructors, although in his particular case he laid claim to being a supply science teacher. While the raffia instructors formed more or less a separate school from Ken and his student-chick acolytes in getting-them-in terms, the two groups did converge to make a rough figure eight, with Lynne, Maggie and one or two other odds and sods bridging them.

The science punter commenced a lecture on asbestos identification that promised to be so eye-glazingly tedious that Maggie gulped back her glass of plonk in one go in the hope that someone, preferably Ken, would come to her rescue by buying her another. Maggie was a gold medallist at the small gymnastic feat of accepting a drink with an imperceptible twist of the body that could transfer her from one person's company to another's without causing offence.

Ken wasn't looking in her direction. The science punter broke off the asbestos lecture to buy Maggie and Lynne a glass of vino apiece but nothing for himself. 'I'll nurse this,' he said, cradling an inch of beer. Mean sod.

'Cheers, Barry,' said Maggie.

'Geoff,' he corrected.

'Mistake at the christening. You're one of life's Barrys.'

She threw her voice in Ken's direction, hoping he'd rise to it but he didn't. She might just as well have been talking to the wall.

Or not:

'Ah, I *see*!' Barry-Geoff nodded with oafish solemnity to show that he understood the game they were playing. 'In that case, my dear, that makes you a Brenda. Yes, definitely a Brenda. Have you met Brenda, Lynne, or may I call you let—me—see, Betty. Betty, this is Brenda, Brenda, this is Betty.'

Oh Christ, the silly sod thought she was chatting him up. Come on, Lynne, drink up and let's get out of it. Giving Barry-Geoff her glassiest smile, Maggie turned to Ken. ''Bye. Nice to meet you.'

'Nice to meet you. Goodbye, my loves.' Loves in the plural included Lynne, probably to Lynne's advantage.

'Have you had him?' Maggie asked bluntly that afternoon as they picked fragments of composition tile out of the lavatory pan.

'He isn't up to the Ls yet,' Lynne said with simulated coyness. 'And remember, our Maggie, L comes before M.'

'Didn't I ever tell you, my name's really Aggie?' Maggie flipped back, unusually arch. Revoltingly arch, in fact. She must have it bad.

She was supposed to be going on the loon with Sean the following lunchtime. She rang from the phone-box at the end of the street and put him off, then took her damson corduroy skirt to the twenty-four-hour cleaners and bought a new pair of tights in a matching shade.

It took three days to get him. Barry-Geoff's thick-headed conviction that he was the one she was chasing didn't help much. On the other hand, Lynne's determination to get Ken first did. The more she chatted him up, the more attention she drew towards her mate Maggie who never left her side and could top every line she uttered in spades. And at the death, even the pathetic Barry-Geoff had his uses. Getting nowhere with Maggie, he turned his attention back to Lynne who was getting nowhere with Ken. If a few sly hints from Maggie that Lynne fancied him rotten had oiled the wheels in any way, she was only too glad to have been of service. What a lark! What next? Make up a foursome, should they? Bit of French kissing in the recreation-ground shelter? Should she ask Ken, 'My friend wants to know if your friend wants to take her to the pictures'?

They did make up a foursome, as it happened. Barry-Geoff asked Lynne if she fancied a bit of nosh at the Spanish-type place round the corner. 'Why don't we all go?' suggested Maggie. Ken nodded and knocked back his beer. She was away to the races. And little Susan, inwardly smirking and standing apart from Ken as she always did, had for once stood apart one step too far and one beat too many. And could smirk on the other side of her innards.

Two bottles of wine later, while simultaneously conducting a spirited discussion on some obscure local council controversy with Barry-Geoff and shovelling back paella with his fork American-style, Ken was groping Maggie under the tablecloth with his free hand. The question was no longer if and when they were going to have it off, but where. He was married, of course, name any non-woofter over thirty who wasn't, so it would all be down to Maggie. No chance of a Box-and-Cox-type arrangement with Lynne: although Barry-

Geoff looked like scoring with her if he was capable of it, which was to be doubted, he was a single punter with his own pad. That removed whatever incentive there might have been for Lynne taking long walks while her flatmate bounced up and down on the bedsprings. Sean lived too far away to make borrowing his place a practical proposition, though he would have lent it if Maggie had asked, which curiously enough she never had. She would have to move.

She had gone off that flat, anyhow. She had gone off Lynne, as a matter of fact, for coming on all best-friendly once she'd realised that Maggie was after something more than a one-night stand. 'What, break my heart and leave it in little pieces, you reckon?' mocked Maggie, after Lynne had warned her for the fifth time that he was in the habit of loving them and leaving them in droves. Lynne pretended to go along with the send-up: 'You're playing with fire, my dear!' she quavered. But she meant it, the silly turd. Jealous as a rat, of course, but she really did think she was doing Maggie a favour in warning her off.

As well as not being a real cleaning lady Lynne wasn't a real friend. Maggie's friends didn't give her advice, they just picked her up and poured her a large drink.

But it was the shared flat that Maggie had gone off most. It would be months, if ever, before the bog ceiling got mended. Meanwhile, you had to sit on the lav and stare up at a quease-making patchwork quilt of laths and black pitch-looking stuff that the guaranteed-non-asbestos tiles had been fixed to or as it turned out hadn't. There were things moving about up there. Maggie had seen one of them—like a centipede it was, only thinner and wrigglier. Bleah. After that she wouldn't enter the lav even for peeing purposes. She used a vase, and on the non-peeing side, did without.

Still, it gave her a funny story, when they had another foursome lunch to follow up the first one. And she told it well. Ken liked funny stories, so long as he wasn't being taken the piss out of personally. She was careful not to put him down.

'If you're seriously looking for another room, one of our girls is moving to Sheffield this weekend,' said Ken, his fingernails delicately scraping the corduroy-ribbed contour of her inner thigh. 'Seventy-three St. Luke's Terrace, just round the corner from where you are now. Don't be put off by the street itself, I know it's a bit rough, but I believe the flat's nice enough and it does have its own bathroom, so I'm told. How much are you paying at present?'

The conversation was murmured so that Lynne, who was being lumpishly chatted-up by Barry-Geoff, wouldn't row herself into the new flat and spoil Maggie's chances. Considering how mundanely they were talking, the effect was curiously erotic.

'I'll certainly have a look at it,' Maggie said, putting her hand on the hand that was on her leg.

'That's you on your own?'

'I should think so, yes.'

Maggie had walked, or in the night hours scampered, along St. Luke's Terrace a few times. 'Bit rough' was the understatement of the year: it was the kind of street even squatters turned their noses up at. If she was prepared to live in that dump just so that a middle-aged lech would have somewhere to get his leg across, there really was no hope for her. She didn't mind a certain amount of old-world grottiness, was all for it in fact, but St. Luke's Terrace went right over the top. Definitely not the kind of thoroughfare that Ken's friends and neighbours from posho Barnsbury would ever be seen dead in. That, of course, was why it came highly recommended. She moved in that weekend, took down the curling Lowry prints that Ken's itinerant raffia instructress had left behind, and pinned up some cheapo anti-slavery and women's suffrage posters she'd bought in Camden Passage. Maggie wasn't a poster person herself, in fact she was a blank wall person, but she thought Ken would like them when he came round as promised to see if she'd settled in, ho ho.

He did. He also, she noted, knew how to find his way to the 'or so I'm told' bathroom without being directed. Still, that was his affair. Or one of them.

He arrived with a house-warming potted plant under one arm and a bottle of plonk under the other. They drank most of the wine and then got on with it. Afterwards, stretched out exhausted on the lumpy single bed and flicking ash into the biscuit-tin lid that served as an ashtray, Maggie reflected that it was easy to see why he was such a hit with those student teacher chicks. Considerate, that would be the word they'd use. What they probably wouldn't realise, not having Maggie's wealth of experience in these matters, was that he spun out the preliminaries to the extent that he did for the very good reason that it took him a long time to get it up, to use a medical term. Still, much Maggie cared. If brewer's droop was what had turned him into a good lover, three cheers for brewer's droop. He was bloody wonderful.

Maggie wondered how long she'd last. Till the potted plant died, she wished impetuously, then wished she hadn't; and for her third wish, that her green fingers weren't all thumbs. She knew sod-all about plants and would probably murder the bloody thing within two days. An azalia, he'd said it was. She went to the public library in Essex Road and looked up the care and feeding of azalias in a gardening encyclopedia.

They established a satisfactory pattern. Meet at lunchtime in the Duke of Clarence, elaborately go their separate ways, then assemble at the flat if he could get the afternoon free, which the idle sod used to manage as often as not. If he couldn't, then it was evenings. All the action groups and committees of one sort or another that he belonged to gave him the perfect cover. That was probably why he'd joined them all.

It wasn't all bed. They found a couple of out-of-the-way restaurants and went out for a nosh sometimes. A little pub on the canal towpath became 'our pub'. Occasionally they swanned up West: it was nice to be able to show off 'her chap' to the faces in the Half Moon.

They talked a lot, or rather he talked and Maggie did a very good listening act. A bit drone-drone he was, and it was a flaming nuisance having to read the *Guardian* every morning to sus what he was going on about, but being with him could be very soothing, like a long hot bath. She seemed to affect him the same way, because he said he found her relaxing. No one had ever called Maggie relaxing before: it was like hearing someone say they found going over Niagara Falls in a barrel relaxing. It must be his influence on her mirroring back at him.

The potted plant died. She'd been going around with Ken for three months now and feared that she must be nearing the end of her run. Come in, No. 99, your time is up. Maggie knew she'd already outlasted the other ninety-eight or however many randy little Susans there'd been, because he'd told her so when they'd swapped true-life confessions, or in Maggie's case true-life generalities. She was glad that he didn't try to keep his screwing-around record a secret or make excuses for it such as his wife's migraines—he was, he freely admitted, a born philanderer. They were in the sack at the time. 'Oh, is that what you've just been doing—philandering?' Maggie asked drowsily. 'Not with you—you're a bit special,' murmured Ken. If that was reassurance, she'd known electrical kettles with better guarantees.

She couldn't bring herself to throw out the dead azalia and it drooped there in its plastic pot on her window-ledge until Ken, on his way home one night, asked if he should sling it in the bin on the way downstairs. She told him at last of the little cross-fingers folk-legend she'd invented for herself, and her fears of their affair dying when the potted plant did. 'Oh, dear, we'll have to do something about that, won't we?' said Ken. The next evening he came back with a rubber plant. Indestructible, he said. Typical: kind of thing he did. Maggie wept a little—the first time on record she'd ever cried from happiness.

They went out for a meal and he talked for the first time about his wife, answering all the questions that Maggie had left unasked. It was a familiar-sounding story that must have been going the rounds for years but it was the first time she had ever heard it first-hand. Married too young, thought they had a lot in common but turned out to be on different wavelengths, drifted along contentedly enough but no excitement in the marriage, on the other hand was never able to relax either, except with Maggie. That night Maggie got relaxed out of her skull. She had really got her act together at last.

It went on for another year before the steam began to run out. They were seeing too much of one another for two faces who weren't shacked up together, but not enough for two faces who never would be. Ken trolled off to Derbyshire and didn't come back. Maggie toed it to Notting Hill. And the rubber plant died.

It was dusk as Maggie turned into St. Luke's Terrace, but still light enough to observe, as she awoke from her sleep-walk, that it could no longer remain at No. 1 in her grottiness top ten. Although it still had a long way to go before there were tubbed bay trees on the front doorsteps, like some of the once-grotty streets in the Bermuda Triangle, it was definitely on the up and up. There were three builders' skips in the street, one of them outside No. 73 itself, and No. 59 was crowned with a canopy of polythene sheeting where they were building a roof extension. It would only be a matter of months now before there were Banham burglar alarms on the re-pointed walls and children called Adam and Emma to be glimpsed in basement playrooms, crayoning pictures of mummy on wads of computer printout paper snitched from the office.

Public midden though she had often compared it to, Maggie thought she preferred St. Luke's Terrace as it had been when she first saw it, when there was a smouldering double mattress in the gutter, plywood up at all the broken windows, and spade kids sitting around in cardboard boxes and picking their noses.

There was her own window, still cracked, still with the potato-sacking-dyed-red curtains drawn as she'd left them when she'd buggered off a year ago. They'd never re-let the room, she'd discovered on previous visits: they were waiting for the tenants to move out or die of hypothermia or gas themselves so they could chuck all the plasterboard into the skip and gentrify the shell back into a house. That made a change. It was the only house she'd ever lived in that hadn't gone from bad to worse once she'd left it, or been blotted off the map altogether like the one around the corner where she'd shared a room with Lynne. Maggie wasn't sure she approved of this tarting-up process, but at least when they'd hung the repro coach lantern and fitted the yellow front door, she could strike pigging Islington off her visiting list.

Pisspots. They'd fitted the yellow front door already. Well, not yellow exactly: varnished imitation-mahogany mock-Georgian, but a new door nevertheless. A new door meant a new lock. Pisspots.

It screwed up the scenario, that did. Maggie had had it all worked out, what she was going to do at No. 73. She was going to sort through all the leaflets and circulars and action-group gunge, and if there wasn't a bijou notelet from Sean, she was going to go up to her old room and sit on the floorboards and have a bit of a sniffle. Seemed a funny thing to be looking forward to, she would be the first to agree, but she really needed that sniffle, Maggie did. And if by any zillion to one chance chance there did happen to be something from Sean—had she ever given him this address? Didn't think so, there was no reason to, but she just might have done—she would take it up to her old room and read it and smile, then have a bit of a sniffle anyway.

She opened her shoulder-bag and jumbled through it until she found a ballpoint. Extracting the envelope belonging to her Inland Revenue letter she rested it against the new front door and wrote: *Please forward any mail for M. Moon to No. 37 Balmoral—*

'Maggie?'

Punter walking a dog: it was cocking its leg at the street lamp outside No. 73 which had just flickered on. She recognised him from somewhere but would need more of a clue than that well-well-it's-a-small-world smirk of his.

'I always forget a face,' Maggie said.

'Geoff.'

'Of course. It's Barry, isn't it?'

Barry-Geoff guffawed. 'You don't change, do you? Long time no see.'

'I've moved.'

'I *thought* you might have done!' exclaimed Barry-Geoff triumphantly, as if she had just given him the solution to a mystery he'd been racking his brains over for months. 'I remember bumping into Lynne, oh, ages and ages ago, and *she* thought you'd moved, but then someone said no, they'd seen you in the Duke of Clarence.'

She wasn't going to tell him that she used to traipse back there from the wrong side of Shepherds Bush three times a week, or he'd guess why. 'I expect I have a double, everyone else has,' Maggie said. Then, not that she gave a sod but to get away from the topic of herself: 'How *is* Lynne? Do you still see her?'

'Good heavens, no! She's married, haven't you heard? Yes, she married. I don't think you'd know him, she's done quite well for herself . . .'

Barry-Geoff commenced five minutes on Lynne's good fortune in marrying a well-heeled punter with his own business of some kind or another, but Maggie wasn't listening. She completed scribbling her note to No. 73's new Fiona and Nigel Tightbum-type owners as she already pictured them, and fell into step with Barry-Geoff as his dog dragged him off along the terrace.

She would have to ask him. If she didn't he would tell her anyway. Or studiously not tell her, which would be even worse.

Why should it be even worse? She didn't want to know. Didn't give a sod.

Not giving a sod, then, it did no harm to ask.

'And how's Ken? Does anyone hear from him?'

'*Well* may you *ask*!' Barry-Geoff smacked his lips, almost slavering in his excitement at having a titbit of gossip. What? Run away with a black lady, has he? Up on a screwing-under-age charge? Divorce? '*He's* married, too,' said Barry-Geoff, being deliberately cryptic.

Don't get it, Barry-Geoff. We know he's married. That's the whole bloody point, isn't it? Or was.

'*I* know what you're thinking,' Barry-Geoff said, thoroughly enjoying himself, as they paused for the dog to have another go at another lamp-post. '*You* thought the same as *we all* thought. That he was married already.'

Yes? And? Of course he was married already. Whole bloody—

Oh. Not married already. Pretending to be married already.

'Maggie,' Barry-Geoff began a bit diffidently it sounded, while staring fixedly at his dog peeing against the lamp-post, 'I don't know how well you got to know Ken in the end, it's none of my business, but it *did turn out in fact* that whereas all of us thought he and Helen were married, *at that time in fact* they weren't.'

'I don't understand,' Maggie said woodenly, just to say something.

'It was what they chose to let everyone believe, in case it affected either of their career prospects, I imagine. But *in fact it appears* that Helen was waiting all that time for her divorce to come through, I don't know the details and don't wish to know. They got married quietly just before Christmas, apparently. I suppose *if the truth be known in fact*, that was why they upped sticks and went to Derbyshire.'

All Maggie was thinking, or all she was dully aware of herself thinking, was that if Barry-Geoff said '*in fact*' once more, she was going to do him some serious damage with her shoulder-bag, whereupon the dog would probably bite her leg.

'I must say you surprise me,' Maggie said. 'I'd always heard they didn't laugh at the same joke.'

She'd been to look at the bitch once, just out of curiosity. Got their address out of the phone book and gone there and stood there.

Helen. Stupid name that it was, Maggie couldn't think of a better one. One of life's Helens. If she'd been called Sharon or Sheilagh or Shitpot, Maggie would have rechristened her Helen.

Helens were passive, trustful, betrayed—and safe.

She even sounded like a Helen, because Maggie had spoken to her once. Being a bit pissed one night, and knowing that Ken was genuinely at one of the meetings he usually genuinely wasn't at, she rang the cow up to hear what she sounded like.

'No, he isn't, I'm afraid. Who's that speaking?'

'The *North London Times*,' said Maggie.

'That isn't Polly, is it, it doesn't sound like her?' Oh shit, she must know everyone on the bloody paper. They probably rang up five times a week.

'No, it's Molly. I'm a holiday relief.'

'I thought I didn't know your voice. Is there any message I can take?'

Yes: would you tell him his fancy woman called, and surely it's not too much to ask that a face of his resourcefulness and experience at leching should be able to organise the occasional dirty weekend, or is that when he services you?

'It's not important. I just wanted to check some dates with him.'

Well, that was what the complacent cow sounded like —like a complacent cow. Now what did the complacent cow look like?

Maggie picked a chilly evening when Ken and Helen were going to the Tower Theatre up the road to see some crap or other—for a couple with nothing in common, a lot of these couple-type arrangements seemed to crop up in their incompatible diaries. She already knew where their flat was, having as it just so happened been going in that direction on one or two occasions but without seeing Helen going in or out.

She stationed herself by the peeling plane tree opposite.

It was bloody uncanny. If she'd rung up Ladbroke's earlier she could have made a fortune. 'What odds will you give me on a woman I've never set eyes on wearing a Marks and Sparks camel coat, sub-Sloane Rangers headscarf, flat shoes, carrying a beige sling bag and putting her arm through her husband's like Barnsbury's answer to Mrs. pigging Miniver?'

Maggie could remember pissing herself when she'd seen that film on the box as a teenage monster: her Dad had bored for England on how she would be giggling on the other side of her face if Hitler had won the war, which the Mrs. Minivers of this world had seemingly prevented him from doing.

She liked the sequel, though, where Mrs. Miniver died. *The Miniver Story.* Good film, that.

She watched Ken and Helen as they came out of the converted Victorian terrace house and waited until they were out of sight, then she crossed the road, marched boldly up the short path to the communal front door and rang all four doorbells. There were no lights in the other three flats but it was as well to make sure: if anyone answered she would pull the *North London Times* trick again.

As if giving whoever she had come to see time to answer, Maggie sauntered casually along the strip of paving stones that ran between the garden and the area railings. Standing on tiptoe, she could just see into Ken and Helen's ground-floor flat. The curtains weren't drawn and they'd left a standard lamp on for the burglars. There were all the many books they'd collected in the shelves he'd probably cobbled up himself, floor to ceiling they were, on either side of a marble fireplace. There were the pictures they'd bought, real watercolours by the look of them, and the good knock-on-wood Heal's-type furniture they'd chosen together. The room stank of good taste. Nobody would ever want to walk out on a room like that, not without getting custody of the fitted carpet.

They had a lot of possessions. Ashtrays. Vases with flowers in them. Potted plants like the one Ken had given her. Staffordshire bloody dogs. An antique sodding solitaire board with original glass marbles that one of them must have gone out and searched for, to please the other one.

Goodness pigging gracious, so this was what a proper real live room looked like, was it?

Peter Pan. That was who Maggie reminded herself of as she perched there on her toes wondering what they had paid for the William Morris-looking wallpaper. Peter Pan when Nana is bathing the kids and the little sod presses his nose to the windowpane. That was another show Maggie had pissed herself laughing at, when she'd seen it light years ago at the Bradford Alhambra. And her Mum, who really should have been told by the authorities that *Gone With The Wind* was more suitable material for a twelve-year-old, had gone spare and sworn never to take her to the theatre again. Nor had she.

Maggie snickered up her knicker-leg at the time but it all seemed poignant now. She walked away, missing her Mum and feeling the cold.

All that gear and they hadn't even been married. Nine kinds of shit, eh? Ken, baby, you've just been decimalised.

'I don't suppose,' said Barry-Geoff as they neared the Angel tube station where, as he would probably put it, he would have to speak now or forever hold his peace, 'you'd like a quickie in the Duke of Clarence for old times' sake?'

'Why not?'

13

Spring in Earl's Court

Legless.

Feeling no pain, she felt terrible. She blamed having had practically nothing to eat. That and having knocked back about a crate of vodka, not to mention the half-bot wine and brandy while toying with her boiled rat earlier.

Finishing up in the sack with Barry-Geoff had been a bit of an error of judgement. She didn't want to do it, he couldn't do it, and he had been put to the embarrassment not only of that but of having to wake her up and ask her to piss off out of it because he didn't want her on the premises when his cleaning lady arrived in the morning. Observing him furtively shoving a fiver into her shoulder-bag, she was about to leap up and clout him round the head with it when he explained that he was stumping up her mini-cab fare. Gent. She didn't want a mini-cab, would probably throw up in it as she had done in Alfie's cab that time, but he'd already phoned for one.

The effort of summoning up the energy she'd thought she was going to need to clout Barry-Geoff with her shoulder-bag had left her dizzy. She lay on his bed with one eye closed, focussing on the overhead light which he'd just switched on to encourage her to get up. When the ceiling stopped swaying she'd start putting her clothes on.

'The mini-cab should be here in a minute,' Barry-Geoff said, squinting hopefully down into the street through the venetian blinds. 'Their office is just up the road and they usually come at once.'

'Where are we?' grunted Maggie.

'Just off Upper Street.'

Upper Street, Upper Street. Oh, yes, Putney Bridge. No,

not Putney Bridge, that was this morning, or was it yesterday? Islington, this was.

'What's time?'

'Getting on for two. Would you like me to help you get dressed?'

The poor bugger was terrified that he wouldn't be able to get shut of her and she was just going to lie there. It was what she felt like doing: she was absolutely knackered. There wasn't a lot he could do if she refused to move. She might just do that, she didn't believe that guff about a cleaning woman arriving at cracko. He wanted to blot her out, that's what he wanted to do. The feeling's mutual, rat-features.

She couldn't half do with a few Zs. She must have been asleep for only a few minutes. What time had they tumbled out of that club they'd gone to after the Duke of Clarence? About one, it must have been. Then they'd come back here and thrashed ineffectively about on the sack for what seemed like light years, then she'd zizzed off. Christ, she did feel terrible.

An important question struck Maggie. Important for Barry-Geoff anyway.

'Where's dog?'

'In his basket, asleep.'

'Thank Christ, thought left it in club.'

'No. We brought him back here before we went to the club, don't you remember?'

No. Yes. But she would sooner have forgotten. That's right: they'd come back here after reeling out of the Duke of Clarence, and he'd put the dog in the kitchen then started groping her on the sofa, but at the death he couldn't get it up, the bloody dog wouldn't stop yapping to be let out of the kitchen and he said it was putting him off his stroke. For some unknown reason this had struck Maggie as funny and she'd burst out laughing, then found she wasn't laughing at all, she was crying. He'd thought it was because he'd got her going, or believed he had, and then couldn't do anything. She'd said no, it wasn't that, it was something personal, but as they were both very keyed up for different reasons, why didn't they just get into kip with a soothing brandy and see what happened when they'd unwound.

Christ, she'd forgotten about having all that brandy on top of all that vodka. No wonder she felt like death warmed up.

He didn't have any booze in the flat and hadn't the first idea where to get any, but she remembered having passed a narrow doorway with a dimly-lit little sign that said 'Members Only', which could only mean a dingy basement drinking club where if you said your name was whatever Barry-Geoff's name was and that you were a life member and couldn't understand why they didn't have it down in the register unless it hadn't been transferred from the old register, they'd eventually let you start buying drinks. So she'd made Barry-Geoff zip up his flies and take her down there, promising him that a couple of brandies would make a man of him. But they hadn't. She'd thought to jolly him up with that bijou epigrammette of hers: those who teach, can't. So then *he'd* started bloody crying. Jesus God, no wonder he wanted to get rid of her.

That undulating ceiling of his really was extraordinarily clean. Wasn't often you got a clean white ceiling like that. Perhaps his non-existent cleaning woman went over it with a feather duster. The whole flat was nice and clean and white. Parquet floors with white shaggy rugs, white painted bookshelves, big white lamps on square white shiny tables. V. Brianish. It was going to be a letdown going back to wherever it was she lived. It had just slipped her mind where she did live for the moment, but she knew it was a shit-heap compared with this place. If she just went on lying there like a fish on a slab until the non-existent cleaning woman came in and found her, maybe he'd think he had to marry her and make an honest corpse of her.

Barry-Geoff was padding neurotically about the bedroom picking her gear up and putting it all in one place on a chair by the bed. He was so anxious for her to go that he had gone to the lengths of getting dressed again instead of putting on his jimjams or nightdress or whatever he slept in; there was no way he intended having anything more to do with this bed until she was well and truly out of it and in that thing, how strange, she couldn't remember the word for the thing you rode about in and paid the driver. Not taxi. Minicab.

Suddenly, though, as he picked up her balled-up tights with her knickers inside them, Barry-Geoff made a lunge in Maggie's direction. She thought for a second that handling her unmentionables must have inflamed him into attempting one last crack at her honour, and so she closed her eyes so as not to see that look of despair on his face when he realised he still couldn't do it. But when she opened them again he had dashed past the bed into the bathroom where, after a moment, she could hear him being horribly sick. Feeling a bit that way herself, and wanting something to take her mind off it, Maggie elbowed herself into a sitting position and began to untangle her tights which he'd tossed on to the bed beside her.

To his evident relief she was dressed, upright, and gingerly finding out what putting one foot in front of the other did for her nervous system when he came back into the bedroom. The sweat was still damp on his forehead and there were bile-flecks on his suede shoes. Poor lamb, and he hadn't even enjoyed himself. Hadn't even got noticeably legless so far as Maggie could remember, had just sat there 'nursing', as he put it, one vodka and tonic for every four of hers, and getting more and more boring as the evening went on. Still, not to grumble: those couple of hours at the Duke of Clarence had had the desired effect of preventing her from toeing it down to the Half Moon. They would all have been picking the bones out of Sean like vultures round a dead sheep, and Maggie would have finished up breaking something on Sid the Squirrel's head. She would have been barred for life this time.

'The minicab's here,' announced Barry-Geoff, peering through the venetian blinds again and completely failing to keep the implied 'thank God' out of his tone. 'I told them Earl's Court but I didn't know your exact address so you'll have to give the driver directions. Do you know the way, because some of these drivers are hopeless and he *probably* doesn't even carry an *A to Z*?'

'I carry an *A to Z*,' said Maggie, able to speak in complete sentences again, provided they were short ones, now that she was on her feet. 'In my head,' she explained, as he began to stutter something about folding it back at the relevant page and showing it to the driver. He was so eager to be of some use to her before she left, having been bloody useless all night, that she felt a bijou wave of affection towards him and gave him a warm goodbye peck on his clammy cheek.

Her memory was going. It really was. Seriously. She was sitting in the back seat of the minicab, they were bowling along a ghost-town-looking sunken road that must be taking her through the Barbican she would say, and she had no recollection whatsoever where she had been.

'Where are you from?' Maggie asked the Asian driver.

'Uganda.'

'No, I mean the minicab firm. Where are you based?'

The driver giggled a great deal, explained at length how he had misunderstood her, and finally orientated Maggie by mentioning Islington. To discourage further conversation she pretended to be even more pissed than she was, not that that overtaxed her powers of persuasion, and closed her eyes.

Yes, Islington. Barry-Geoff. She could be forgiven, she hoped, for not remembering the unmemorable. But she still couldn't remember leaving his flat and getting into the minicab, or whether he'd come downstairs to see her off. Probably had, he was a born cab-door-opener, Barry Geoff was. All he was good for.

If she was suffering from alcoholic amnesia, how come she could remember nearly everything else about that life-long day?

Hearing about Sean. Meeting Aliboo outside her little marzipan cottage. Being cross-examined at the Portakabins. Signing the babe away. Snivelling in front of Alfie's mum. Her Dad getting married. Ken getting married. Dad marrying Alfie's mum, and Ken marrying Jenny, with Sean and Maggie as the witnesses. And the babe wouldn't stop crying . . .

Pulling up abruptly at a red light the minicab shook her awake. She rubbed the condensation off the window with her sleeve and looked out. Cromwell Road, were they on? Or not.

'Where are we?'

'New King's Road,' said the driver.

Bloody con-artist. Or raving idiot, one or the other. They'd have finished up in pigging Wimbledon if she hadn't woken up. 'The New Kings Road,' said Maggie, sitting upright, 'doesn't take us to Earl's Court.'

'I know it doesn't take us to Earl's Court. You said Parsons Green.'

'I said Earl's Court. I want Balmoral Gardens.'

'You didn't say Balmoral Gardens, you said Gaspar Road, Parsons Green.'

Really? Freudian slip of the bloody year, that must be.

No it wasn't a slip. She'd given him Riggsy's address on purpose. Hadn't been able to remember her own.

The minicab had slowed down. Without looking round at her the driver, who had clearly by now got her down as a nutter as well as pissed with it, said, 'Do you want Earl's Court or Parsons Green?'

'Parsons Green.'

It took a long time to get Riggsy out of bed. The Garden Flat didn't have a doorbell and Maggie didn't like to bang on the knocker for fear of rousing the punters upstairs. Instead she tapped on the basement window with a coin for a few seconds, then positioned herself on the area steps so that when Riggsy woke up she would be able to see that it wasn't her friendly neighborhood rapist making an early morning call.

After she had repeated the performance a few times Maggie saw, through the ill-fitting curtains, that a faint pinkish light had appeared at the far end of the living-room. Judging rightly that Riggsy had opened the bedroom door and was shuffling blearily to the window, Maggie stood on the area steps and began to gesticulate ingratiatingly at herself, to indicate that it was only Maggie. The curtain twitched. Then a light was switched on behind the ribbed glass of the outer door and she heard Riggsy sliding back bolts and unfastening chains. There seemed to be a great many of them.

'Maggie, are you going to make a habit of this? Because if you are I shall simply have to find another flat. I can't have it, Maggie, and I won't have it.'

Christ, she wasn't half in a stew. Wide awake she was, but looking as if she'd been fast asleep. Not caught in the best of moods.

Accusing Maggie of making a habit of it was going over the top a bit, though. It was nearly a year ago since that pantomime with the Amazing Albert and Pam and she hadn't done it since.

'I'm sorry, Riggsy, did I wake you?'

'You know very well that you woke me. Now *I'm ill*, Maggie. I've had a bad attack of flu and I'm *very run down*. I can't take this, I must be left alone!'

Granted that she'd been dragged out of bed and it must be

around three in the morning, she was reacting a shade shrilly, wasn't she?

Must be telling the truth about being ill, though. That would be why Maggie hadn't seen her around for a few days. She looked, to use one of her own favourite words, *ghastly*. Staring out through four inches of doorway like a mad thing, with her tatty kimono tugged round her scraggy frame and her dead straw hair all over the shop and her white face all fallen in as if she took her cheekbones out at night, she was more raddled than Maggie had ever seen her. Beat all raddling records, this did. If Maggie was going to look like Riggsy at forty, this was how Riggsy was going to look at seventy.

'I know it's late, Riggsy, but do we have to talk on the doorstep, love?'

'I don't want to talk to you *at all*. I want you to *go away*!' Riggsy was trying to talk in a forceful whisper but her blacktreacle voice wasn't suited to it. And Maggie could never remember to keep her voice down when she'd had a few. They would have the neighbours tuning in if they went on like this.

'It *is* urgent, Riggsy,' she pleaded.

'What's urgent? Urgent for you, you mean! What's so urgent that you come pestering me at this hour?'

Yes, what? What the hell was she doing here?

She'd come to talk to Riggsy, hadn't she? Her mate. Sit on her rickety wickerwork sofa and swig the last of her gin and talk.

'Can't I explain, Riggsy?'

Riggsy shuddered and pulled her skimpy kimono around her as the raw night air seeped in on her. The silly cat was going to catch pneumonia if she stood there much longer.

The same thought evidently occurred to Riggsy. On impulse she opened the door wider and pulled, almost dragged, Maggie into the bare little hallway. Pushing the door closed with one hand, she kept hold of Maggie's sleeve with the other.

'No, this is as far as you're going, my lady. You *do* have some explaining to do, then you'll hear what I have to say, and then you'll leave. Now I want you to tell me why two council social workers should have come here this evening looking for you, and I want to know exactly which people you've given this address to as your own, and why.'

Jesus. They didn't piss about on the Jenny-Miss Roberts network, did they? They hadn't half got their skates on. Those sods up there on the wrong side of Shepherds Bush must have got on the blower as soon as she walked out of the Portakabins this afternoon.

'Oh, God, Riggsy. I didn't think they'd really actually turn up here, and certainly not so quickly, or I'd have done something about it. I would, truly. I just gave your address to this one person in a panic, not to anybody else, I swear it. I wanted to get them off my back.'

'And on to *my* back?'

She was right. 'You're right, Riggsy. Oh, Christ. Look, I'll get in touch with them first thing in the morning and give them my proper address. Promise.' And then move to Kilburn.

'Why did they want to see you, anyway? Why were they so worried about you? You haven't been doing anything silly again, have you?'

Maggie didn't have the chance to provide an answer, not that she had one ready. Riggsy, raising a bony, nicotine-stained finger, cut in quickly: 'No, don't tell me, Maggie. If you have problems, they're your own problems. I don't want to be involved.'

I know, Riggsy, that's why I'm here. I've just realised.

Aloud, Maggie, said, 'Can I ask you what you told them?'

'Give me a cigarette,' demanded Riggsy brusquely.

Grateful for the small social contact it afforded, Maggie dug out of her bag a new pack of Rothmans that Barry-Geoff must have bunged her during the evening, offered Riggsy a cigarette and lit it, then lit one herself. There was no ashtray in the hall that she could see. If she took a few drags, then asked Riggsy where she could put out her ciggy, she would be in with a good chance of getting into the living-room. Then they could sit on the wickerwork sofa and drink the last of the gin and talk.

'I told them,' said Riggsy, expelling smoke angrily, 'that you didn't live here and *never have* lived here, and that if you're going around telling people you *do* live here then you must be in need of medical help. I must say they seemed to agree. They asked me what I knew about you and I said I didn't know anything about you at all, which is perfectly true.' Good girl, Riggsy. 'But now, of course, I'm worried sick in case they try to trace your whereabouts from the police and find out about that cock-and-bull story you involved me in last year.'

'They won't do that,' Maggie said with confidence, more to reassure herself than Riggsy.

'I just don't know what you've been playing at, Maggie. You've caused me a lot of distress this evening, do you realise that?'

'I honestly didn't think they'd come round here. It won't happen again.'

'It most certainly will not happen again, because if it does I shall consult my solicitor, Maggie, and I *mean every word I say*. I shall take out an injunction against you if necessary. All right: last year I can just about understand, you were in a particular state at a particular time, but there's absolutely no excuse for it now. If there's something on your mind that makes you do these things then you should go to a doctor or psychiatrist or talk it over with a close friend or relative, but *don't drag me* into it. I'm very sorry, but I have enough problems of my own.'

I know you have, Riggsy, and I don't want to hear about them, just as you don't want to hear about mine. That's why I want to talk to you. Not to a close friend, I don't have a close friend any more. To you, Riggsy. You be my friend.

Maggie tapped ash into the palm of her hand, hoping that Riggsy might take the hint. She didn't. Her own ash spilled unheeded down the front of her kimono.

'Can't I talk to *you*, Riggsy?'

Riggsy's usually deep voice had become unnaturally high. 'Maggie, *no*! I simply *can't see* why you want to *attach* yourself to *me*! Just because we have a joke and a laugh in the Half Moon occasionally, it doesn't mean—' Floundering angrily, Riggsy dropped her cigarette and ground it into the lino with the heel of her slipper. Slut. That was that chance gone, then. 'There must be a dozen people who know you better than I do, Maggie. Why try to involve *me*! I don't understand!'

Oh, come on, you old boot, you *do* understand. We know you don't want to be involved but that's what it's all about, isn't it? *I* don't want you to be involved either, Riggsy. Either you with me or me with you. You're the same as me, don't you see, Riggsy? That's why I like you. It's what I respect about you.

Is someone being like yourself a reason for respecting them, then? Maggie couldn't answer that one. But she knew it was why she'd come here. To be among her own kind. And her own kind, being the same kind as she was, wouldn't have her. That was a fine bloody petard to be hoist with at this hour.

'Oh, shit, Riggsy, I'm sorry. I keep saying that, don't I? Sorry. There we go again. Bit pissed. Sorry.'

'But you see you *don't* keep saying you're sorry, Maggie. You haven't said it at all, for the trouble you've caused me tonight.'

'Haven't I? Sorry. Sorry sorry sorry.' She shouldn't have admitted to being a bit pissed. Admitting it made her feel terribly pissed.

'All right, Maggie. I'm going to ask you to leave now. *Now*, Maggie. No, not that way. Come along. Please, Maggie. Please. Please.'

Riggsy must have opened the door because there was cold air wafting around Maggie's ankles. Did cold air, when mixed with vodka and brandy, make you more pissed? It must do. Riggsy had become a blurred figure, as if seen through the ribbed glass of the door she was holding open.

'There hasn't been a letter for me, has there?' asked Maggie thickly.

'A letter? What letter?' Riggsy sounded very harsh.

'From Sean. You know, Riggsy—Sean.'

'Why should Sean write to you here? Why should *anyone* write to you here?'

She wouldn't have heard about Sean. Been off ill, hadn't she? Out of touch. Don't tell her, Mags.

No, quite obvious, he wouldn't have written here. Couldn't have written here. Not on the milk round. Not on the Monopoly board. Bit pissed. Sorry, Riggsy. Forget it.

'Sorry, Riggsy. Forget it. Bit pissed. Where can I put out ciggie?'

Another fine grand exit she couldn't remember making. She was walking up Gloucester Road now, stone-cold sober. All right—call it well on the way to being stone-cold sober. She couldn't remember leaving Riggsy's place but she could remember every step of the way from Parsons Green. New King's Road and King's Road to World's End, up Thingy Walk to Fulham Road, up Thingy Gardens to Old Brompton Road, turn left into Gloucester Road. Not all that far, really. The old plates ached a bit but at least she'd walked off the vodka if not quite the brandy.

Dead lucky she'd been with it, too. Not accosted once, not harassed by the prowling panda car, no friendly-menacing meths drinkers lurching suddenly out of the mews turnings off the wide safe-looking streets. A chance to think, that long walk had given her, though what she had been thinking she couldn't bring to mind just now. Something important, though, it was something important. Walking up Fulham Road before turning into Thingy Gardens, Maggie had thought something important. Or not, possibly. If it was as important as all that, it would come back.

The Waiters' Club rented the front basement of what Maggie would always think of as a fly-by-night hotel, except that hotels couldn't fly by night, could they? They seemed to be doing well enough, though, because recently they'd treated the whole place from top to bottom to a paint job in pale blue gloss. Since then, in order to get through the blue-gloss gate set in the blue-gloss area railings to go down the blue-gloss fire-escape-type metal steps leading to the blue-gloss door of the Waiters' Club, you'd had to push really hard, because it stuck. Maggie was pushing really hard, and nothing was happening, when a cab horn hooted briefly from the road behind her. You could always tell a cab horn from a car horn, it sounded muted, as if you were hearing it through fog. It did mean at this hour of the morning, whatever hour of the morning it was by now, that you could risk turning round without getting indelicately propositioned by a smashed-out-of-his-brains kerb-crawler. Maggie risked turning round, and recognised the apple-dumpling features of Alfie leering benignly from behind the wheel of his shuddering cab.

'You'll be lucky, sweetheart! Closes at three, don't he? Invariable.'

Know that, Alfie. Not entirely unfamiliar with the London scene, you know. 'What's it now, then, Alfie?'

'Ten to five. No use pushing at the flaming gate, it's locked.'

So it was. Maggie noticed the chain and padlock for the first time.

'Didn't realise it was so late. I just came out for some ciggies.' And if you believe that, Alfie baby, you'll believe anything.

Now why was she glad to see Alfie though not glad to see him? Was very unglad to see him because she was making a right nana of herself rattling the gate of the Waiters' Club at ten to five in the morning, and also for some other reason, oh yes, oh Christ, his Mum on the concrete path to the Portakabins this afternoon, or yesterday afternoon as it had now become. That was the bad news, and the good news was what?

Her letter. Her last bijou notelet to come from Sean. He had it. How could she have forgotten, or if not forgotten, not remembered?

Alfie was saying something about hopping in the cab and he'd drop her back at Earl's Court. Something about her taking a chance being out on her own at this time. He always said that when he came across her wandering the streets.

Come on, Alfie, stop pissing about, give me the pigging letter.

'I'll be all right, Alfie. I'll go down to the all-nighter and have some coffee. It'll be light soon.'

No risk of him driving off without giving her the letter, because he had something to say to her, hadn't he? 'Suit yourself. I'll tell you what, though,' said Alfie. 'That was a right flanker you pulled on my old lady. You was definitely out of order there, Maggie. And I'm having to tell you out in the street what I wanted to tell you private in the cab.'

Yes, Alfie. The street does happen to be deserted as it just so happens, so you can call me every kind of pig without causing offence or embarrassment. But can I have my letter?

He handed it over at last, shuffling it all dog-eared and grubby out of a stack of dog-eared and grubby documents that he kept loose in his inside pocket. Sorry it was a bit creased, but he'd been carrying it about. Meant to have left it at the Half Moon but had been off with his back. Hoped it wasn't urgent but she was out of order having mail sent to his Mum's. Yes, Alfie. Thank you, Alfie, won't do it again, Alfie.

Tell you what, Alfie. Might buy you a crocodile wallet for Christmas.

She got away from him at last by saying she must spend a penny at the all-night coffee-shop and heading in that direction. As soon as she heard Alfie's cab moving away, though, she stopped, turned, made sure he'd driven off, and crossed the empty road to the twenty-four-hour launderette. It was deserted, which the coffee-shop never was. Didn't want anyone to see her reading Sean's last bijou notelet.

Maggie sat on a slithering plastic bench under the hard fluorescent light, opposite the silent battery of washing machines. She ran her thumb along the top of the crumpled envelope and took out the crumpled piece of card and smoothed it out as best she could and read it.

KITTEN. NO REGRETS ARE WORTH A TEAR. I LOVE YOU. SEAN.

All those full stops. Kitten stop. No regrets are worth a tear stop. One of his sayings, that. I love you stop. Sean stop. Like a telegram. It should have been waiting for her, if all had gone according to plan and she'd gone round to Alfie's mum's for sweet tea and biccies after signing the babe away.

It was quite short, but violent, her last bout of weeping. It came on like a bad fit of sneezing, with the same kind of impetus, the same kind of distortion of her skin as the anguished face muscles tugged at it, and the same kind of noise. She stumbled across to one of the machines and put some coins in and switched it into rumbling life so that no one chancing to pass by would hear the dreadful row she was making. Soon she stopped and wiped her face with paper tissues. They were drenched, as if she had just dried herself after a good wash. There, Maggie. There. She was glad no one had seen her.

I love you too, Sean. It's bloody obvious when you think about it for a sec, isn't it? Of course I love you. Always have done, always will. Never loved anyone else, ever. It was you. It always will be you. Sorry, ducks, but you can't get out of it just by chucking yourself under a train. You're lumbered. I love you. Finish.

Maggie got up and walked quickly out of the launderette as an Indian punter entered, humping his washing in a Royal Borough of Kensington and Chelsea trade-disposal-only rubbish sack. He gave her a stare. She must look a terrible sight. Or maybe he thought she was on the game.

She walked briskly now, not in her usual sleepwalking way, along Gloucester Road towards the Old Brompton Road. The long way home: it would be light by the time she got to Balmoral Gardens.

She heard the rumble of a train in the morning quiet, couldn't be the first tube yet, it was too early. Goods train probably, or as Sean had always insisted when they'd heard one together at this hour, the nuclear waste train on one more lap towards the holocaust-type accident that statistically, according to Sean, it must finish up having.

Now she remembered the important thought she'd had while walking up the Fulham Road before turning into Thingy Gardens. She'd heard a train then, as now, and thought how if Sean had been there he would have said it was the nuclear waste train; and she'd begun to think about survival. Why she'd survived so far, when by all the rules she should have gone under. And she'd realised that it was because that was what she was for. It was *all* she was for, nothing else. She was programmed for survival. If and when that day ever came when there was nothing left but ruins, she would be one of those few who came crawling out as the dust blew away, and started again. And just given that ruin to crawl in and out of, she could look after herself better than anyone she knew. Better than Aliboo with her gardening wellies in the hatchback, better than Alfie's mum with all her earth-mother lore, better than Jenny and Miss Roberts with their back-up team support, better than her Dad with his Black and Decker drill, better than all of them. They weren't made for it, she was, like the giraffe is made to eat the topmost leaves.

Sean would have been a survivor too, if he'd survived to be one. Shame you didn't, Sean. Could have put a great act together.

Perhaps it wasn't such a very important thought she'd remembered having after all. None of that stuff was going to happen, was it?

Don't know, though, Mags. Sometimes feel that it's happening already.

She turned right into the Earl's Court Road from the Old Brompton Road. It was already busy with juggernauts delivering fork-lift trucks of junk-food to the hamburger joints and sawn-off supermarkets, and the Asian greengrocers setting out their pavement displays of fruit. The bleached April sun was rising now, far behind her over Sloane Square tube station. Soon it would be over South Ken, following the District Line to Earl's Court where the station porter was pushing back the trellis gate dividing the galleria from the piazza, and where a handful of punters lingered, waiting for the first train of the morning or the last rent-boy or hooker of the night. It would rise high above Parsons Green and set somewhere around Hammersmith. It was going to be a fine Spring day and Maggie would get through it. It was light now and she could go home to bed. A survivor. She wasn't kidding. Anyone who could get through yesterday could get through today. And it wasn't even raining.

THE END

A SELECTED LIST OF CORGI TITLES

While every effort is made to keep prices low, it is sometimes necessary to increase prices at short notice. Corgi Books reserve the right to show new retail prices on covers which may differ from those previously advertised in the text or elsewhere.

The prices shown below were correct at the time of going to press.

☐	11660 2	PRINCESS DAISY	*Judith Krantz*	£1.75
☐	11730 7	PORTRAITS	*Cynthia Freeman*	£1.95
☐	11775 7	A WORLD FULL OF STRANGERS	*Cynthia Freeman*	£1.95
☐	11698 X	LOVE'S SWEET AGONY	*Patricia Matthews*	£1.75
☐	10494 9	LOVE'S AVENGING HEART	*Patricia Matthews*	£1.95
☐	10737 9	LOVE FOREVER MORE	*Patricia Matthews*	£1.95
☐	11181 3	LOVE'S MAGIC MOMENT	*Patricia Matthews*	£1.50
☐	11553 3	LOVE'S RAGING TIDE	*Patricia Matthews*	£1.75
☐	11149 X	IMOGEN	*Jilly Cooper*	£1.00
☐	10878 2	PRUDENCE	*Jilly Cooper*	£1.00
☐	10717 4	OCTAVIA	*Jilly Cooper*	£1.00
☐	10576 7	HARRIET	*Jilly Cooper*	£1.00
☐	10427 2	BELLA	*Jilly Cooper*	£1.00
☐	10277 6	EMILY	*Jilly Cooper*	£1.00
☐	11575 4	A NECESSARY WOMAN	*Helen Van Slyke*	£1.95
☐	11321 2	SISTERS AND STRANGERS	*Helen Van Slyke*	£1.50

All these books are available at your book shop or newsagent, or can be ordered direct from the publisher. Just tick the titles you want and fill in the form below.

CORGI BOOKS, Cash Sales Department, P.O. Box 11, Falmouth, Cornwall.

Please send cheque or postal order, no currency.

Please allow cost of book(s) plus the following for postage and packing:

U.K. Customers—Allow 45p for the first book, 20p for the second book and 14p for each additional book ordered, to a maximum charge of £1.63.

B.F.P.O. and Eire—Allow 45p for the first book, 20p for the second book plus 14p per copy for the next 7 books, thereafter 8p per book.

Overseas Customers—Allow 75p for the first book and 21p per copy for each additional book.

NAME (Block Letters) ....

ADDRESS ....

....